DARKMOUTH

WORLDS EXPLODE

SHANE HEGARTY was a journalist before becoming a full-time writer. He lives on the east coast of Ireland, in a village not unlike Darkmouth. Only with no monsters. That he knows about.

Follow Shane on Twitter: @shanehegarty

Discover more at: www.youtube.com/Darkmouth

Books by Shane Hegarty

DARKMOUTH

DARKMOUTH: WORLDS EXPLODE

DARKMOUTH: CHAOS DESCENDS

DARKMOUTH
WORLDS EXPLODE

SHANE HEGARTY

Illustrated by James de la Rue

HarperCollins *Children's Books*

First published in hardback in Great Britain by HarperCollins *Children's Books* in 2015
HarperCollins *Children's Books* is a division of HarperCollins*Publishers* Ltd,
1 London Bridge Street, London, SE1 9GF

The HarperCollins website address is: www.harpercollins.co.uk

1

Copyright © Shane Hegarty 2015
Illustrations © James de la Rue 2015

HB ISBN: 978-0-00-754573-5
TPB ISBN: 978-0-00-813944-5

Shane Hegarty asserts the moral right to be identified as the author of the work.
James de la Rue asserts the moral right to be identified as the illustrator of the work.

Printed and bound in England by Clays Ltd, St Ives plc

MIX

For Oisín

THE INF

DEAD FOREST

CAVE

CLEARING

DEAD FOREST

Previously in Darkmouth
(AND THE MESS THINGS WERE LEFT IN)

It was, everyone on the Council of Twelve agreed, a bit of a mess.

Actually, it was a *lot* of a mess. In fact, 'mess' understated things a little. It was more of a disaster really. A catastrophe. A complete catastrophe.

It was, everyone on the Council of Twelve eventually agreed, a complete catastrophe.

What was the worst part of the catastrophe? There was so much to choose from.

Darkmouth was the last town left on Earth where Legends of myth still invaded, but Hugo the Great, the only active Legend Hunter left to fight them off, was lost on the Infested Side.

As if that wasn't bad enough – and it was very, very bad – Darkmouth had been left in the hands of his son Finn, a boy still almost eleven months away from his thirteenth birthday when he would become Complete as a Legend Hunter.

Worse yet, this boy was not exactly top of his Legend Hunter class. Which was some achievement given he was the *only* boy in his Legend Hunter class.

Somehow, that wasn't even the end of the mess.

The Twelve had managed to plant a spy in the town. Steve, a Half-Hunter from a long line of Legend Hunters, had never properly hunted until he arrived in Darkmouth. It turned out he had never properly spied either, as his cover was blown by Finn, the very boy he was supposed to be keeping a close eye on.

There should have been a positive in the form of Steve's daughter, Emmie, who not only befriended Finn, but also showed a desire and heart for fighting Legends that the boy lacked. Except it was increasingly clear that her enthusiasm would cause trouble someday – and that day came when she helped a Legend, Broonie the Hogboon, escape back to the Infested Side from which all Legends come.

And then, just to add icing to the whole cake of catastrophe, Darkmouth turned out to be harbouring a traitor. Mr Ernest Glad was supposed to be a Fixer, a helper, a lifelong friend to Hugo. Instead, he was collaborating with the Legends and helped them invade. And he ended up opening a gateway to the Infested Side and pushing Finn's mother, Clara, through it. Eventually, Clara was rescued by Hugo, but he became trapped in the world of the Legends.

Yes, Finn did shove Mr Glad into the gateway, trapping him and turning him into a million points of light. And yes, he did admittedly defeat a Minotaur and stop an all-out invasion of Legends.

But buildings were destroyed. People were hurt. Every goldfish in Darkmouth disappeared. Hugo the Legend Hunter was gone.

And it would not help matters at all if the boy tried to get him back. No, that would only end in further, final catastrophe.

Or something far worse.

'The Arrival of the Human'
From *The Chronicles of the Sky's Collapse*,
as told by inhabitants of the Infested Side

When the human stepped into this cursed world, the sky changed colour. A gateway had opened from the Promised World. There were two voices, that of a human boy and a man. But when the gateway closed only the man remained and, as the army arrived to capture him, the sky went from its usual bleak grey to an entirely different shade of abysmal grey.

It is true that all of this was witnessed and described by one of the ancient Graeae sisters, and it is also true that it was not her turn with the single eyeball they shared between the three of them. She could sense it, though, she insisted, just as she could sense the advancing army. She had felt their tremor through her only tooth. Just before it fell out.

The army followed the fleeing human across the dead earth. Shimmering armour covered his body, yet by the time the chase was over he had suffered wound after wound until the redness of his flowing blood was vivid against the desolate land where even the soil desires vengeance.

Escaping deep within the scorched forest, the Legend Hunter glanced behind to see if they were closing on him, only to stumble at the edge of a crater in the earth. He grasped desperately at a petrified branch, but, when it broke, the crack echoed across the land.

The human fell.

The army converged.

Through the wood, creatures of every sort crept forward. Two-headed and goat-backed, serpent-tailed and poison-tongued, scaled and leathery, hairy and fire-scorched. They moved as one, encircling him, howling, snarling, barking, yelping, expressing their bloodlust in a thousand voices.

The human hauled himself to his feet, pain obvious in every fighting breath, and turned, slowly, to take in the full scene and absorb the great futility of his situation. Having done this, he then did something most surprising.

He smiled.

At this time of all times. In this place of all places.

It caused a momentary hesitation, a brief quietening of the army.

What did he know?

They pushed away their doubts and closed in on him again, crawling, creeping, flying across branches, screaming through mouths rimmed with teeth, heads rimmed with mouths, necks rimmed with heads.

This human would soon become one more pile of bones in a forest of the dead.

"Stop!" demanded a voice.

Every creature did, standing aside as a giant pushed his way through their ranks.

He was a Fomorian, armoured and fierce. Holding a spear, he moved forward steadily, circling the human, letting the fear sink in, until he stopped in front of him and pressed the spear against the intruder's chest.

"I command this army in the name of the great and mighty Gantrua," the Fomorian told him. "And you have wandered into the wrong world."

The human slowly scanned the Legends around and above him, then leaned in close to the mighty giant towering over him and spoke.

"Actually, this is exactly where I wanted to be."

The army howled, leaped, roared. The Fomorian

raised a hand to calm them again. "Choose your next words very carefully, human. They will be your last."

The Legend Hunter lifted his chin and declared, "They call me Niall Blacktongue. I come from the Blighted Village of Darkmouth to find someone, but not anybody of this world. And I wouldn't press that spear too hard if I were you."

"You mean like this?" The Fomorian applied just the tiniest pressure to the spear, but enough to pierce the armour until a dribble of blood ran down Niall Blacktongue's chest plate.

The human flinched. Then sparked, like the ignition of a match in the moment before the flame consumes it.

"I did warn you," sighed Niall. Then he exploded.

I

THIRTY-TWO YEARS LATER

Finn's father had told him to go to room S3 in the house.

Then he'd pushed Finn out of the Infested Side, back through the buckling gateway to their own world and safety. Finn's dad had gone to the Infested Side to rescue Finn's mam, and Finn had gone there to rescue both of them. The last time he saw his dad, he was stepping towards the onrushing Legends and the human who led the charge – Hugo's own father, Niall Blacktongue.

So, once the gateway had closed, trapping his father on the other side, Finn ran straight to room S3 in the Long Hall. All he found there was a plain box. Inside it was a handwritten note with a simple instruction: *Light up the house*.

So Finn did. He switched on every lamp and light bulb from the library to the bedrooms, from the bathrooms to the storerooms. He replaced spent light bulbs. He filled empty sockets. He lit up rooms he'd spent hours training in. Rooms he'd never been in. Rooms he'd hardly even noticed.

By the time he'd finished, the house must have been visible from the moon.

"Find the map," his father had also said.

So Finn found maps.

Lots of maps. Two weeks of hard searching later, he hadn't found his father, but he was still finding maps.

They were now stacked in piles the length of the Long Hall, under his ancestors' portraits lining the wall. One mound of maps was overseen by the painting of a meek, almost shameful Niall Blacktongue that Finn could hardly bring himself to look at since losing his father.

Pages were heaped up across the circular floor of the high-ceilinged library, scattered about the device in the centre of the room that his father had built to desiccate Legends, but which Mr Glad had used to awaken them for the invasion. And, at the very spot where Glad had been trapped by a collapsing gateway and scattered into light, there was a small mountain of maps, sorted, discarded, ruled out or held on to for further investigation. Finn sat on one of its slopes.

But he wasn't alone.

"I'm guessing we can ignore *The 1956 Guide to Norway's Best Pudding Restaurants?*" he asked Emmie.

"*The Great Scourge of 1886: A Map of Missing Legends,*" she read from where she stood by a half-ransacked section of the vast shelves that ringed the room. "How many Legends went missing? And how can there be a map of them if no one knows where they are in the first place?"

They had spent a fortnight leafing through books of maps, fold-out maps, laminated maps, two braille maps, even a jigsaw map of Ireland that Finn used to play with as a child. That very afternoon, they had put the jigsaw together and become very excited when they discovered the piece for County Tipperary was missing.

"It *must* mean something," Emmie had said excitedly, until Finn remembered that he'd almost choked on Tipperary when he was very young and the piece had been thrown away as a safety precaution.

He and Emmie continued sifting through the maps in the hope that something might jump out at them. Although, given that they were surrounded by the desiccated husks of Legends, shrunken and frozen but not at all dead, they quietly hoped that nothing would *literally* jump out at them.

Since his father's disappearance, no alarms had wailed. No gateway had opened. No Legends had come through. Instead, it had been all about the maps, with the problem being that even if they found one that looked right they didn't have a clue what it would lead them to.

A weapon? A person? A Legend with its mouth wide and teeth sharpened? Maybe it would be a convenient path to the Infested Side, and they would skip their way along it to find Hugo sitting in a room somewhere, grinning at them.

With the way things had gone so far, that seemed unlikely.

"We'll know it when we see it, I guess," Emmie said, apparently sensing Finn's despair. "I'm sure that at some stage the map we're looking for will just drop out of something like…" she looked at the book she was holding, "…*An Illustrated Atlas of the Last Stands of Slain Legend Hunters*. OK, bad choice."

Finn was flicking robotically through another book, *The Happy Rowers' Guide to the Inlets of Southern Sweden, 1974 edition (Now with Added Coves)*.

"Dad wouldn't have told me about it if he didn't think we could find it," he said, trying to convince himself as much as Emmie. "And he told me he knew I wouldn't give up. So I won't. Except..." From the book he was holding, a small, red, frayed hardback notebook dropped to the floor. "...we've been doing this for weeks now, looking for something we mightn't even recognise."

"We'll find it soon, Finn," said Emmie.

"I'm not saying we won't," Finn replied, picking up the notebook. On the inside cover were the initials NB, and he scanned its pages of hand-drawn mathematical symbols, diagrams and shapes, the writing so small it was like a spider had fallen in an inkpot before scampering across the page. *NB*, he thought. *Niall Blacktongue?* Was it possible this notebook belonged to—?

A crumpled-up bit of paper bounced off the side of his head. "Earth to Finn?" said Emmie, with a sympathetic grin.

Finn blinked. "Oh. I'm not saying we won't find it, I'm just afraid we're looking for the wrong thing in the wrong places."

Which was the exact moment he found a map.

2

Low evening sunlight flooded the small Darkmouth alley, forcing Finn to pull his visor down to block its glare. He crept low along the narrow laneway, brushing the high walls on either side, the butt of his Desiccator pressed into his armoured shoulder, ready to protect him against whatever he might find. Whenever he found it. Whatever it was he was looking for.

He backed along a wall, the armour of his clattering fighting suit screeching across the stone. Keeping out of sight, he took a hard right into another alleyway of high glass and nail-rimmed walls in a town built for defence. Gouges and missing chunks in the brickwork were a reminder of the invasion only two weeks before, of the chaos and near catastrophe wrought by multiple Manticores, a Minotaur and those trying to hunt them down.

He scuttled down the laneway where Mr Glad's

burnt-out shop stood behind a criss-cross of police tape warning trespassers to keep out, a blackened reminder of the traitor who had opened a hole in Darkmouth through which Finn's father and mother had gone and only one had come back.

Where the lane bisected another, Finn stuck his head round the corner. From a parallel alley, the barrel of a weapon emerged, followed by a helmet and a flurry of exaggerated hand signals.

Palm out flat. Knuckles curled. A swirling motion.

Finn flipped open his visor, squinting against the sun as he tried to properly convey his bemusement. "What?" he mouthed.

Steve pushed his visor open and repeated the gestures, this time adding some kind of pumping fist motion.

"Lie down?" asked Finn. "Hop?"

Steve gritted his teeth with obvious frustration. From behind his back, another head appeared.

Emmie, her helmet propped on her head, tight red hair avalanching from it, waved at Finn. He waved back.

Her father gently but firmly pushed her behind him and then, pressed against the wall, crab-walked towards Finn. Emmie followed, no Desiccator in her hand. She wasn't allowed one. Her sole weapon was an eagerness that almost burst from her.

The three crouched at the wall. Finn's fighting suit was pushed up uncomfortably at his neck; his kneepads dug into the top of his shins. He shifted awkwardly and loudly as Steve spoke.

"We're to follow that lane north for another forty metres," said Emmie's father, pointing ahead, "then west for twenty metres. That's where we'll find our target."

Finn narrowed his eyes to see. "But that's the wrong way," he said.

"No, it's the right way."

"It's not," Finn insisted, pointing instead at the sliver of alleyway directly ahead of them. "I'm sure that's what the map tells us."

An old man cycled towards them, whistling a tune that he left hanging in the air as he saw them, crouched, in armour, and wielding their fat silver Desiccators. He stopped, turned his bike clumsily in the narrow alley, climbed back on to the saddle and cycled away in the direction he'd come from, mumbling curses as he went.

They watched him go, then resumed their planning. "It's the correct way, Finn. It's the only possibility."

"I know these streets. My dad made me memorise them."

"Look, Finn, I am in charge here. Those are the orders, so that's just the way it is, whether we like it or not."

Steve didn't just like it, he loved it. That was obvious. Since the Council of Twelve had ordered him to stay on in Darkmouth and act as temporary Legend Hunter, he'd been practically giddy with authority, and even more disappointed than Finn that a gateway hadn't opened since.

"Finn does know them, Dad," said Emmie, pushing open her visor to reveal her face. "Trust me."

"Do you want to go back to the car?" Steve asked her.

"No," she answered.

"Then let me deal with this. We almost got killed in this town because of invading Legends. This is serious stuff."

"But you said I could do a bit more, Dad."

"Yes, you can observe more."

"Come on, Dad. I just want to help."

Steve rooted through a pocket of his fighting suit, pulled out a set of car keys and held them out to her.

Emmie let out a deep sigh.

Content he'd made his point, Steve pushed the keys back into his pocket and again turned his attention to Finn, who had already stood up to cross the road in the direction he knew they needed to go. Steve pulled him back down by the shoulder and eyeballed him. A shudder went through Finn's fighting suit. It was tough to exude ferocity when sounding like a wind chime.

"This is the right alley," insisted Steve, rising to move forward. "So, follow me and let's see what's down here."

It was the wrong alley.

A dead end.

"They must have put this in after making the map," said Steve, coughing to hide his embarrassment. Finn and Emmie's silent response said it all. Steve eventually cracked.

"OK, let's go the way Finn thinks we should," said Emmie's dad and the three of them moved back towards the other laneway. "And let's hope he's not wrong."

Finn felt his frustration rise sharply, but kept it to himself.

They moved through the jagged shadows of the laneway's cobbled defences, past houses of chipped paint and gouged windowsills. They ducked past old, dirtied walls dotted with fresh brick, like fillings in a tooth.

It eventually led them to a wooden door, the entrance to a backyard. As was standard in Darkmouth, its wall was ringed by broken glass, nails, tacks, sharp stones, anything that might keep a Legend out. Softened by decades of rain, though, the splintered door pushed open easily, revealing a yard half filled with blue plastic barrels and large bins.

Finn felt a jolt of uncertainty: this wasn't right at all.

Before he could speak, Steve held up his hand and began counting down with his fingers. Finn drew his Desiccator to his shoulder and followed him. Emmie stood behind them and tried to look as tough as she could before remembering to snap shut her helmet's visor.

They edged forward, between bins and barrels and the occasional waft of something rotting, until they reached the back door.

Steve placed his hand on the handle.

"This is ridiculous," Finn's mother, Clara, said from the yard behind them, causing each of them to almost jump clean out of their fighting suits. They spun round. "What do you think you're going to find here?" she asked.

"We were just about to discover that before you interrupted," answered Steve, deeply frustrated by this disturbance.

"Give me the map," demanded Clara, hand out.

"Keep your voice down," Steve hissed.

Finn snatched the map from where it was tucked into

the utility belt on Steve's fighting suit and, despite the man's protests, handed it quickly to his mother.

Clara held it up. "Do you really think it would be on a beer mat? You don't think that *just maybe* Hugo would have told Finn to 'look for the map on the beer mat' if he wanted you to find it on an actual beer mat?"

She turned it over in her fingers. On one side was an image of a full and frothy glass (*Widow Maker – as refreshing as a kick from an eight-hooved Sleipnir*). On the other, the print had been picked clean off and on the soft white cardboard a pen had been used to scribble what seemed to be a criss-cross of laneways, with an X at one corner.

"It's the best map we've come up with," said Steve, his Desiccator wilting somewhat.

"Better than when you thought you'd found the right one, but ended up bursting into Mrs Kelly's crèche at nap time?"

"The mark on that map seemed legitimate," said Steve, flipping open his visor.

"It was a coffee stain. And you set a dozen toddlers' toilet training back a month."

"We're trying our best, Mam," said Finn.

"I know you are, Finn. This isn't your fault. I just don't

like to see you being led around blindly while carrying a dangerous weapon."

"Oh, that thing's not even loaded," said Steve, motioning at Finn's Desiccator. Registering the shock crossing Finn's face, he added, "Come on now, if you had to use it, you'd probably do more damage to yourself than anything else. But it kept you quiet to think it was working."

The door behind them swung open with a clang.

Finn and Steve spun round, their raised Desiccators almost scratching the nose of the man who stood in the doorway, wearing a white apron and holding an open-topped blue barrel. He thrust his hands in the air, dropping the barrel so that everyone had to leap out of the way while water and slices of potato washed across the concrete.

As he turned and stumbled back into the building, Clara crouched down and picked up one of the raw chips. "It didn't occur to you that maybe Hugo had just doodled a map to the nearest takeaway on a beer mat?"

"But our files say Hugo doesn't drink alcohol," said Steve.

"No, but he eats food," she said sternly. "Especially fish and chips. He loves fish and chips."

Steve and Finn both slumped, almost simultaneously. Steve rubbed his eyes with his gloved hand. Finn hung his head and sagged against the wall. Emmie hovered, toeing the ground. Clara stood between them all, arms folded, head tilted back towards the orange sky.

"I'm sorry, Mam," said Finn.

"It's not you who should be sorry," she said. "Steve's supposed to be the grown-up here. Honestly. We need to find whatever Hugo wanted us to, but this carry-on has to stop."

"You don't think I'd rather be anywhere else but in this place, sorting out your mess?" said Steve.

"No, I don't. A Blighted Village of your own? It's clearly your dream come true."

"I'm getting out of here at the first opportunity," insisted Steve. "It's pretty much all I talk about at this stage. Even Finn will confirm that."

"I…" hesitated Finn.

"You don't need to say anything, Finn," said Clara.

"Tell her, Finn."

"Ignore him, Finn."

"I…" stuttered Finn.

"Ahem," said a strange voice.

A young man stood at the entrance to the laneway.

So tall and lanky that he seemed almost to stoop in case his head bumped the sky, he was dressed in a shiny grey business suit, a crisp pink shirt and a lime-green tie that knotted tightly at his neck. A briefcase sat on the ground beside him.

Everyone looked at him and, after a few seconds, the man seemed to finally remember why he was there. "Ah yes, hello there. My name is Estravon Oakbound, Assessor to the Subcommittee on Lost Hunters, as appointed by the Council of Twelve. And, under section 41, clause 9 of the 1265 Act of Disappearance, I am here to assess and ultimately assist in the case of the missing Legend Hunter of Darkmouth, Hugo the Great."

He held out a greasy, fat, brown paper bag. "Excuse my manners. Would anyone like a chip?"

B ack across town, at the end of a nameless street lined with buildings whose doors had been unopened in decades, windows boarded up or black with grime, was Finn's ordinary-looking house. An unassuming brick building, it was tucked in behind a low stone wall, a patch of grass and a flower bed into which daffodil stalks were slowly turning into mulch, a couple of weeks after being crushed under the foot of a very angry Minotaur.

On a sofa in the living room, the visitor loomed over Finn and the others even though he was sitting down, his suit jacket flapping loose from his bony frame, his knees rising higher than his waist.

Finn and Clara sat opposite him, separated by a low table on which her tea stood untouched and cold. Finn could see his mother's mouth was pinched, as if she was trying to prevent rash words from escaping.

Behind them, Steve paced slowly and a little nervously. He hadn't been given any tea and had arrived late, having been delayed persuading a stubborn Emmie that she couldn't be part of this and would have to return to her house.

"Darkmouth's a hard place to find," said Estravon Oakbound, dipping a biscuit in his tea and failing to catch it as the damp half broke away and splashed into the cup. He fished it out with his fingers, gobbled it. "But I am so glad I made it here. This place is famous."

He checked his wristwatch, licked his fingers clean of tea and crumbs, then reached into the briefcase by his feet and pulled out a clipboard and a pen. "It may be just case number 4526-dash-U, as far as the filing clerks back at Liechtenstein HQ are concerned, but to me it's a privilege."

Estravon looked up to see that his enthusiasm was not appreciated, so switched to a more sombre tone as he ran the tip of his pen down the page on his clipboard. "Let's see. Let's see. Ah yes, here we are. The map."

He waited. Eventually, Clara responded.

"The map?" she asked.

"Yes," said Estravon. "I believe you've been looking for it. As an Assessor, I work directly with the Council of Twelve to examine and, well, assess cases relating to Legend Hunters or their villages. That's why I'm here." He looked at his watch again. Finn noticed its hands were curved rather beautifully, like daggers. "For a precious few hours anyway."

He sat forward, looking towards the window as if expecting someone to be eavesdropping, then spoke almost conspiratorially. "We could probably have done a lot of this over the phone, but it wouldn't be the same at all. Now what did it smell like?"

Finn was baffled and silent until he realised the Assessor was talking to him. "Excuse me?" he said.

"The Minotaur that crossed over into Darkmouth. What did it smell like? Rotten, I'd imagine. I believe the local sergeant was lucky to survive the old..." He raised a finger in a stabbing motion while making a squelching noise.

"Horrible big thing. The Minotaur, obviously, not the sergeant. And real. So very, very real…" The Assessor seemed briefly lost in a daydream. Finn, meanwhile, still felt suffocated by how Sergeant Doyle had been so badly injured two weeks ago because he'd come to help himself and Emmie.

"We need a rescue party," interjected Steve.

"That's why I'm here," said Estravon.

"You're the rescue party?" asked Clara.

"No." He blurted a laugh, then became more serious. "But I'll have a great say in what happens. And I think we can put a good case forward for some very positive action here." He paused. "Do you know about the six hundred scorpions?" he added, turning to Finn.

"Scorpions?" said Finn.

"At your Completion Ceremony. Sorry, I shouldn't be giving away any surprises. Let's just hope it goes ahead now. The chance to become the first brand-new, true, active Legend Hunter in many years. Not a mere Half-Hunter like the rest of us. And then this happens. Shame. I'd already chosen my suit."

The Assessor fingered his jacket, clearly hoping for a compliment. He seemed a little deflated when he didn't get one.

"You were going to say something about the map," prompted Clara.

"Ah yes." He ran his pen down his list again. "The Infested Side. That's one thing that wasn't clear in the report."

"I wrote everything down," said Steve.

"And very detailed it was too, thanks, Steve. So, you were all there on the Infested Side…" He went into his daydream again. "I can't even believe I've had a chance to say those words. So few have visited, never mind returned alive. I can think of only a couple, and Conrad Single-Limb's name says everything about the condition he came back in. Of course, according to the prophecy, you will be going back there some time, Finn. But let's not dwell on that."

Queasiness hit Finn and he didn't know if it was in his body or his mind. "You know about that?"

"Of course I know about that. Everyone knows about that. Any of us around the Twelve anyway. Didn't you grow up hearing about it?"

Estravon noted the embarrassment creeping across Finn's face and the displeasure on his mother's. He guessed what they meant. "You really didn't know?" he said.

"Not till recently," said Finn.

"The Legends are rising, the boy shall fall," recited Estravon. "Out of the dark mouth shall come the last child of the last Legend Hunter."

"There's no need to—" said Clara.

"He shall open end the war and open up the Promised Land. His death on the Infested Side will be greater than any other."

"—hear it again," she finished, irritation flushing through her cheeks.

"It's nonsense anyway," said Estravon, busying himself with his clipboard again. "Rubbish. Could mean anything. I wouldn't worry about it. We don't. Not at all."

"You don't?" said Finn in surprise.

"Well, more or less. Not too much. Only sometimes." Estravon tailed off and, in the few heavy seconds of silence, Finn thought he could hear the dust falling through the air.

Finally, Estravon announced, "Anyway, to the matter at hand. How did your father get trapped on the Infested Side? It says in the report that you were the last to see him, Finn, that you were with him, and Steve and your mother came through the gateway ahead of you. Yet only your father was trapped. How?"

"He pushed me through."

42

"He pushed you through?" Estravon made a note.

"And the gateway closed. Suddenly. Behind me."

"Closed. Suddenly. Behind you." Estravon was focused on the clipboard, writing every word down. "But he told you about the map?"

"Yes," answered Finn as calmly as he could through a head swimming with guilt. "He shouted it at me."

"We've been through all this," said Clara. "Can we just get the help now?"

"Let me get this straight, Finn," said Estravon, placing the pen across the clipboard and concentrating on Finn. "The gateway was closing as a swarm of Legends descended so your father pushed you through, shouting to you as you fell. And then the gateway closed. He therefore simply became stuck, Finn. Trapped there. For no other reason than bad timing?" Finn felt sweat moisten his brow. "Yes," he said, his tongue like sandpaper. "Bad timing, I suppose."

The Assessor stared intently at him, his face expressionless for what seemed to Finn like an age, but can only have been a few moments. Then he suddenly snapped into a grin. "Well, that's all good then."

He clicked the pen, pushed his clipboard back into his briefcase. Relief surged through Finn. A moment ago he'd wanted to jump out of a window and escape. Now he had to fight the urge to punch the air in delight. He wanted to ask if that was it, if they actually believed all of that, but managed to wrestle that idea away from his mouth before he said it.

Estravon checked his watch again. "I can't believe I'll have to go so soon after getting here. But I wouldn't want to impose on you here in this house." He looked at Steve. "So, I'll stay the night in your house instead."

Steve gawped a little.

"But what about the map?" asked Finn.

"Oh yes, the map," said Estravon.

"Can you help us find it?"

"Well, that's the thing, I'm afraid," said the Assessor. "There is no map."

"No map? Of course there's a map," insisted Clara. "Hugo said so."

"I'm afraid he was mistaken, Clara. May I call you Clara?" He didn't wait for a response. "The existence of any map, Clara, was thoroughly investigated after the death of Niall Blacktongue although no one really likes to talk about all of that. Nevertheless, what I can say, quite sincerely, is that there is no map. There never was. It was searched for. It was not found."

That information settled in the hush of the room.

"So that's it?" said Steve.

"Not at all," the Assessor said as he stood up suddenly, triggering Finn and Clara into doing the same. "I will report back to the Twelve, to make a recommendation. I feel confident there'll be some progress as a result of this."

He glanced once more at his watch as if in a hurry and, seeing Finn look at it again, unclasped it from his wrist and dangled it at him. "Please. Take it."

"I can't do that," Finn said politely.

The Assessor insisted. "It would be an absolute privilege for me to know that it was being worn here, in Darkmouth."

Finn looked at his mother, who nodded in encouragement while looking as if she wanted this man out of her house as soon as possible. So, Finn took the watch and strapped it on his wrist. "Thanks," he said.

Estravon leaned into Finn and whispered, "They're standard issue anyway. I have a drawer full of them at home."

"I worry we've very little time," said Clara pointedly.

"I do understand." The Assessor picked up a biscuit. "But there is time at least for one more of these before I have to leave."

Fully aware of the intense irritation now radiating from his mother, Finn distracted himself by looking at his new watch, admiring how the delicate curves of its steel hands caught the light of the fat moon flooding through the window.

Outside, the sky was clear and still. Another night falling on a world without his father.

4

The next morning, sun crept into Darkmouth and an early summer breeze travelled across the sea, tickling the low waves that ran up to the raggedy shoreline and warming the fat rocks that littered the small crescent of beach at the town's southern edge. Reaching the wide mangled cliffs that separated Darkmouth from the rest of the world, the breeze rose up until it ruffled the grass lining the top.

A basset hound scampered across the stony beach, stopping briefly to sniff a pebble, pee on it, then move on again.

"Yappy!"

The animal's owner, Mrs Bright, scrambled after it, struggling to keep her footing on the shifting layer of stones.

"Yappy! Come back, Yappy, you stupid animal."

She stopped for a moment and looked back along the

beach. It curved away into the early morning haze, its stones kissed by the sun-sparkled sea that lapped at the long sweep of the bay. Inland, the houses of Darkmouth huddled together, as if cowering from some unseen danger, but, in this clear morning light, it looked like a normal town. You couldn't see the shimmer of broken glass on walls, the dull glint of bars on windows, the tight squeeze of the town's mazy alleyways. You could only see the painted house fronts, the wooden shop signs, the little playground of swings and slides. It was almost, in fact, a thing of beauty.

I really hate Darkmouth, thought Mrs Bright.

Mrs Bright wasn't supposed to be living here at all. She had made the mistake of marrying a man from Darkmouth who had come not only with a dog she couldn't stand, but a promise that they would live in the town for exactly one year, and no more, before moving on to any place of her choosing.

He died suddenly eleven months later.

She was left with a house she couldn't sell and a dog she didn't want.

"Yappy!" she shouted. "Where did you go, you useless mutt?"

She scanned the beach for the dog again. No sign. She

moved towards the corner of the cliff, where rock jutted towards the water and the shore narrowed. Squeezing herself carefully round the base of the looming cliff to the beach on the other side, she could still see nothing of her tiresome pet.

"Yappy! I'll leave you here, don't think I won't."

From somewhere she heard a muffled yap.

She stopped. Listened. Heard it again.

Squinting at the black stone of the cliff, its layers of rock turned in on itself as if it might collapse at any moment, Mrs Bright realised there was an opening. It was small, a fissure not much taller than herself, and bent over as if buckling under the weight of the land above it.

She had walked this part of the beach many times and never noticed a cave before. Loose soil and stones were scattered at the entrance, apparently freshly fallen. *There must*, she thought, *have been a rock fall, maybe caused by the heavy rains that accompanied the recent invasion of those* things. Another reason why she wanted out of Darkmouth at the earliest opportunity.

There was another bark from inside the cliff.

Mrs Bright sighed, stepped carefully over the rubble at the opening, manoeuvred round a large rock and carefully made her way inside.

It *was* a cave, its walls narrowing as she moved deeper into it, the roof sloping down so that she needed to stoop as she called again for the dog.

"Yappy!"

Her shout echoed back at her just as she squeezed through a gap and into a chamber that stretched high into the blackness above her. The cave was so dark that Mrs Bright could hardly see the ground at her feet.

She gave one final call for the dog and heard nothing but her own breathing and the sound of trickling water.

As Mrs Bright turned to leave, she realised she could see now. A flickering crimson light crept across the hollowed-out rock. Then something else occurred to her: the light was coming from *inside* the cave.

From somewhere in the direction of that light, Yappy yapped.

Mrs Bright peered towards it. She made out a smudge of deep red, the soft edge of a light obscured by a fold in the cave wall. Cautiously, she edged towards it.

"Is that you, Yappy?"

It most definitely was not.

Mrs Bright's strangled scream echoed through the high cavern.

*

Many dogs are intelligent, perceptive beasts with an almost supernatural sense of danger.

Yappy was not one of those dogs.

A couple of minutes later, he emerged from the cave, stopped at a large stone at its entrance, sniffed it, peed on it, sniffed again. He dropped something from his mouth, a curved pink and white object, sniffed around a bit, licked between his legs, sniffed around some more, picked up the object again and scuttled away down the beach. The sun climbed above the horizon into a sky of near unbroken blue. But, if anyone had been looking up at that moment, they would have seen the merest hint of a cloud cross the sun, dimming it almost imperceptibly before burning away again.

And they would have presumed it was just a trick of the light that the cloud briefly appeared to change, solidify and form the shape of a howling face.

5

Finn waited at the front door of his house, his father's hulking car parked outside. Black with a few old scrapes scoring the paint, its familiar sleekness had been dulled by the dust slowly settling on it as the days and weeks went by. It was becoming a spectre and a reminder of Finn's failure to find his father.

In those last violent moments before the gateway closed and he turned to face the approaching army of Legends, Hugo had told Finn he believed in him, that he knew he'd find a way into the Infested Side. Finn the Defiant he had called him, and Finn had carried that faith with him through the first few days following his father's disappearance. Yet each speck of dust on that car was a reminder of every day, every hour, every second of failure since. His father believed in him. But Finn was struggling to. All he knew for sure was that he'd been unable to stop Mr Glad pushing his mam through a gateway and his father had been lost while rescuing her. He felt that guilt as heavily as if a Hydra was squatting on his chest.

The morning breeze picked up for a moment, spreading goosebumps across Finn's arms. He grabbed his backpack, a dead weight that needed to be hoisted with a grunt on to his back. An arm of his fighting suit fell loose from its open zip.

He was in the habit of carrying the armour every day, just in case it was required, and would sit in class with an eye on the weather outside the window. The merest spit of rain – it always rained when portals opened from the Infested Side – was enough to give him the jitters.

Finn twisted in an awkward effort to shove the arm back into his bag. Out of the corner of his eye, he saw something move. An animal was scampering up the street. It was a dog – a basset hound – stopping occasionally to sniff a paving stone or to pee on random parts of the street.

Even from a distance, Finn could see its coat was sodden and it appeared to be carrying something in its mouth. He only half watched the dog approach, his mind still largely occupied by the awful thought that he might never find a way to his father, and partly distracted by his continued inability to stuff the fighting suit arm into his bag.

The next thing he knew the hound was sniffing at his leg. Finn looked down, the dog looked up and Finn realised it was wearing false teeth. Not false teeth for dogs, if there even were such a thing, but human false teeth. Large pink and white gnashers, crammed into its mouth so that it sported the widest, most surreal grin he had ever seen.

The dog had a tag round its neck. *My name is Yappy*, it read. *If you find me, you can keep me.*

Yappy shook his wet coat, spraying salty water and tiny stones in every direction as Finn jumped out of the way.

He recognised the dog. He had met its owner about the town, spotted her coming in and out of her house over the years, had seen her walking through the town with a headscarf and a scowl as she barked at the dog.

He had a flashback to meeting her a few weeks ago, the day the Minotaur first came through. She was huddled in a doorway on Darkmouth's main street, Broken Road, while the Legend rampaged through the town. She hadn't been particularly confident in Finn's chances of stopping the creature. She'd had a point.

The dog had been in the doorway too. It didn't have those teeth then. Finn was pretty sure he'd have noticed a thing like that.

"Your owner's name is Mrs Bright, isn't it?" he said to the dog. Accepting a tickle under its sodden chin, Yappy looked up at Finn. The teeth glinted in the bright morning light.

It coughed out the dentures and, following another violent shake of its hair that left Finn's knees flecked with tiny pebbles, it trotted away, stopping only to pee at the corner before disappearing.

Finn picked up the teeth.

"What's that you've got?" asked Emmie, coming down the street, schoolbag slung over her back, woollen hat forced down over her hair.

"I'm not sure," said Finn. "I mean, they're false teeth, but I don't know why a dog had them."

"A dog had them?" she said as she reached him.

"Yeah, in its mouth."

"And you're holding them now?" said Emmie, disgusted. "Lovely."

Finn felt the slippery teeth in his hand and shuddered. He found a wad of tissues he had stuffed in his jacket, wrapped the teeth up and put them in his pocket.

"That's even lovelier," observed Emmie.

"I know who owns them," he said.

"How? Did they write their name on the gums? 'If found, please return to the mouth of whoever.'"

"No. I recognised the dog that just dropped them here. It belongs to Mrs Bright. We'll call in on the way and hand them back."

"Make sure you tell her to put them through the dishwasher first. By the way, you should brush down your trousers. You've got half the beach on them for some reason."

Finn gave them a quick scrub with his thumbs, then frowned. "Do you reckon my trousers smell sort of seaweedy?"

Emmie sniffed him. "Nah, you're OK."

"Sure?"

"Nah. I mean, yeah. There's no smell."

Finn suspected Emmie was lying just to make him feel better. Which she was.

M rs Bright wasn't home.
They knocked on her door, rang the doorbell, but she did not come out to reclaim her teeth.

"He likes Chocky-Flakes," said Emmie, leaning against the wall of the house.

"Who likes Chocky-Flakes?" asked Finn.

"The Assessor. He loves that cereal. Ate about three bowls of it last night and another three this morning. He went for a walk and came back with an ice cream and a giant grin on his face. Then he just disappeared to his room where he said he had to file his report."

Finn tried to peer through the net curtains behind Mrs Bright's barred front window. "She's not home," he said, but knocked one last time anyway.

"And he talks in his sleep. I could hear him through the bedroom door. 'Snuggles,' he said. 'Come here, Snuggles.'"

"Snuggles?" wondered Finn.

"Snuggles," Emmie confirmed. "I'd say it's his cuddly toy."

From the house neighbouring Mrs Bright's, there came the sound of locks and chains being undone. *Clank. Rattle. Clunk.* The door opened and a man popped his head out to greet Finn with a lukewarm, "Oh, it's you."

"Have you seen Mrs Bright?" Finn asked.

"No. Saw her yesterday with that dog of hers. Not since then. She's probably walking. She likes walking. Well, she does a lot of it anyway. It's hard to tell if she actually likes it. Hard to tell if she likes anything at all really."

Finn considered handing the teeth to the neighbour and asking him to hold on to them, then decided that troubling him with another person's well-worn dentures probably wasn't the right thing to do.

"If you do see Mrs Bright," Finn said, "please let her know I have something that belongs to her."

"What is it?" the neighbour asked.

"I think she'll guess. She can find me at—"

"She'll know where to find you. Everyone does. Speaking of which, any sign of your father yet?"

"Not yet, but he should be back any time soon."

The neighbour raised an eyebrow at that. "I'm Maurice Noble by the way," he said. "I went to school with your father as it happened. I wasn't at your house."

"Excuse me?" asked Finn, confused.

"That night the monsters invaded. I didn't protest at your house with all those other people. I didn't agree with it. There are still a lot of us here who would prefer to have you lot around to protect us."

"Thank you."

"Although it's true that there have been no monsters since your father disappeared."

"Well—"

"Not a single one."

"That's right, but—"

"And I'm not sure what to make of that. No one is."

Finn stuttered again, but Maurice Noble ignored that and glanced at Emmie instead, who was hanging back on the edge of the footpath. "Still, better the devil you know, I suppose. We could do with getting him back."

"We all could," said Finn.

"I'll be honest, I was hoping for something a bit more positive than that. By the way, you have a leg sticking out of your schoolbag." He disappeared back into his house, followed by the sound of locks slamming shut.

Clunk. Rattle. Clank.

Finn turned round so that Emmie could shove the leg armour of his fighting suit back into the backpack. The other leg popped out instead.

7

Finn sat in school, alongside Emmie, at a desk in a rear corner by a window, but he might as well not have been there.

His eyes and mind weren't on the whiteboard or his teacher, Mrs McDaid, nor were they on the schoolbooks flapped open in front of him. They were instead concentrating on the slight darkening of the day. Was that rain?

Under the desk, he pulled his bag closer with his feet, feeling the weight of the fighting suit stuffed into it, ready to be worn if necessary.

From the desk beside him, Conn Savage leaned over and whispered out of the side of his mouth, "Oh, looks like a couple of drops of rain out there."

Manus Savage stuck his head out from the far side of the desk, a cruel grin on his face. "Must be time for you to steal our bikes and wreck the town again."

Since the attack of the Manticores, and the Minotaur's rampage, the twins had felt a little less deadly to Finn. He had survived something worse than them. A bit worse anyway. But he did still owe them a new bike each, having commandeered theirs for himself and Emmie when being chased by the Minotaur.

He had returned the old ones, even if they were missing a few spokes. And wheels. And most of the other parts that make up a bike.

Still, Finn had prepared a really smart and funny response to the twins' jibes and was ready to slay them with it. "Well, I—"

"Quiet, Finn!" said Mrs McDaid from the other end of the room. And that was that. His teacher spared him any real anger because of what she occasionally called his "special circumstances", but Finn's face flushed nevertheless.

He reverted to staring out of the window until Emmie slid a doodle under his nose. It was of a cross-eyed Minotaur with knotted horns.

"...isn't that right, Finn?" asked Mrs McDaid.

Finn looked up to see his teacher staring at him from behind her desk, and quickly hid Emmie's notebook under his textbook as he answered. "Yes, miss."

The class murmured.

"No, Finn, it is not right. You really need to pay attention, even though we all have great sympathy for your *special circumstances...*"

This turned out to be one of the better moments of Finn's day.

Later that afternoon, Finn and Emmie wandered home again under clearing skies, through the sullen Darkmouth streets, past people with their heads down, except for when they gave accusing glances. They walked up Broken Road past its row of dusty shops. The dummies in the fashion store that looked like they'd been dragged from a skip before being dressed. The dusty bookshop with the little gathering of dead flies in the corner of the window.

They passed the damaged dental surgery where Finn's mam should have been pulling teeth, fitting crowns, removing dead nerves, and all the other things she did that Finn loved to watch.

Except his mother wasn't there. The rebuilding hadn't even begun and probably wouldn't until she had helped find a way to get Finn's father back.

They stopped for a few moments at Darkmouth's pet

shop – *Tails and Snails* – where Finn stared wistfully at its window of flapping budgies and curled-up snakes. He felt he was being dragged as far away as possible from whatever hopes he had of being a vet.

They passed the police station with the now-dead flowers left at its entrance for Sergeant Doyle, grievously wounded saving Finn and Emmie, and who now lay in a city hospital, having finally got out of Darkmouth – but not in the way he would have liked.

The town had been sent a replacement, who hid out so effectively that most people were still unsure whether the new sergeant was a man or woman, bearded or clean-shaven, brave or scared.

"I should've stopped Mr Glad," said Finn, idling at the front of the police station.

"You did," said Emmie.

"Not in time to stop Sergeant Doyle getting badly hurt, though. Or half the town destroyed."

"Seriously, you fought a Minotaur. You went to the Infested Side. You've really got to stop beating yourself up over the whole thing." She jumped at him and, laughing, gave him a friendly punch on the arm. "That's *my* job."

Emmie ran on ahead and Finn followed, rubbing his arm and wondering how much more it would have stung if it had been an *unfriendly* punch. When they reached the corner where their streets met, Finn saw that Estravon the Assessor was parked up at the front of his house, talking to his mother.

"Maybe it's good news," said Emmie.

"It's not," said Finn as they approached slowly.

"How do you know?"

"Because he hasn't even got out of the car," said Finn, "and he's kept his engine running. I think he's ready to leave here quickly."

They arrived to hear the Assessor methodically reading the words on a piece of paper stretched across his lap. Even with his face down, his head was crammed up against the roof of the car.

"The Council of Twelve has read the Assessor's report and met again on this matter," Finn heard him say as he and Emmie arrived.

"If this was something positive, you'd be inside tucking into the biscuits," said Clara. "So, just get on with telling us whatever bad news is on that page."

Estravon cleared his throat and continued, clearly hoping that he'd be allowed to do so without interruption so he could just make his escape. "Before this tragic occurrence in Darkmouth, Hugo the Great was due to become a member of the Twelve, a true reward for a real hero. This is our loss as much as yours."

"You really think so?" Clara asked.

"The Council of Twelve has accepted that Hugo acted out of the highest bravery, which will be duly noted in a later, official capacity, according to section 19, clause..." The Assessor looked at them out of the corner of his eye, noted the impatience on the faces of his audience and skipped on a little.

"Nevertheless, it is with the deepest regret that we must conclude that Hugo is most likely..." Estravon cleared his throat, "...dead."

Finn's mouth flopped open.

Emmie's head dropped.

Estravon paused, as if expecting a reaction or a follow-up question. All that came was a calm, stern instruction from Finn's mam.

"Just keep reading," she said.

"Under rule 123a, paragraph 14, it is required that an appropriate time must pass before a lost Legend Hunter is officially declared dead and a full-time replacement Legend Hunter brought in."

"And the appropriate time is?" asked Clara.

"Forty-eight hours."

Finn's mouth flopped open a little more, so that his jaw felt like it might fall from its hinge.

"Two days?" exclaimed Emmie, but Clara simply put a hand up to quieten her, as if she was keeping her fury snarling behind a locked door for when she really needed it.

"A little less than two days, to be accurate," said Estravon. "You know, with the gap between the news being passed to me and then me delivering it onwards to yourselves."

"And what happens to us?" asked Clara.

"Reassignment," said Estravon.

"Reassignment?" said Finn. "To another town?"

"No, no. Another house in Darkmouth. Where Steve and Emmie are at the moment."

Steve appeared round the corner, a bounce in his step that suggested he had absolutely no idea what had just happened. "You all sunbathing?" he asked.

Clara's glare hit him like a blastwave.

"What?" Steve asked.

"You wanted a Blighted Village to call your own and you finally got it," Clara said to him, still remarkably calm on the surface even though her anger was so very clear.

"Actually," said Estravon the Assessor, bumping his

head on the car ceiling, "that's not quite how it works."

"Someone is going to have to rewind this conversation and start from the beginning," said Steve, "because I have no idea what you're going on about."

"All those years of living with their rules, of living with their demands and restrictions," added Clara, "and this is how we're repaid. Eviction."

"Reassignment," clarified Estravon.

Clara ignored him. "So, congratulations, Steve; unless Hugo comes back within forty-eight hours, we're swapping houses. I hope you like vacuuming corridors because you're going to be doing a lot of it."

Calculating that this was his moment to escape, Estravon took his chance and put his foot down so the car lurched on to the quiet road, paused at the corner and, with a belch from the exhaust, disappeared from view. They could hear the engine fading away into the town, the fumes of its exhaust still acrid in the air.

Finn had already gone into his house and was heading straight for the library. He had less than two days to find the map. To find his father.

8

It was the next morning, but Finn had no idea what time it was exactly. Neither did he notice Emmie's arrival. He was at the door between the main house and the Long Hall. It was propped open with books, and the whole corridor to the library was strewn with pages, piles of paper arranged in haphazard order.

As Emmie approached, Finn disappeared into a side room before emerging with another armful of candidates to work through. Not able to see where he was going, he tripped over a mound of atlases, sending himself one way and paper the other.

"Have you been awake all night, Finn?"

Finn picked himself up, shaking off her helping hand, swatting a small hardback off his shoulder until he stood staring at the mess he'd created.

"No, of course not," he said, sifting through the pages of tattered, yellowing books that had disintegrated as they hit the floor.

"Did you sleep here, though?"

"No! Well, a bit," he admitted. "My mam forced me to bed eventually. I got up early. We've only three days to find something." He stopped himself, looked at the watch given to him by the Assessor, the tiny daggers slowly working their way round an ivory face. "Actually, not much more than a full day now."

"But you've been in the library pretty much since the Assessor said your dad was, you know, erm..."

"You can say it," Finn said tersely. "You can say 'dead', Emmie. Go on. Because it doesn't matter. It's not true."

Emmie didn't say the word. "You must be exhausted."

"I can't stop," he said, biting his lip. "Dad told me I wouldn't. I can't."

Above them, a strip light flickered and died. Finn tutted and immediately headed to the narrowest door in the corridor which had S4 hand-painted on it. Emmie followed, hovering outside the door while Finn rooted around fretfully in search of a new bulb.

"We're out. Do you have any bulbs at your house?" he asked.

"Come on, we'll get breakfast before school," said Emmie.

"We need to keep the place lit up, so we don't miss anything," he replied.

"Finn—"

"Can you get me a bulb from your house or can't you?"

Emmie looked up at the Long Hall's ceiling. "Doubt it. These are strip lights, like you'd have in an office or something. I live in a normal house. Not a *crazy* house like this."

Silence.

They both paused for a moment to appreciate the inadvertent clumsiness of what she had said and the words that were left hanging there: she didn't live in a crazy house like this *for now*.

Emmie coughed.

Finn felt his hopes sink even more.

Emmie looked at the lettering on the door and pushed her head in to find a room crammed with boxes, tools, dusty and rusting equipment. "So, what does S4 stand for anyway?"

"It's a storage room," explained Finn.

"Just junk and stuff?"

Finn stood with hands on hips, looking around, admitting defeat in the search for a new bulb. "Yeah, and stuff. Do you think I should just give up searching?"

"No, there must be one here somewhere," said Emmie, squeezing past him and rooting through the overcrowded shelves. She pushed aside some boxes to see what lay behind before she belatedly realised what Finn had actually meant. "No, Finn, I don't think you should stop searching for the map."

"What if the Assessor's right, though? What if there is no map?"

"They didn't *find* one," said Emmie. "There's a big difference." She kept rummaging through the clutter, as much to move on the conversation as in the hope of finding any light bulbs. She pawed at a couple of things as she went. A ship's wheel with rusted wrenches taped to each handle. What might have been a satellite dish made out of a roasting dish, tinfoil and a spoon.

She knocked against something propped on a shelf and just about caught it before it hit the floor. A tin box attached to a circuit board, it had a couple of old brass light switches fixed on to it and what looked like an egg whisk protruding from one end.

"What's this, Finn?"

"An egg whisk, I think."

"No," said Emmie, "what is this whole thing? What does it do?"

"Actually, my dad loves this," said Finn, taking it from her and examining it. "It's a Legend Spotter. It was used years ago, before they invented scanners to track Legends down. Come on, I'll show you."

He headed quickly to the library, pushing the door through a carpet of papers and books, and carefully picked his way to the centre of the room. Emmie followed.

"Wait there, by the wall," Finn told her while he found a switch on the Spotter's underside and thumbed it for a moment. "Now turn off the lights. All of them."

Emmie flicked off each of the dozen or so switches, section by section, until the library was in total darkness. She promptly fell over a pile of maps as she tried to return to Finn.

"You OK?" asked Finn.

"This had better be good, Finn. I think I've broken a tooth."

"It is. I promise." He pressed the button and the device's whisk glowed a weak orange, hardly enough to illuminate his chest.

"Wow, great trick," said Emmie, her sarcasm carrying across the darkness. "Halloween must be a blast in this house."

"Just wait."

Then it began. It was hard to perceive at first, but across the span of the room, on its shelves, in spots along the floor, they began to make out dull smudges of orange light. Quickly, each flicker grew in intensity until the room was lit solely by the glowing balls of Legends caught over the decades and now scattered across the shelves and floor of the library. The unbroken jars, which each housed a desiccated ball of a creature caught invading Darkmouth, were like glow-worms in a cave, the still lights fostering an eerie calm.

"That is pretty cool actually," Emmie said.

"If something's been on the Infested Side or in a gateway, this will identify it," Finn explained. "We use scanners now, so this hasn't been used to track down a Legend in years, but Mam and Dad sometimes have their dinner here on Valentine's Day. My dad calls it 'the

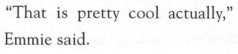

Planetarium'. Apparently, this is how he asked Mam to marry him. He spelled it out on the floor in glowing desiccated Legends."

In the galaxy of orange lights, Emmie picked her way across the floor to where Finn stood and they enjoyed the silence and surprising beauty to be found in the glowing husks of savage creatures from a parallel world.

"I can see why they found it romantic," said Emmie.

Finn moved away a step, a flush of heat running through his face. "I'll turn the lights back on."

He started back towards the wall and its light switches, while he looked again for the on/off button of the Spotter.

"Wait," said Emmie, looking at him. "The orange."

Finn looked down at himself and for the first time realised he was lit up; a radioactive glow was spreading across his skin, emanating from his chest, but pushing out of his sleeves, the neck of his sweater, the gap between his trousers and socks.

"That's weird," he said, holding his hands out to examine them. "But I was there, on the Infested Side, so I suppose that's why I—"

"No," said Emmie, "not you. What's that beside you?"

Finn looked around, unsure for a moment what she was referring to. Then he saw his schoolbag propped up on a chair beside him, where he had left it the day before. From inside leaked a bright orange glow.

He put the Legend Spotter down, reached carefully into his bag and pulled out Mrs Bright's false teeth. Directly under the device, their orange was deeper, more vivid than any other in the room. The colour had the newness of fresh paint.

"I don't get it," said Emmie. "What's that mean? That Mrs Bright was a Legend?"

Finn thought of the grains of sand that had clung to Yappy's paws and the damp fringes of its coat. He tried to make connections where none seemed obvious. All the while, the tiny echo of a message began to intrude on his thoughts.

Light up the house.

"Is it possible that Mrs Bright…?" he muttered. "Were her teeth…?"

Light up the house.

"Is that what the message really means?" he continued, only half audible to Emmie. The connections were forming in his mind, solidifying out of mist.

"OK, Finn, you're going to have to make a bit more sense because I don't—" Emmie stopped, eyes growing wide as she worked it out too. "*Oh,*" she said.

Finn began to wander the room, waving the Legend Spotter up, down, left, right, diagonally, sweeping across the floor.

"*Light up the house,*" he said as he passed Emmie, holding it above his head. "That's what the note from my dad said. But maybe we've been lighting it up in the wrong way. Maybe it's been about this all along." He held the Legend Spotter upright.

Still, Finn couldn't quite figure it out. "It just seems to be the usual desiccated Legends here. Mrs Bright's teeth must have been on the Infested Side somehow or touched it in some way. Maybe she got caught up in the Manticore attack. Half the town would probably light up if we waved this at them."

"Or she could have got caught up in a gateway," suggested Emmie. "Except there's been no gateway in weeks."

Finn ran the Spotter across the curving length of a shelf, where the petrified Legends glowed a little brighter as he passed, dimmed slightly as he left them behind. "I just don't see anything out of the ordinary," he said.

"But this is only one room, Finn," said Emmie. "The note in the box said to light up the house."

"You're right!" Finn strode past her towards the door

to the Long Hall and began sweeping along the walls, the ceiling, the doors, and waving the Spotter into each room they passed.

Still, they nearly missed it. It was weak, almost imperceptible, a tiny smudge in the dark registering in the corner of their vision. But Finn noticed it first and his heart rapped on his ribs when he did. He nudged Emmie to follow him to the wall.

The closer they got, the brighter it glowed.

Squinting, unable to quite make out any detail, Finn reached out a finger and placed it on the spot. He felt the slight bend of canvas, the roughness of paint.

"Turn on the lights, Emmie."

She palmed her way across the wall until she found the switch. The bulbs flared in a race along the corridor, Finn's and Emmie's eyes briefly recoiling at the sudden intrusion of bright light. As they refocused, Finn kept his finger on the painting for a moment more.

Niall Blacktongue gazed directly at Finn's fingertip.

Finn pulled his finger away to reveal a painted table on which were scattered a few objects, including books, a magnifying glass, a compass, a small mirror.

In the mirror was the reflection of a map.

On the map was an X.

Finn looked at it, then back to his grandfather's face. Where there had only ever seemed to be meekness, a sagging under the weight of responsibility, now he looked relieved, unburdened, free finally of a great secret kept for so many years.

Finn forgot to breathe for a moment and, when he finally remembered, it came with a quiet utterance of relief.

"Found it," he said.

'The Arrival of the Human'
From *The Chronicles of the Sky's Collapse*,
as told by inhabitants of the Infested Side

THIRTY YEARS AGO

Humans smell.

It is a bad smell. It is not like the intoxicating sweetness of a Pantera, whose scent lures victims to its lair, the horror its victims feel as they are eaten alive offset only by their fervent hope that it bites off their nose last of all because its fragrance really is that delightful.

To be fair to humans, they don't smell as putrid as the vile Nuppeppō, those blob-like creatures whose odour was in ancient times compared to rotting flesh until it was realised that covering yourself in rotting flesh was far preferable to getting close to a Nuppeppō, not that anyone has been close to a Nuppeppō in a millennium. They are forced to live high in the mountains, far from the rest of us, under strict orders to stay downwind at all times.

No, humans smell of damp skin; of the cheese on their feet and the dandruff on their shoulders; of the oils in their hair and food in their teeth. They smell of fear, panic, inevitable death. And sausages.

They all smell of sausages.

Stooping to enter the cell of the human, Niall Blacktongue, the great and ghastly Gantrua inhaled. He drew the air molecules past the metal grille across his face, and deep into his cavernous lungs, because he wanted to taste the very Promised World he would one day take as his own. Only then did he speak. And only two words.

"Shut. Up."

But the human did not shut up. Instead, he kept babbling, words tumbling from his mouth in a torrent, just as he had done for the two years since he arrived there.

"Ljensboytareskypartljensboytareskypartljensboy tareskypartljensboytareskypartljensboytareskypart…"

"He is still like this?" Gantrua asked of the Hogboon guard half squashed against the wall by Gantrua's bulk.

"Yes, master," replied the guard.

"The same nonsense over and over?"

"And over. And over. Every day for the two years since he came here, Your Hulkness," confirmed the Hogboon. "Even as he eats, which is rarely. Although

I'm not sure what's not to like about a plate of juicy scaldgrubs."

On the ground, a plate of fat, spiky maggots writhed untouched.

"Ljensboytareskypartljensboytareskypartljensboy tareskypartljensboytareskypartljensboytareskypart," continued Niall Blacktongue.

Gantrua listened. Closed his eyes to take in the sound. Licked his lips to ingest any vapours of the Promised World. "He must stay here," he said finally.

"I hadn't planned to take him anywhere else, oh most gracious and wise and muscly sire."

"Ljensboytareskypartljensboytareskypartljensboy tareskypartljensboytareskypart."

Gantrua bent low, the creak of leather and armour filling the room, and with a crooked finger lifted Niall Blacktongue's chin and pulled a talon across the skin that had melted in the human's great explosion, when energy had burst forth from his seemingly puny body and annihilated half of Gantrua's army. He looked into Blacktongue's eyes, where the colour had been blasted away. Sighing in frustration, he released the human's head to flop back into his chin, stood and ducked to exit the cell.

The human recommenced his mantra.

"Ljensboytareskypartljensboytareskypartljensboy tareskypartljensboytareskypartljensboytareskypart."

"You must do everything in your power to keep this human alive until he is better," Gantrua instructed the Hogboon.

"Aye," said the shaking Hogboon.

"And, when he is better, I will kill him."

Gantrua left the tower, knocking a chunk from the stone frame of the door as he emerged into the world outside. It was just another gouge in a tower already mutilated and crumbling where its roof touched the sky.

At its entrance, two Fomorian guards stood to attention. Gantrua ignored them, instead mounting the back of his Sleipnir, which snorted and bucked until he grabbed it firmly by the throat to calm it, then dug his heels into its flank to spur its eight legs onwards.

He rode away from the tower, through a long rank of heavily armed Fomorians. Then another.

And more still. Each parted to make way, until he was gone, leaving behind hundreds of Fomorians, armed, nervous, massed in wide rings of might round the tower and its single human prisoner.

9

Finn shaded his phone's screen from the morning sunshine, covering it with the palm of his hand to better see the picture of the map on it. He zoomed in, moved the image around, then lifted his head again to scan the grassy cliff he and Emmie were standing on. Ahead was spread out a glistening green sea. Away to their left, the buildings and walls of Darkmouth huddled up against each other as if afraid. And, below their feet, lush but uneven ground.

Nothing else.

"There should be something here," said Finn, disappointment tightening his voice. "The X says it's in the centre of this area somewhere. See?" He pointed at the picture.

Emmie squinted at it. "No. Sorry."

Since finding the clue hardly an hour ago, Finn had

feared another dead end. They had been wrong so many times already. So, they had agreed they should check this clue out alone, to say they were off to school as always, an illusion of normality even when their world had been turned upside down. No worrying Finn's mother. No raised hopes. No drama. No Assessor. No Steve. No one to disappoint but themselves.

The two searched again, Finn's bag jolting on his back, the clatter and clash of the fighting suit stuffed inside, as he marched through clumps of grass, pushed aside weeds with his feet, carefully lifted knots of thorns.

They criss-crossed the cliff, looking for something, anything.

"Anything?" Finn shouted to Emmie.

"Nothing!" she shouted back.

The table in the painting had featured some objects that had seemed relevant and a few that didn't. There was the mirror and its map obviously. There was also a compass pointing south-east, which happened to be the direction from the house to this crest of cliff. There were two books without titles, but one looked quite like the thin notebook Finn had found which had Niall Blacktongue's initials on it. He had brought that notebook with him this morning, just in case it helped.

But there were other things in the painting. A magnifying glass, some coins, a feather in an ink pot. They could have meant anything or everything. Or nothing at all.

Yet the map itself, while spare in details, seemed clear. This was where they were supposed to be. Maybe.

On the cliff edge was a crumbling stone hut, which locals called the Look-out Post, but only because "Look out!" were someone's last words before being grabbed by a Legend here a hundred years ago.

Emmie joined him, wincing at the stench of wee in the hut. Finn looked inside the simple old shelter, then outside it, where an orange life jacket and a solid buoyancy ring were placed in case someone fell into the sea.

"You sure this is the right place?" Emmie asked.

Finn wasn't sure at all. "Yes," he said.

Heads down, they made another sweep of the terrain. Finn could feel his breath growing laboured with stress, the nagging sense of anger that he'd fooled himself into believing this was it. He stopped at a patch of grass and weeds, darkened as if from some old campfire or splash of poison. Poking at it with his fingers, he caught himself

on a thorn which scratched his right wrist and tore free a coloured rope wristband he'd once made for himself when he was supposed to be doing his homework.

He was licking at the scratch as he met up with Emmie again.

She put her hands in her pockets, glanced around so she didn't have to catch his eye. "We could always—"

"We're not telling your dad, Emmie."

"OK. Then maybe—"

"Or my mam. Definitely not my mam."

They remained on the same spot, Finn half hoping something would just come to him.

"Maybe it's hidden," said Emmie. "Or buried and grown over."

"If it is, the map isn't very precise," said Finn, kicking at the hard ground with his heel. "We'd probably dig up half this cliff before we found anything."

A sound drifted across the breeze and reached their ears.

Yap.

It was coming from some distance away.

Yap. Yap.

It was coming from *below* them.

Yap. Yap. Yap.

"Do you hear that dog?" Finn said to Emmie as he marched off towards the edge of the cliff.

He jogged to where the grass began to rise up to meet the plunging edge, then dropped on to his belly and peered over the cliff at the crescent of rock-strewn beach at its base. Emmie flopped on the grass beside him. Finn pointed at a mound of rubble. A buckle in the cliff. The glimpse of a large hole crumpling under the weight it shouldered. And a basset hound peeing at the entrance.

"That's Yappy, the dog with the teeth," Finn said.

"That's why he was covered in salty water and bits of sand," said Emmie.

The giddiness of hope rose inside Finn again. "That's it. Whatever we're supposed to find, it's in there."

inn and Emmie followed the sound of running water. Finn rummaged through his bag, pushing aside the miscellaneous objects stuffed in there – fighting suit, a radio, his lunchbox, fruit, books. He fished out a torch. Under its narrow light, the two of them shared a look that meant they had heard this sound before. But there had been no water then. Only the fizzing light of a gateway between this world and the other.

They squeezed through the ever-narrowing rock, ducking a little as the roof came down to meet them. The sound encouraged them to keep moving forward. It was the sound of promise, of a way to Finn's father. To Finn, it was not just the sound of magic. It was the sound of hope.

In fact, it was just the sound of water after all. Nothing more. Nothing less. At the back of the cave, the most meagre of waterfalls was leaking through the rock and running into a small pool at the foot of the wall.

Finn threw a groan about the chamber, his deep frustration bouncing about every corner of the cave, echoing back at him for a while after he closed his mouth, as if his frustration was so intense it had become bigger than him, taken on a life of its own.

Excitement left him and weariness flooded in. Another dead end. The deadest of ends.

He sat back against the cave wall, sliding down to his haunches, the torch dropping by his side and leaving them in near-total darkness, save for the muted beam of light creeping across the floor. Catching the edge of something. A reflection. Low down and small, but sharp.

Emmie spotted it.

Without explaining, she picked the torch from the floor and pointed it towards the reflection. Light glinted back at them. A sparkle.

Finn's expression turned from one of defeat into curiosity. He pushed himself to his feet and together they moved to a hollow low in the wall, worn away behind a large stone.

Growing in it was a small crop of crystals.

"Could they be...?" asked Emmie.

"The same crystals that make gateways?" queried Finn. "They can't be. They only grow on the Infested Side, don't they? These have to be just ordinary, everyday crystals."

"Ordinary, everyday crystals in a cave marked on a map hidden for decades in a missing Legend Hunter's painting?" she replied.

"OK, maybe not," admitted Finn.

They lay flat on the ground to examine the crystals more closely, and saw that these didn't have the diamond purity of the ones that had been brought to Darkmouth by Legends. Their reflections were instead dulled by the coating on each of them, a thin layer picked up from growing through what seemed to be fine dark red dust in the hollowed-out rock at their roots.

But, under the torchlight, another quality became apparent.

"It's alive," said Emmie, pressing her beam up to the tallest crystal. Inside was a smokiness that writhed slowly, rising to the top, falling gently again, in constant motion.

Finn reached out to pull at the crystal.

"Should you do that?" asked Emmie.

Finn shrugged. "I don't know what more could go wrong."

Actually, in his head, he had a lengthy list of things that could go wrong, but thought twice about sharing it.

Finn took hold of the crystal. He expected it to resist,

but instead it came away easily, softly releasing itself from the cave wall as if ripe, like an apple ready to be plucked.

He stood up straight, holding the crystal high under the torchlight. Within it were tendrils of smoke, gentle in their movement. The finest coating of scarlet dust clung to the sweat of his palms. He touched the dust with a finger: it seemed dried in, more like clay than sand.

Emmie lay beside the hollow for a few seconds longer before pushing herself up from the cave floor too.

"Do you think these might open a gateway, to help us get to Dad?" asked Finn, still examining the crystal.

"It's probably impossible," said Emmie, pointing her torch up under Finn's chin, so that long shadows were cast from his ridged brow. "But we should definitely try it."

"Maybe we should bring it back to the library," he suggested. "Dad went through a gateway there and that would open it to the same spot on the Infested Side. He might be waiting there for us. But you can't tell anyone, Emmie. Not a soul."

"I'm afraid that's a bit too late," said a voice in the darkness.

11

"**B**esides," the voice went on, "I can't begin to tell you how many rules it would violate."

Emmie swung her torch and illuminated Estravon the Assessor.

"Well, I *could* tell you how many rules it would violate, but we'd be here all day," he said. "All that matters is that you have to hand that crystal over. Now."

Estravon stepped forward so quickly that Finn hardly had time to close his grip on the crystal, and instead found surprisingly strong fingers prising it from his grasp. Finn felt immediate shame at the struggle being so short, his prize so easily lost.

"You can't take that," protested Emmie.

"I *have* to take it," said Estravon, indignant, "according to rule 43b of section 5 of the, oh, stop rolling your eyes, young lady. The rules matter. There'd be anarchy without the rules. There'd be people running around doing

whatever they wanted without recourse to the proper procedures and, if you doubt me, then just have a look at where we've all been led this morning."

"I need that crystal," said Finn. "It might help me get to my dad."

Estravon stood back, examining the crystal under his torch's light. He appeared genuinely curious, as if this discovery was as much of a surprise to him as it was to Finn and Emmie. "Well, that is an odd one. Some town this, isn't it? Full of surprises. I found that ice-cream shop on the harbour too. Tasty. They do an amazing nutty chocolate sauce."

"How did you know we were here?" asked Emmie.

"Finn told me," answered Estravon, still closely examining the crystal. "Well, his watch did. There's a tracking device in it."

Finn felt the fat watch on his wrist and then disgust ran through him at having fallen so easily for the Assessor's camaraderie. Finn had led him right to them. He really needed to be more careful in future.

"I'll be honest," Estravon continued, "I wasn't sure you would find anything, but when doing an assessment it always pays to be a couple of steps ahead just in case. I did have to sleep in my car on a country lane outside the town while I waited, though. A mission like this requires a little subterfuge, you see. And a measure of discomfort and physical sacrifice. Plus, the only hotel in Darkmouth has been closed for years so I didn't have much choice."

Estravon pulled a small plastic bag from his suit, placed the crystal into it, zipped the bag shut and put it back in his jacket pocket. He then looked at his hands and the blood-red residue left behind.

"Do you think it's one of the gateway crystals?" asked Finn, feeling helpless now, and switching to a softer approach in the hope of persuading the Assessor to let him try it out. "Because there are more. We could use them to send in a rescue party."

"More of the crystals?" said the Assessor, interest piqued.

Finn had immediately failed in treading more carefully.

The Assessor motioned them to move aside so he could stoop to examine the hollow in the rock. "There's only one more here," said Estravon.

Finn frowned – but Emmie shot him a look while putting a finger to her mouth.

Bending down, Estravon pushed at the crystal with his bare finger, examining the powder on the tip of his finger. "Did you ever have sherbet?" he asked them, a grin filling his face. "I doubt this tastes too good, though. There we go."

He eased the jewel-like object from the rock with little effort. The hollow was bare of crystals now, except for a couple of tiny buds poking through the film of red dust that clung to the rock.

"So?" asked Finn. "Do you think we should use them to send a rescue party?"

"Oh, I doubt it," Estravon said cheerily. He took the plastic bag out and added the crystal to the other, before tucking them both away again in his suit jacket. "Aside from the specific risk-assessment regulation forbidding rescue parties, I'm not sure it's going to matter anyway. Yes, they're crystals, but they're probably just standard ones with nothing at all to do with gateways. After all, if crystals were to just pop up and open gateways all the time *that* would be a health-and-safety nightmare."

Holding the torch under his armpit, he inspected the dust on his hands before giving them a clap in an effort to be rid of it. He didn't appear satisfied so took out a small bottle of hand soap, squidged it on his palms, gave them a clean and then grabbed his torch again to point it towards the way out.

"We have to see what the crystals do," insisted Finn.

"Don't worry, we'll run tests just to be conclusive," said Estravon. "Although, when I say *we* will run tests, I obviously don't mean *you*. Now it's time to go. Your co-operation would be appreciated. For the report and all of that."

Sulking, angry, Finn started for the exit, with Emmie and the Assessor following. They emerged into the daylight at the base of the cliff, where Yappy sniffed busily at the stones littering the entrance. Narrowing their eyes to the brightness, they made their way unsteadily across the stones, where crashing waves splashed at them, until they rounded the small rocky headland. There, Emmie walked closely alongside the Assessor.

"You know I came here to Darkmouth with my dad," she said. "We spied on Finn's family."

"Yes. I appreciate that," said Estravon. "Now we do need to get a move on."

"I haven't stopped spying, you know," Emmie continued. "Actually, there are a couple of things I could tell you about what's happening here that you really should know."

"Watch your step," he said, holding her elbow. "Seaweed."

"Number one," she said, pulling her arm away. "That dog that was sniffing about at the cave? Its owner was in contact with the Infested Side. Definitely. And she's been missing ever since. That has to be important."

Somewhere behind them, Yappy yapped.

"I'm not sure that's very likely," said Estravon.

"Number two," Emmie said, walking on. "Has it occurred to you to ask us how we even found that cave in the first place? Surely that's quite important for your assessment."

Back towards the cave, out of sight, the dog was yapping incessantly. "I had fully planned to investigate that particular..." The Assessor stopped and looked around, distracted.

The dog kept barking.

"Where's the boy gone?" he asked.

"Oh yeah," said Emmie. "Maybe there's a third thing I should have mentioned. It's about the crystals."

A smile crept across her face as she held a palm up to display the red, dusty residue clinging to it. But she wasn't holding a crystal. "There might have been three of them," she said.

Estravon ran back towards the cave.

"Shush, Yappy," Finn begged the dog as he clambered over the mound at the cave entrance.

Yap, replied Yappy. *Yap. Yap. Yapyapyap.*

Pushing towards the darkness, Finn wished he hadn't given his torch to Emmie. As any natural light became choked off, he had to trust his hands, the feel of the walls as they narrowed either side. His head scraped the roof of the cave, causing him to wince in pain.

In his pocket was the crystal that Emmie had shoved into his hand as they were leaving the cave. She had distracted Estravon while rounding the headland, and Finn had dashed back, the waves drowning out the clatter of the armour in his bag, but not the drumbeat of his heart in his ears.

Finn knew he would need to make this count. It was his only chance. He was going to try and open a gateway with the crystal. At least they would know there

and then if it would work.

He felt the cave wall open up in front of him, sensed the sound suddenly released to bounce round the high roof of the chamber. He gripped the crystal tight, making sure he didn't drop it in the near-total darkness.

As his eyes tried to adjust a little, Finn recalled what he had seen when Mr Glad had opened a gateway, the day his father disappeared. He remembered how Mr Glad had searched for a snag in the air on which to attach the crystal. Broonie had done the same thing, reaching up and scraping down an invisible divide until he found one and opened a way into the Infested Side.

From outside the cave, he heard Yappy yapping and Estravon shouting.

Hurriedly, Finn pushed the crystal into his palm. It felt sleeker than the dust coating suggested it would, a little greasy compared to the clear crystals he'd held before. Yet his grip felt more secure, and the crystal stayed in his hand so that he could relax it a little, hold it out flat and run his other hand down the empty air in search of something in nothing.

The scramble of feet coming through the cave grew louder; the intrusion of torchlight began to dance in the chamber.

Finn searched for a snag. No luck. He tried again. It still wouldn't take.

Light flared fully into the room.

"This will all go in my report—" shouted Estravon.

"Wait!" Finn shouted. "I've got it."

He had caught the crystal on something. Slowly, he spread his fingers and opened his palm to let the crystal go, while keeping the other hand cupped underneath, ready to catch it should it fall. But it didn't budge from its invisible hook.

Under the white light of two torches, Finn could see the edges of the crystal become agitated, the smokiness accelerating inside. Where his skin met the crystal, it felt almost ticklish, as if it was writhing into position.

Briefly, he laughed at the impossibility of that while turning his head to Emmie, whose eyes were wide with encouragement. Estravon stepped between them, sporting a look of deep unhappiness. "That is not good," the Assessor said. "That is not good at all."

The tickle turned into a crackle on Finn's palm. He moved his hand to separate it from the crystal, but it didn't come away. His skin felt glued to the air.

Finn stopped laughing. "Erm, Emmie..." he said.

She stepped towards him, halting as the crystal sparked a little.

Finn felt heat flow through his right hand. With his left, he pulled at the stuck wrist, but couldn't release it.

"What's going on, Finn?" enquired Emmie, torch lighting up his panic.

The red crystal crackled, fizzed in his palm, like a trapped firework ready to explode.

"Put that crystal down," demanded the Assessor.

"I can't!" shouted Finn.

"Put. It. Down. Now."

"I'm trying to!"

A judder of energy shot up his arm, through his torso, sparked through his backpack, wracking his body, contorting him, sending a shock through him so total he couldn't even scream. It felt like his body had been taken hold of by an injection of fire into his shoulder, his chest, into every vein, every cell of his arm.

With the crack of a detonation, Finn was fired across the chamber and into the opposite wall. For a moment, he was out. Gone. As if he'd been switched off.

Then he jolted back into consciousness, winded, gulping for air. And his vision was dominated by a pulsating glow of red.

He shook his head. Out of the corner of his eye, he saw Emmie and Estravon standing rigid, gawping. But they weren't looking at him.

They were looking at the great blood-red gateway Finn had opened in the cave.

13

This gateway was different to any Finn had seen before. It wasn't just that its colour was red when gateways were usually golden. It was the way the energy moved at its edges, grinding rather than groaning. It didn't sparkle and flow, but writhed. Thick jagged tendrils poured back into the opening as if the gateway was consuming itself, feeding off its own energy. It was as if the effort of staying open caused it terrible agony.

Estravon looked like he couldn't decide if he should be annoyed or astonished by this turn of events. "That. Is. Incredible," he said, a palm to his forehead. "And terrible. And something I never thought I'd see in my lifetime. And you two are in so much trouble."

Shading his eyes from the red light, Finn picked himself carefully off the ground and pushed away from the rock wall he had been flung against. He ached, but luckily his backpack had taken the force of the blow.

Emmie stepped forward to help him, but touching him sent a burst of static through her fingers, repelling her. "Well, that's weird," she said. "Are you OK?"

That was the truly strange thing. Right at that moment, Finn felt better than OK. He felt extraordinary. He felt wonderful. Amazing. Fantastic. Like nothing could ever hold him back again. It was a glimpse of perfection. Of ecstasy. Of strength he had never experienced before.

Then he felt really, really awful.

A headache hit him like a frying pan and he held his head because he felt it was about to explode. Or implode. Or both at the same time.

As Finn watched the gateway, even the tiniest movement made his head feel like it was a car in a crusher at the precise moment all its windows explode.

"You are *not* going into that gateway," said Estravon, manoeuvring between Finn and the open portal.

"I don't want to—" Finn tried to reply weakly.

"And you had better hope nothing comes *out*," added the Assessor.

In Finn's backpack, his radio clicked. A ripple of static.

"We don't know if that is a gateway to the Infested Side," said Estravon. "It's not like any I've ever read about."

The gateway's tendrils writhed at its edges, slowly, steadily eating itself so that it shrank gradually but noticeably. Finn couldn't quite believe he had opened a gateway – a very strange gateway – but it had worked. He hadn't really thought about what should happen next.

"What do we do?" started Emmie.

Finn's radio crackled again. Hearing it, with some effort Finn pulled the backpack forward, fumbled inside it.

"What do we do?" Estravon responded to Emmie, over the noise of the groaning gateway. "We hope nothing comes out. There's not much else to do. We're certainly not going in."

Another crunching from the gateway. Another burst of static from the radio in Finn's hand. "I don't want to go in," he said again.

"It would be a really stupid idea anyway," said Estravon. "Although I'm beginning to think you might specialise in stupid ideas."

"I just needed to know if the crystal worked," said Finn, every word stabbing at his mind.

The gateway continued to feed on itself, a scar in the world, puckering and ragged but diminishing.

"I think it's getting smaller," said Emmie.

Finn tried to stand, but his legs buckled and he collapsed to his knees, exhausted. Emmie tried to catch him. A bristling electrical charge forced her away again. Finn sank further, defeated, in the fading light.

There was a crackle from the radio.

A voice.

Distant. Buried under static.

Finn pressed the radio to his ear, tried to catch the words.

"I'm going to need a lot of extra pages for this report," said Estravon.

The voice came back again. **"This— is——"**

"A couple of different colour pens, I'd imagine."

"Quiet!" demanded Finn, turning up the radio to its highest volume and holding it outwards so they could all hear the voice almost lost beneath an electronic *hiss* and the grinding of the gateway.

"Hew— of Dar—outh— If you hear this—"

Then there was only static again. Uniform. Undisturbed.

"Dad?" said Finn, pressing the button, croaking into the handset. "Dad? We're here. Dad, answer me!"

No response. The only sound in the chamber was the grumble and suck of the gateway as it finally began to give up its fight to stay open. The radio was silent, the message cut off.

Finn hauled himself up, pulled his backpack on. He'd been scared before. He'd been scared by small things, big things, things he knew he shouldn't be scared of and things he knew he should be really, really scared of. And he was scared now.

He didn't know what he should do next. Go in. Stay out. Wait. The gateway was shrinking fast now. Time to make a decision.

"You're not going in," Estravon told him.

"You heard my dad," said Finn. "You know he's alive now. We have to help him."

"We will try, after—"

"I just wanted to test the crystal," said Finn, clarity pushing its way through his headache at last. "To see if it worked so we could get him."

"OK," said Estravon. "I'll admit that might have been Hugo on the radio. That he may be alive over there."

He looked at the gateway, which was flexing more wildly now, apparently exhausting itself.

"Promise him you'll do your best to get his dad," said Emmie.

Estravon rubbed his chin. "I'll try."

"Promise," repeated Emmie.

"Right, I promise I'll do what I can. No more silly tricks. No more sneaking around. And, for heaven's sake, no more rule-breaking, got it?"

Finn contemplated that. He had heard his father's voice. He was alive. Finn would be able to tell his mam that, give her some good news finally. Help would come. They would rescue him. "I need to get Dad back. And you'll keep your promise to help?"

"I'll help," said Estravon. "As long as you promise you won't go jumping into any gateways."

The gateway cranked, pulsed, shrank almost out of existence before finding one final throb of energy to stay open.

Finn looked at it, then at Emmie. "I promise I won't jump into any—"

The gateway burst.

With shuddering violence, scarlet tendrils shot into every corner of the chamber before disappearing suddenly and completely. All that was left was a tiny blood-red smudge drifting in the darkness.

But there was no one in the cave to see it. Finn, Emmie and Estravon had disappeared too.

I n the last embers of the gateway's light, droopy-eyed Yappy appeared, sniffed around the floor of the cave, cocked a leg and scampered away again.

Above, a fine residue of energy floated towards the roof of the chamber, through the rock, souring the soil above it, staining the roots knitted into it, the grass that fringed the clifftop.

The energy rose further into the wide sky, its particles at first drifting apart, then slowly coming together again, binding, cohering, until high above Darkmouth a shape appeared. It was a face, with empty eyes and a mouth distorted in anguish, that stretched across the sky before evaporating. It was similar to that which had appeared on the day Mrs Bright had disappeared, but this time there was a hint of shoulders, a smear of a body below. As if it was growing each time a gateway opened in that cave.

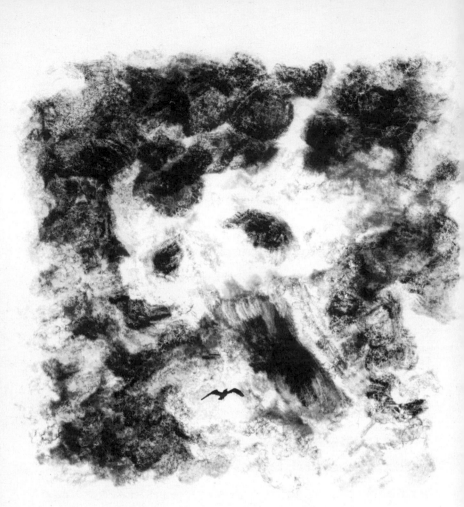

However, the only witness to this strange apparition in the sky was a lone seagull who had the misfortune to fly directly into it.

The bird was dead long before it hit the ground.

Finn felt every moment of time there ever was and ever will be, every possibility, every certainty, every passage of every molecule that has ever existed in two worlds.

Which was impressive given he crossed the gateway in under a quarter of a second. Or, more accurately, was sucked across it.

As soon as it was over, he noticed that his crippling headache was gone. Then he realised he was completely and utterly blind. He could hear voices. Well, heaving. And coughing.

"Oh, for the love of—" That was Estravon's voice, interrupted by a splash of what Finn presumed were the Chocky-Flakes the Assessor had had for breakfast.

"That was incredible!" yelled Emmie with clear delight, obviously dealing with any travel sickness far better than the Assessor.

The strange thing was that Finn felt all right too. At least he felt all right compared to the last time he'd taken this return trip. Sure, he was on his knees and in a state of great horror, but his body was perhaps the tiniest bit less wracked than the last time he'd passed through a gateway; his mind had reassembled just a tad quicker. It was awful, but not quite as awful.

Except he still couldn't see. At all.

"Emmie?" he called.

"I'm here," she said. "I think. What just happened?"

Finn reached out and felt the coarse wool of her school uniform's sweater. All he could sense were the sounds of Emmie and Estravon, and a rising stench that he realised was meeting one that already existed here. But his vision was gone and panic grabbed him. He had opened a gateway using a clearly unusual crystal, without thinking through the consequences, and had not only stranded himself and Emmie on the Infested Side, but had destroyed his eyesight in the process.

"I can't see," he gasped. "I've gone blind!"

A flash of light briefly stabbed at Finn's eyes. Then it was dark again except for the afterglow in his vision.

"You're not blind," coughed Estravon, followed by another flash, accompanied by the sound of a camera shutter. "And, if you were, that'd be the least of your worries."

Emmie turned her torch on and, as the flare gradually cleared from Finn's sight, it became apparent that Estravon had a camera in his hand and that they were still in the cave.

"We're still here," Finn groaned. "Maybe the gateway was too weak. Or it warped in some way, bringing us around and back again."

"I'm not so sure it *is* the same cave," said Emmie slowly, scanning the chamber with her torch. The beam fell upon an interior riddled with spikes of rock. Most were tiny, but only a couple of steps ahead of him one reached from the floor almost to the roof. "We would've noticed those stalactites before."

"Stalagmites," Estravon corrected her. "They grow up. Stalactites hang down."

"And there's *that*," said Finn, pointing above them. Estravon turned his torch on and directed it upwards to where some kind of goo ran along the cave ceiling and walls. The goo was a dull golden colour that sparkled weakly under the torchlight. In places, it hung in long strings until their weight tore them to the ground with a splat. It was these that were creating the stalagmites, building them slowly and surely into hard, pointed structures.

With the camera in his other hand, Estravon took another photo, the flash less of a shock now that torches lit the chamber.

"Should you be doing that?" asked Emmie as she ran her fingers through the ooze on the wall nearest them. Sticky, it glued her fingers together where they touched. She sniffed it, whipping her head back in reaction to a pungent odour.

"I have to do it," said Estravon. "It's my job. I'm an Assessor. I am assessing so I can reach the obvious conclusion."

The words didn't need to be said, but Finn said them anyway. "That this is the Infested Side?"

"That this is a mess," said Estravon. "And yes, that we're on the Infested Side. I cannot begin to imagine how many regulations we're breaking just by standing here. Actually, I can. There's regulation 34, governing the misuse of crystals. Regulation 68-slash-3 on the correct uniform when engaging with the enemy—"

"We heard Dad's voice," interrupted Finn. "The signal came through the gateway. We should try him." The radio was still in his hand, gripped tight throughout his brief journey through the gateway. He pressed the talk button. "Dad. Come in, Dad."

"There's the breaking of regulation 21 on proper radio protocols," continued Estravon.

"Try again, Finn," Emmie suggested.

"Hugo," said Finn, even though it felt odd to use his father's name like that, regardless of the circumstances. "Come in, Hugo. It's Finn."

There was nothing from the radio except mild, uninterrupted static.

"*A good chance to see the famous Darkmouth*, I thought," mumbled Estravon, now looking through his pockets. "*A break from the norm*, I thought. Except we find crystals, or whatever they are, in our own world. Ah, here we are. And, if I'm right, this here in my pocket is about to confirm that we're in..." He held a bag of dust up to the torchlight, with its fine red powder and the crumbled residue of what had been solid crystals. "...a whole heap of trouble."

"You can't bring crystals through gateways. Not without attaching them to living flesh," explained Finn.

"I know that," said Estravon. "I *did* spend three years studying Applied Gateway Chemistry. I was thinking more of what the loss of these two crystals *means*. Which is...?"

"That we did go through the gateway," said Emmie. "And now we have no way of getting back."

"Exactly," said Estravon.

Finn didn't say anything. If they were really stuck on the Infested Side without any crystals, they were in an extraordinary amount of trouble. The only thing distracting him from calculating exactly how much trouble was the intermittent spasm through his arm, which felt like a lingering aftershock from the ignition of the red crystal.

"Are you OK?" Emmie asked him. "You went flying across the cave when the gateway opened."

Finn shook his arm out, let the spasm dissipate, then looked around again. "This cave is like a near mirror of our world, as if they'd been divided right here."

"They're not identical, though," added Emmie. "All that goo and the awful smell. But maybe it's just coincidence we're in another cave."

"Like the way a gateway can lead from open ground in our world to open ground here?" added Finn, trying to stay as calm and reasonable as possible, even when his mind was telling him he'd made a massive mistake. "I suppose it's possible."

Estravon stepped forward, his torch trained on a shadow that suggested a gap in the wall.

"We can't stay here," he said through clenched teeth.

"But we can't go on either. It's too dangerous."

"What do your regulations say?" replied Emmie breezily.

"Please don't sneer at our regulations," said Estravon. "Regulations keep you safe. Regulations keep you from ending up in screw-ups like this one. Except, unfortunately, on this occasion."

"If we want to talk to Dad, we need to get a better signal for the radio than this place," said Finn. "The rock and stalactites must be blocking the radio signal."

"We could look for an exit," suggested Emmie.

"Firstly," Estravon said, "when I say that we can't stay here, I don't mean that we go out there. And, secondly, they're *stalagmites*."

Ignoring him, Finn and Emmie walked a few steps towards the gap in the rock.

"And thirdly," continued Estravon, his voice rising so he could be heard, "I am wearing a suit. Not a fighting suit. An ordinary *suit*. Italian tailoring, as it happens. Brand-new. And you two are wearing school uniform."

"My fighting suit's in my bag," said Finn. "There's no helmet, but at least it's something."

"There are three of us," said Estravon, stretching up to his full rangy height. "And I haven't been your size since

125

about a week after I was born."

Finn took the fighting suit from his bag and it fell with a clatter that echoed away from them.

"Why don't we just light up a flare to alert the Legends that we're here?" complained Estravon. "Maybe post them some invitations to dinner."

Finn held the quivering, clanking pile of metal, rubber and leather out to Emmie. "You have it."

"No, I've a better idea," she said. "Let's split it."

Finn felt it best not to argue, so gave her the torso and took the legs for himself. Emmie pulled her part of the armour over her head, then tightened the clasps at her shoulders and along her sides, before turning round a bit to show it off. "I don't even mind that it's smelly or anything," she said with a grin. "Don't they give you something to protect yourself?" she asked the clearly disgruntled Estravon.

"They give us pens. Until now, they've proven sufficient for most jobs."

Finn felt claustrophobia closing in on him. They were here, without much option but to move on in search of his dad. And it was getting more helpless by the second. "We have no weapons," he said.

"Actually," said Emmie, with a mixture of guilt and

giddiness, "that's not entirely true."

She dropped her schoolbag to the floor, unzipped it fully and pointed her torch into it. Finn and Estravon watched from over her shoulder. Inside was a hotchpotch of devices of various sizes, shapes, mostly dark green or tin grey, scuffed and blackened in parts. They looked like the guts of a disassembled machine. "Since Mr Glad's shop blew up, my dad's been grabbing bits and pieces from the ruins. But they were just sort of sitting around at home."

"Just sitting around?" asked Estravon.

"Well, sitting around in his safe. Anyway, I thought I should grab a handful, just in case."

"It didn't occur to you they could have gone off at any moment, killing you and anyone standing close by?" asked Estravon, incredulous. "Or, worse, killing *me*."

Finn picked out a rectangular object with spikes at one end. "Do you know what any of these do?"

"Nah," said Emmie, closing the bag again and swinging it on to her back. "But I'm sure we'll figure it out."

Estravon grabbed her shoulders, turned her round abruptly and zipped open the bag. He picked out a spiked ball and a fat little pistol. "This looks like a Grappler, slightly modified, but in working order." He next took out something that looked a bit like a metal pineapple,

Knock-out Box

with clasps on its side. "This is probably a Knock-out Box. Crude but effective." He pointed at a thin strip that resembled a firework. "That's a Roman candle. Handy for a firework display; not much use in a fight."

Finn and Emmie were both staring at him.

"You learn a lot in two years of Advanced Weaponry Class," explained Estravon.

They kept on staring.

"What?" he said, hurt by the implicit disbelief about his knowledge. "We don't have much else to do at the Council of Twelve other than study, you know. *You* try spending your life in the headquarters of the world's Legend Hunters when there are no actual Legends to fight any more. The days need to be filled somehow."

Finn took a deep breath, wished he hadn't filled his lungs with the stench, then pulled the torch from Emmie's hand and decided he had no choice but to head forward through the gap. "Let's go," he said. "No one in

Darkmouth knows we're here. And the only person we know on the Infested Side is Dad. If we're going to escape from this, we have to contact him."

Emmie agreed and together they made their way through the jutting stalagmites. After a few seconds, Finn heard the rule-quoting grumbles of a very unhappy Assessor follow behind them, his complaints bouncing about the high roof of the chamber where a hole high in the wall leaked in grey light and a glimpse of the Infested Side beyond it.

"Here's the plan," said Estravon. "We use the radio, try and contact Hugo, and we don't go further under any circumstances."

He almost walked into the back of Finn, who had stopped suddenly. "What's wrong with you now?" he asked.

Finn pushed Estravon's torch down and pointed towards the smudge of light in the cave wall. Something moved there. A silhouette in the dull light. Accompanying it was a low growling that made Finn's heart find a whole new rhythm of distress.

"Turn the torch off," he whispered to Estravon. "Turn. It. Off."

Estravon killed the beam.

That's when they saw the eyes.

16

Whatever it was that was staring at them had only two eyes. Not four. Not a dozen. Only two. At least only two eyes that they could see. In the circumstances, this was the only comfort Finn could find. Because whatever Legend was attached to those eyes was staring right at him.

He could feel his brain wanting to shut down and fill his head with happy thoughts. He felt woozy, and the tremor returned to run through his arm. He tried to push it all away and concentrate on not moving until the Legend stopped looking at him.

"Can it see us?" whispered Emmie, at his shoulder.

"I think it can see Finn," Estravon whispered in response.

In the light of the cave's opening, the creature curved its back, appeared to stretch. Its eyes, vivid yellow with black slits, rose as if whatever Legend belonged to them

was craning to see better. Then they disappeared. Its silhouette shrank and the gap in the wall widened. Finn, Emmie and Estravon stepped back reflexively. They could not see the Legend, but knew it was still in the cave with them.

Estravon pushed his hands out in self-defence. Emmie carefully began to remove her pack of weapons from her back and pull quietly at its zip.

Finn tried to keep calm and not think about prophecies and spectacular deaths or any kind of nastiness, but they all just kept flooding into his thoughts.

Estravon turned the torch back on, giving Finn and Emmie a fright.

"It might be able to see in the dark," he said through gritted teeth. "But we can't."

At the edges of the torchlight, on the floor of the cave, something glinted. Gold. Finn carefully reached down to pick it up, still keeping an eye out for the Legend. Whatever, and wherever, it was.

He took hold of a chain, short and snapped, as if it had been torn away. Holding it under Estravon's torchlight, he worked it through his fingers until he came to a fat locket. With his thumb, he sprang it open. Inside was a picture – faded but well preserved – of two people on their wedding day.

Finn had no idea who the man in the picture was, but after a couple of seconds he recognised the woman. She had aged over the years, but her scowl was unmistakable.

He handed the locket to Emmie so she could examine it while Estravon peered at it over her shoulder.

Then he turned and almost jumped with fright.

"It's Mrs Bright," said Finn.

"You should wash your hands after touching that," said Estravon, rummaging in the inside pocket of his suit jacket. "I have hand soap here somewhere."

"*No*," said Finn urgently. "Mrs Bright. She's here."

Emmie and Estravon looked up to see a woman, a floral scarf pulled across her head, standing a few metres away behind a waist-high stalagmite, staring at them with a look of frozen concern.

"Yappy," she said. "Is that you, Yappy?"

"Mrs Bright," Finn called, taking a step towards her. "Are you OK?"

Estravon gripped his elbow and out of the corner of his mouth warned, "Careful. She could be booby-trapped."

"She just looks petrified to me," said Emmie. "Are you OK, Mrs Bright?"

Mrs Bright didn't move, just called out again meekly.

"Yappy? Is that you, Yappy?"

"It's OK, we're all Legend Hunters," said Emmie. "We'll be able to help you."

"Something about this doesn't feel right," said Estravon. "And we're not official Legend Hunters, so you shouldn't introduce yourself as such."

"We're going to have to do something," said Finn, seeing the blankness of Mrs Bright's face, probably made rigid by fear. He felt he needed to help her, to comfort her. "It's OK, Mrs Bright. It's me, Finn. Hugo's son. You're safe now."

He offered a hand to help her across the rough cave floor towards them. Mrs Bright reached out, almost robotic. Her hand touched his. It was stone cold.

Finn smiled at her. Mrs Bright's face broke from its blankness, forming a smile. But it was almost unnatural, as if she was practising one for the first time.

"I'm not sure that's actually—" began Estravon.

"Duck!" shouted Emmie.

Finn didn't have time. Something fizzed by his ear, causing him to jump sideways, away from Mrs Bright, and, when he looked at her again, the blinding white fire of a Roman candle was glued to the wall by her forehead, burning fast and spitting sparks.

Mrs Bright looked at it, flinched as the sparks showered across the side of her face. But she didn't scream. Or drop. Or run. Instead, she began to grow, her back mutating, pushing outwards, her body rising, limbs thickening, headscarf disappearing, hands bursting into claws, skin into dirty green fur, until a Legend emerged, a rough mass of hair, limbs, claws and those yellow and black eyes.

Beside it, the fizzing, sticky sparks cast a flickering flame on stone, stalagmites, dripping golden goo.

And no humans whatsoever. They were already gone, the only trail being the echo of Estravon's last shouted word before they ran.

"Shapeshifter!"

Shapeshifter

17

They crashed through a gap in the cave wall and into a narrow corridor, the beams of their torches bouncing around them as they searched for a way out.

Finn led the way, the legs of his fighting suit scraping the stone as he pushed through. "How did you know it wasn't Mrs Bright?" he asked Emmie, who was following right behind him.

"When she smiled, the end of the gold chain was still stuck in her teeth," she panted, forcing her armour through the gap. "Stuck in *its* teeth. Whatever. It was as if it had bitten into it. Or that she had been bitten into, I suppose. The light caught it and I just knew."

"We need a strategy," said Estravon from behind Emmie. "We can't just run away in a random direction."

From somewhere in the cave came the echo of a long, rattling growl.

They reached the end of the tunnel, Estravon's head bowed beneath the low ceiling, with Emmie complaining as the long skirt of her uniform snagged on a shard of rock. She paused to unsnag herself, while Estravon waited impatiently behind her, urging her to hurry.

"I'm trying!" Emmie was saying as Finn pushed on through and emerged alone into a cavern and gloomy light.

Here he found two things.

The first was a way out. The second was standing in his way.

Someone he had never, ever expected to see, here or anywhere else.

Himself.

18

Still bickering, Emmie and Estravon arrived a few seconds later to find a cave entrance half blocked by rocks, with long filaments of goo dripping from the ceiling on to a carpet of jutting stalagmites.

They couldn't see what was beyond because blocking their view, standing with their backs to the half-light of the entrance, were two Finns. Same height. Same school sweater. Same oversized fighting suit round their legs. Same cowlick of hair. And both rigid with bemusement as they stared at each other.

One of the Finns was the real one. But both of them reacted with panic when Emmie hurriedly produced a chubby pistol with a spiked metal ball lodged in its barrel and pointed it straight at them.

"No, no, no, Emmie," Finn said in panic. "Don't. I'm me."

"No, Emmie," insisted the other Finn. "*I'm* me."

The real Finn felt indignant about this, disgusted at the brazen lie. He also felt more than a little embarrassed at how weedy he looked in half a fighting suit.

Emmie switched her aim from one Finn to the other, no idea which was which.

"That is astonishing," said Estravon, glancing from Finn to fake Finn and back again. He spluttered a half-laugh in admiration. "They're identical. He even sounds like Finn. Or Finn sounds like him. Whichever. This is incredible because Shapeshifters are extraordinarily rare. They feed off the likeness of other animals through touch."

"That doesn't sound too bad," said Emmie, still moving her weapon between the two Finns.

"And then they feed off their flesh," finished Estravon.

"Oh," said Emmie.

"What?" exclaimed the real Finn.

"Help me, Emmie," said the fake Finn.

"Hold on, help *me*," said real Finn, increasingly aghast at this impersonator and how he managed to act just as horrified.

"What do we do?" asked Emmie, getting more agitated by the moment while waving a weapon of unknown power at the Finns.

A flash lit up the cave as Estravon took a picture.

Both Finns flinched at the white glare.

"Stop," said real Finn, trying to rub the flare from his eyes.

"Stop," said fake Finn, doing the same.

"I'm recording this," said Estravon. "For the report."

"No, don't stop," said Emmie and, still moving the weapon rapidly between the two Finns, she snatched the camera from Estravon's hand.

"Oi!" complained Estravon.

"Smile," she told them.

"What?" the Finns said.

"Smile or I'll shoot."

So, under about the least jolly of circumstances imaginable, the two Finns attempted a smile. Emmie pressed the button on the camera and the flash burned through the darkness.

"I thought I'd see which had the gold chain in their mouth," she said. "Neither of them do. But I saw something else."

Estravon's eyes widened. "I saw it too," he declared. "That smile. It's not human. That's *not* Finn."

Emmie pointed the weapon. Right at Finn. The *real* Finn.

"No!" he gasped, raising a hand reflexively as she squeezed the trigger. Suddenly, she switched to the fake Finn and fired.

The fat spiked ball shot from the weapon's barrel, wedging itself between the plates of armour at the fake Finn's knee.

"Emmie?" it said, disbelieving, as it staggered forward. With its first step, the spiked ball burst open with a *phip* and piano wire whipped round its legs, up round its shoulders and round again. It pulled at it, stumbled, pleading, "Emmie?"

"Oh no..." she said.

"It's the wrong one!" said Estravon. "I told you."

The unharmed, relieved and very real Finn dashed forward and grabbed the weapon from Emmie and quickly shot his doppelgänger again. The ball wedged itself in a shoulder this time. More wire shot round the Shapeshifter's torso. Finn's doppelgänger looked straight at him, its eyes glowing yellow.

"Oh, thank goodness," exclaimed Emmie.

"I was never in doubt," said Estravon.

"That feels really weird," said Finn, dropping the weapon to the ground. And it did. It felt utterly wrong. Like looking in a mirror only for the reflection to start

141

snarling and slashing at you. "How did you know it wasn't me?"

"Easy," said Emmie. "I haven't seen you smile once since your dad disappeared. I think you've forgotten how to. So, I figured the one with the weird smile was you."

"That sounds like a guess to me," said Estravon. "We cannot afford guesses in this place."

"Thanks, Emmie," said Finn. "I think."

"No worries," said Emmie, grinning.

"You know we didn't even have to do that," Estravon pointed out. "A Shapeshifter can only speak the words it's heard its prey say. All we had to do was ask a few quick questions of the two Finns and we would've found out quickly enough."

"The fun way worked out OK, though," said Emmie.

"Fun?" spluttered Finn.

Before them, the Legend's shoulders pulsated, mutated, thick bottle-green fur bursting out. The Shapeshifter's lower half reverted to its hairy, horrendous original state. Its arm was that of a woman. One leg was a giant rabbit's leg for some reason. And its head was a deformed version of Finn's, with a headscarf wrapped round it.

It collapsed between stalagmites, a half-formed mix of so many things, all of them on their own enough to keep

Finn in nightmare material for the rest of his life.

"I didn't need to see that," said Finn, yet unable to quite take his eyes off it. "And I'm not sure how to feel about the fact that looking miserable turned out to be a good thing."

The three of them remained somewhat dumbstruck by the sight of the Shapeshifter morphing into various forms in an attempt to escape. Each time it shrank, the wire only tightened its hold on it.

"We'd better go," said Estravon.

"I thought you didn't want to leave here," said Emmie.

"The situation has changed."

They made their way to the exit, round the struggling Legend, a ghastly combination of people and creatures which occasionally fell quiet for a few seconds to regain its strength before thrashing about again.

Finn realised his horror was being undercut by something else: sympathy. He hadn't given the Legend a chance; instead, he'd been part of another exercise in shooting first and asking questions later, just like humans had always done. Another reason for Legends to hate them.

"It looks like it's in awful pain," said Finn. "Maybe it didn't really want to hurt us."

The Legend snapped one of the wires and lunged at them, using its free arm to start dragging itself towards the three of them, biting and foaming.

"Still think that?" asked Estravon and they hurried away, scrambling through the opening and into the fetid, grim air of the Infested Side that they never thought would be so welcome.

19

H*ssssss*
    Finn held the radio close to his mouth and called his father's name. Clearly but quietly.

"Finn to Dad. Come in, Dad," he said.

The only response was unbroken static.

Finn called him again.

Hsssss.

They were hunkered down a short distance from the cave on a ground of cracked stone slabs on which tendrils of dull blue lichen clung. The area bordered what seemed to be dense woods, although its trees could barely be described as such. They had definitely been trees at some point in their history, and the tallest had grown to dizzying heights, great giants with long branches that suggested they were once wild with growth and renewal. But no longer. Now they were bare, petrified remains on the edges of a forest that appeared frozen mid-agony.

Above them, the sky was a uniform, unending grey, squatting low over the world. So low, in fact, that the tallest trees in the dead forest disappeared into the layer of cloud as if they had simply been snipped off cleanly at their tops.

"So this is the Infested Side," Estravon said and sniffed. "It smells awful."

It really did. Finn had noticed it too – it was impossible not to. "It's sort of like feet. Feet wrapped in fish or something," he said.

"No," said Emmie. "It's more like the worst morning breath ever. But everywhere."

"Just try the radio again," Estravon instructed.

"Finn to Dad," he said. "Can you hear me, Dad?"

Hssssss.

Finn's spirits sank. He had brought them here. He hadn't meant to. Hadn't planned to. He was supposed to be bringing his father *back*, not going in to find him. That didn't matter now. His impulsiveness had dropped them into the Infested Side and now they were stuck here, in the full knowledge that it was a world full of things that wanted to kill them. Or worse.

He wondered what his father would say. What his mother was going to do when she realised he was gone.

The fear brought on by all those thoughts crowding his mind felt as intense as those inspired by the world around them.

"Finn to Dad. Are you there, Dad?"

Hssssss.

He looked at Estravon, who was clearly keen to say something.

"You need to say 'over'," said Estravon. "That's the standard radio protocol."

"Finn to Dad," Finn repeated. He glanced at the Assessor and reluctantly muttered, "Over."

Hsssss. Click.

"Fi—" *Sqwuack. Chquiiilth.* "—**mus**t—"

Hsssss.

Finn held the radio tight, not wanting to let go of his father's voice. It was distant, drowned in white noise. But it was him. It was his dad.

"Dad. It's me," Finn said, excitement rippling through him, making his armour quake. "I'm here. Dad. We're here to get you. Over."

Chwachlsck. His father's voice returned, caught in a loop of deepening distortion. "*meme*meme*me* *mememe*ME**MEME**MEM" It cut out again. "—ountain nnn**nnnn**n."

Sqwushch. Hssssss.

Far ahead, in the distant haze beyond the trees, they could just make out a great mountain range slicing high above the horizon, snowcaps gripping like talons to their peaks. The carpet of cloud hugged the landscape until it reached them, where it rose, matching the slope of the mountains, almost as if to accommodate them.

"Is he saying we need to go to the mountains?" asked Emmie.

"No," spluttered Estravon. "We avoid the mountains. Clearly, he meant we stay *away* from the mountains."

"Dad. Come in, Dad."

"—toWerrrr**rrrrrrrr**rrrrrrrrrrrrr—"

Hssssss.

"Towels? Do we have to bring towels, Dad?" asked Finn.

"He said tower, not towel," said Estravon. "What is wrong with you? *Tower.*"

"Dad. Can you hear me?"

Hssssss.

"Dad. Come in, over."

That was it. Finn tried again. Stopped, gave it a few moments before giving it another go. His father had gone, finally overcome by static. But Finn savoured the sound of his father's voice for a little while longer before focusing on what he had said. Because, whatever the words meant, that they had been spoken at all made one thing very clear.

Hugo was out there somewhere. He was alive. And Finn had no choice but to find him.

How they were going to do that was a whole other matter.

'The Execution of the Human'
From *The Chronicles of the Sky's Collapse,*
as told by inhabitants of the Infested Side

There are many ancient sayings that refer to our greatest enemy.

"A human may run very quickly, but it cannot escape its legs."

"If you prick them, they shall bleed. But slashing is more effective."

But there is one saying that every young Legend is taught, and must know by heart, for the day will inevitably come when they will be faced with its truth.

"There are many ways to kill a human, but there is only one type of human to kill."

It means they are a species which does not vary greatly. Some are large, some small. Some wear ink on their bodies; others are covered from head to toe in steel. But they are generally all the same: they have two legs, two arms, one head, and will not sprout another should any of them be cut off.

So, while there are many ways to kill a human, it is considered best not to overcomplicate things. The best way to kill a human will generally be the same way you killed the last human. And the one before that. And before that again.

On the day of Niall Blacktongue's death, the executioner was keeping it simple. The hooded Fomorian had built a platform in a scorched clearing. The centre of the platform was hollowed out and the human was made to stand at its edge. Beneath it was dug a pit which had been filled with writhing death larvae.

Below that again had been placed fifty rows of daggers. Just in case keeping it simple didn't work. The human's head was bowed, and the dark words that used to tumble from his mouth like the acid waterfalls of the Deep North had stopped many months before. Suddenly. Finally. Not uttered since, despite efforts to pull them from him along with his fingernails.

As Blacktongue struggled to stay upright on the wobbling platform, Gantrua stood before him, the jagged edges of his grille sporting several extra layers of teeth since the human had first stepped into this land from the Promised World. If Blacktongue had cared to examine them, he would have recognised at least one of those teeth as having once belonged to him.

Death Larva

In Gantrua's hand was a struggling half-lizard. "Do you know this place?" Gantrua asked him, looming over the human even though the prisoner stood some way off the ground. "This is where we first found you. This is where you saw fit to use your power to lay waste to half an army."

Blacktongue did not react.

Gantrua looked around. "You know that some of these fools thought you brave when you came here? In truth, I thought so myself briefly. Here was this saboteur, sacrificing his life to destroy us. We know more now. We know you were discarded by the humans, a piece of flotsam washed up in this world because you were of no use to your own kind. And now you are of no use to us. At least your corpse will be of some value to something."

He dropped the squealing half-lizard into the pit. It was consumed in a frenzy of death larvae.

Gantrua turned his back on Niall and began to walk away, his sword carving a scar through the burnt earth.

"Kill him."

There was a murmur from Niall Blacktongue. Gantrua heard it, the human's whimpering a mere tremor in his ear.

The executioner lifted a rod, weighed it in his hands for a moment, then planted his feet firmly in the ground as he swung it behind his shoulder.

Blacktongue spoke louder.

The executioner swung at the platform.

Blacktongue shouted. "I have seen the end!"

The executioner struck the platform with such force it splintered instantly, releasing Blacktongue into the void.

But the human did not fall.

Gantrua had a hand wrapped round his neck, holding him between life and death.

"This had better be worth it," he snarled.

Through the crushing grip round his throat, Blacktongue forced words. Lines so throttled they did not carry beyond the ears of Gantrua.

The hushed Legends saw Gantrua tighten his grip. They saw the prisoner splutter and gag. A fleck of

spittle arced in the grey light.

Below, the death larvae were in a frenzy.

"You humans break so easily," said Gantrua.

But he did not let go.

20

Finn's plan was falling apart.

Not that he ever really had a plan.

He had no idea what they were supposed to do next and neither did Emmie or Estravon.

Opening the gateway had seemed a perfectly logical thing to do, until Finn had actually opened the gateway. Now they each had only half an idea of where they were supposed to go, only an inkling of where his father might be.

And they disagreed on that anyway.

"He told us we need to go to a tower in the mountains," said Finn.

"No, he said the words 'mountains' and 'tower'," clarified Estravon, "but it doesn't mean we hotfoot it there."

"Finn wants to go there," said Emmie. "Isn't that right, Finn?"

"I'm not really sure—" he started.

"So, we go there," concluded Emmie before he could finish.

They were still on the edge of this forest scoured of all its leaves, a landscape of arboreal skeletons grasping for some unreachable mercy. Above it was a sky stripped bare of comfort and colour.

It was not the most welcoming of places.

For the first time since arriving, Finn felt the chill of the Infested Side on his skin. He was a bit shaken by the encounter with the Shapeshifter. It had not merely been like looking in a mirror, but rather something far more revealing.

"Is that what I look like in this fighting suit?" Finn asked Emmie as they crouched by a dead tree. "All that armour round my legs, but not much of me inside it?"

"It's better you're inside it than outside," said Emmie, trying to cheer him up.

"How long were we here before we were attacked?" asked Estravon. "I'll tell you how long. Three minutes and forty-two seconds. You do realise that you matter, Finn? You're actually quite important in the grand scheme of things. You need to get out of this place alive because they don't do Completion Ceremonies for the dead. At least not since all that trouble over Jeremy the Eviscerated."

"Are you saying that I don't matter?" asked Emmie, insulted.

"No," said Estravon. "Of course you do. But not like he does. So many of us have bought our suits, for crying out loud. Ties. Souvenir cufflinks."

"Souvenir cufflinks?" wondered Finn, baffled.

"Obviously, that's not the only reason your Completion matters, but they weren't cheap all the same." He took a notepad out of his pocket, unclipped the attached pen and began to scribble.

"Are you coming up with a plan?" Finn asked him.

"I'm making notes for my report." Estravon seemed to sense Finn and Emmie's bemusement at this because he addressed them without even looking up. "It'd be a bit strange if I didn't take notes. 'So, what did you do after the giant red gateway sucked you into the Infested Side?' 'Oh, nothing much, Council of Twelve. We grabbed some soil samples and hopped back home.'" Estravon stopped writing for a moment and considered that. "Actually, we probably *should* grab some soil samples."

"Make sure you spell my name right," said Emmie.

"I will. I promise you. I'll save a whole subsection of

the report just for you. Footnotes as well."

"May all your pens be dry of ink," Emmie responded, pleased with herself. Estravon looked mortally irked at that insult and at his inability to come up with a snappy response.

Finn thought it best to see what might be in the immediate vicinity before deciding what to be most afraid of.

He pulled his bag round to take the blocky scanner from it. Except for a dent along one edge, the device appeared largely undamaged after being flung across the cave when the gateway had opened. He turned it on and it worked immediately, and he watched as it got a fix on the landscape around him.

What emerged was unfamiliar. This was not the usual image of Darkmouth he was so used to. Instead, varying contours infused the screen, their edges softening until they settled into a palette of brown smudges with occasional beige patches. Finn examined it carefully. He had no idea what any of it meant.

On the side of the scanner was a button that – when pressed at home anyway – revealed any nearby life signs. Legends showed up as pulsing green dots on the screen, after which they could be tracked down. This time,

Finn would need to use the scanner to *avoid* any passing Legends.

Pushing the button, he waited for a moment while it blinked, warming up.

Emmie stood at his shoulder, peering at the screen. Estravon broke off from his note-taking to stand at Finn's other shoulder and they waited silently for something to show on the screen.

A green dot appeared towards the lower left corner.

Scanner

Finn looked round in that direction. "There must be a Legend over there somewhere."

"The Shapeshifter?" wondered Emmie.

"I don't know. I'm only really used to seeing a map of Darkmouth, so I'm not sure exactly where it might be."

"Well, that is just super," sighed Estravon. He made a note, then stuffed his notepad back into his pocket.

"It's only one Legend," said Finn. "I'm not sure exactly how far away, but look – we're these red dots at the centre of the map so we just need to keep some distance from whatever that one green dot is."

Another green dot appeared at the top right of the screen. Finn took a deep breath. "And that one too," he said.

A third green dot appeared behind them.

Four. A green pulse beside the third.

At least the Legends didn't seem to be too close. *If we're careful,* Finn thought, *we can avoid…*

Five. Six. Seven.

"Maybe it's an error with the reading," he said hopefully.

"Give it to me," said Estravon, grabbing the scanner from Finn. He gave the screen a flick with a knuckle.

The scanner blinked off.

On.

Off.

It did not come back on.

Finn grabbed it, tapped it again. Slapped it. "There was no need to break it," he grumbled.

"I'm upgrading our current status from Super to Just Bloody Fantastic," said Estravon.

"Come on," said Emmie. "We're here, we're still alive, Finn's dad is close enough to talk to on the radio and we're not just on a Legend hunt, but a Legend Hunter hunt. This is going to be exciting, isn't it, Finn?" She slapped him cheerily on the shoulder.

"They'll notice us missing from school pretty soon," Finn said. He put the malfunctioning scanner back in his bag and chewed on his lip while he tried to figure out what they should do next, secretly hoping someone would just tell him. He looked up at Emmie. "Although it was double geography anyway, so..."

"I have to walk away from this," said Estravon. "This contravenes so many protocols that, frankly, I think we've exceeded the number of protocols there can possibly be."

A look of realisation crossed Finn's face. "You're wrong," he said. "I've done my apprentice Legend Hunter studies. I know there's a rule about this, which means you have to help us. Section 46a or something."

Estravon considered this. "Section 46a? 'That no Legend Hunter may eat spaghetti with their hands at formal dinners?'"

"No," Finn said. "There's another one. That apprentice Legend Hunters must be allowed to make their own mistakes with the guidance of any adults present. Or something."

Estravon's eyes narrowed. "That's section 64a, and I really think it's more a guideline than a hard-and-fast rule."

"I didn't think the Council of Twelve liked to leave things too loose," said Finn.

"OK, it's a rule. But it states that it can only be acted upon if there's reasonable cause."

Emmie stepped forward, the crown of her hair tickling Estravon's chin so that he had to tilt his head back. "I would've thought an apprentice rescuing his father would be reasonable cause," she said. "Especially if his father is the last active Legend Hunter on Earth."

Estravon picked a speck of dust off his tongue. "There'll be a tribunal about this when we get back, trust me. A *big* investigation."

"Great!" declared Emmie, genuinely delighted with events. "Then we're heading for the mountains."

A tremor ran through Finn's arm, and he wasn't sure if it was the cold or the aftermath of the crystal or fear. He didn't want to have to go anywhere other than home. But he was here and so was his dad.

Finn the Defiant. Again, he seemed to hear those words his father had spoken to him before he'd been lost. *Finn the Defiant.*

He trained his eyes on the depths of the dead forest ahead of them, and his mind replayed the last image on the scanner before it had stopped working. All those green dots. There were Legends all around them.

Well, *almost* all around them.

Because, in that last image, there had been a path ahead. Clear. Not yet Infested.

"I need to find my dad," he said. "If we move on, maybe we'll reach clearer ground to talk to him, and we can get to the mountains and the tower he talked about."

Estravon shook his head.

Emmie rubbed her hands in excitement.

The three of them stood there. A man in a tailored Italian suit. A couple of twelve-year-olds in school uniform and half a fighting suit each.

No Desiccator.

A malfunctioning scanner.

A half-working radio.

A bag of cobbled-together weapons that might be dangerous.

"Oh, come on," said Emmie, skipping on ahead. "We've faced worse, haven't we, Finn?"

"I'm not sure that we have, to be honest," he said, but he followed slowly. Anything that might bring him closer to his father was better than standing around doing nothing.

"I expressly order you by the provisions of the 1912 Act on Misdirected Searches..." said Estravon, but Emmie and Finn had already disappeared into the forest.

21

Finn moved forward. Step by step. Trying not to think about how easily the clank of his fighting suit carried across the Infested Side. And trying not to think about the stories of those who had travelled to here in the past.

Liam the Perished. Shaun the Lost-Hunter. Lucinda the Missing.

He managed not to dwell on their destinies. Pushed them to the back of his mind. Stayed positive.

Unfortunately, Estravon took great pleasure in relaying each of their dreadful fates. In great detail. Then added some new ones.

"You know about Lucas the Half-Escaped?" he asked as they walked.

"We probably shouldn't talk too loudly," said Finn.

"He was a French Legend Hunter," Estravon continued, addressing Emmie as her armour clanked in tune with

Finn's. "It's a great example of how you're never safe until you're back home, tucked up in bed, drinking cocoa. And even then only if the cocoa's hot enough to burn the eyes of any attacker who might jump into bed with you."

They separated to round the fat, blasted trunk of a tree, with Estravon taking up his story again once they came together on the other side. "Anyway, Lucas chases a Cerberus right through a gateway. The gateway shuts behind him. He's gone."

Finn stopped for some water, leaning against a tree stump as he did so. The bark felt slick and glassy to the touch, a couple of what might once have attempted to be buds but never grew, were now razor-sharp. He felt the frigidity of the air tickle his face, but there was no breeze at all, only a staleness. It was as if this world had been robbed of all dynamism.

Emmie sat beside him. "This armour isn't made for hiking in," she said. Wiping her brow created a noise like a bin being emptied.

As Finn took the water bottle from his bag, he accidentally pulled out the red notebook and it flopped on to the flat tree stump.

Estravon took it almost without thinking and flicked

through it absent-mindedly as he continued his story. "Anyway, as the weeks went by, it became clear that Lucas was injured, but still alive on the Infested Side, fighting his way through in the hope of finding a path back home. So, the Council of Twelve captured and bribed a sprite Legend, a Kobalos, to return to the Infested Side, find Lucas and bring him back."

"This story is not going to end well," said Emmie.

"Surprisingly, the Legend was true to its word and three days after being released back to the Infested Side it returned, pushing Lucas through a gateway ahead of it." Estravon slowed his flick through the notebook's pages. "It was only when the Kobalos followed Lucas through and saw the look on the humans' faces that it realised it had underestimated the severity of the wounds Lucas had received in his battle to escape. And all it said was, 'I did think it was strange that all of you had legs, but he had none.'"

Finn gawped at Estravon.

"Is it in the rules that you have to be constantly gloomy?" asked Emmie.

"Just passing the time in a manner commensurate with our situation," said Estravon, blowing air from his cheeks.

"Well, maybe you should do it a bit more quietly," she responded.

Finn brought the bottle to his lips again, felt a spasm run through his hand, veins pulse, a tremor chase up his arm. The aftershock of the force that had thrown him across the cave still running through him. He lost his grip on the bottle and Emmie caught it before too much was spilled.

"Are you OK?" she asked him.

"Just cold, I think," he lied as a bead of sweat crawled from his matted, damp fringe down his cheek. "Maybe we should keep moving."

He forced himself to stand, holding the radio in his hand, resisting the temptation to try it again. Its battery felt like the most important item he had.

"This notebook isn't yours, is it?" said Estravon, flicking through it again.

"It is," said Finn, a bit feebly. "Well, I found it. At home. I think it might have belonged to Niall Blacktongue."

"Niall *Blacktongue*? We're not supposed to talk about him. But why would you think that?"

Finn gestured at the notebook. "It says NB on the inside."

"Hardly persuasive."

"Plus, he was my grandfather and I found the notebook in my house."

Estravon frowned. "Well, all right. Anyway, whoever wrote it knew a lot about gateways," he said. "These calculations, these diagrams, they're almost like a guide to creating them. Different types of them. Stuff about different crystals too. You just found it lying around?"

"Yeah," said Finn, passing the water to Emmie.

"It's also a guide to what *not* to do." Estravon held open a couple of pages with a drawing of what looked like two gateways, one with a skull and crossbones at its centre. "Like, for example, not opening one gateway on top of another. Someone put a lot of thought into this. And you just happened to find it? And then a cave full of crystals? I really can't decide if your luck is good or bad."

Finn took the notebook from Estravon, put it back in his bag. "Come on," he said. "We'd better go."

"Yes, wonderful," said Estravon. "Let's march on towards our doom, in whatever form it comes."

"And again that's cheerful," said Emmie.

"Statistically, we shouldn't have survived even this long. Especially you," Estravon said to Finn. "What with the prophecy and all."

Finn felt a shiver at the idea of the prophecy – and its

prediction that he would die on the Infested Side.

Here.

Now?

"The prophecy's rubbish anyway," he shrugged crossly.

"You think so?"

"I've been on the Infested Side before and survived. The prophecy means nothing."

"*The Legends are rising, the boy shall fall,* it says. *The last child of the last Legend Hunter, and all that,*" said Estravon.

"Yes, yes, you don't need to recite it again," said Finn.

"*His death on the Infested Side will be greater than any other,*" finished Estravon. "It's been around for years, you know. Long before I became an Assessor. Long before you were born even."

"Can't this wait until we get home?" complained Emmie. "It doesn't matter right now."

"Actually, seeing as I'm currently trapped on the Infested Side with a girl in patent shoes and a boy whose very fate has been the subject of rumour since before he was even born, it matters quite a lot, don't you think?"

"What do you mean it's been around since before I was born?" asked Finn.

"It's been around a lot longer than any of us," said Estravon. "Decades. Since around the time that, well, you-know-what happened."

"We-know-*what* happened?" asked Emmie.

"Since my grandfather disappeared," guessed Finn. "Not that I've ever been told why."

"No one likes to talk about it," Estravon repeated and pulled his suit lapels tight against the chill. "We should move on."

"Hold on," said Finn, grasping Estravon's arm.

"Don't grab me like that. I can't be held responsible for my violent reflexes," said Estravon. "Four years of Advanced Combat. Deadly."

"Are you saying that there's a connection between my granddad disappearing and the prophecy starting?"

"I am merely stating the facts as we know them," replied Estravon. "Or, at the very least, the facts about a very strong rumour. The two events coincided. Whether that is accident or design is way above my pay grade. Which is grade 3, by the way, and not too bad for someone of my age."

"But it doesn't have to be about Finn," said Emmie.

"Why's that?" asked Estravon.

"Because it doesn't say it's me," Finn said. "It says it's the last child of the last Legend Hunter, but it doesn't actually say it's *me*."

Estravon flicked some dirt off the lapel of his suit, straightened his cuffs, looked further into the bare, foreboding forest ahead. "I don't know what to think frankly. I don't know if the prophecy is real or not. I don't know if it has anything to do with Niall Blacktongue, although we *really* don't like to talk about that. But I feel increasingly sure that there is something about you that makes you very different from any other human who's ever been here."

"Why?" asked Finn.

"Because you've survived a visit to the Infested Side once before. Because you're here again. And, most obviously, because we've got this far into this forest, with so many Legends out there, and they haven't attacked us yet." Estravon bent to glare at him. "Don't you find that a bit odd?"

Finn felt it again. That tremor through his arm, a flash in his veins. Brief but sharp. He turned away as he winced, urging it to pass.

He took a furtive peek at the back of his hand. Veins were raised, a glowing network spreading from his fingers to his wrist. He pulled a glove on to cover it.

For weeks, he had dwelled on this rumour about his fate, one he knew was spoken of by Legends on the

Infested Side as well as Legend Hunters back home. It had begun to seem only a matter of time until the prophecy was fulfilled, meaning that every step he took brought his death closer.

The thing was he didn't know which way to go to stop it from happening, or if he was just locked into a destiny he couldn't avoid.

He decided to add that to the growing list of things he shouldn't think about.

Deep in the trees, there was a cry. An animal cry. Distant but clear.

"They're out there," said Estravon. "So, why haven't they come for us yet?"

"We're doing the right thing, aren't we?" Finn asked Emmie as she handed him the water back.

"You're going to have to stop asking that, Finn," she said. "After all, you're the only one of us who's been on the Infested Side before. That's got to count for something."

Finn wasn't sure that it did. Before shoving the water bottle back in his bag, he took a last swig. Liquid leaked down his chin, dropping to the ground. They moved on again, stepping carefully over sharp brambles and shattered leaves.

Behind them, where the drops of water had fallen, the

soil writhed, hungry for a purity it had not tasted in aeons.

And, within the leafless trees, the Legends crept after them. Keeping their distance.

Waiting.

22

Thump. *Thump.*

Thumpthumpthumpthumpthump.

"OK, OK, OK, I'm coming." Steve half fell down the stairs of the small house, two steps at a time, a sweatshirt tight round his torso, coconut-themed Bermuda shorts flapping at his knees. As soon as he unlocked the door, his nose was almost broken by Clara pushing through. She had a cuddly toy in her hands.

"Be careful," he complained, "we only rent this place."

"Where is he?" she demanded.

"The landlord will keep our deposit if there's damage to the house," said Steve, examining the scrape in the paint on the wall where the door had slammed into it. "Anyway, where is who?"

She threw the cuddly toy at his head. "What the...?" he exclaimed.

"Finn's gone. Start talking."

He picked up the toy and took a note from where it had been skewered on one of its soft fangs. It read:

Mam, we found a map. Maybe it's nothing and I don't want you to worry about me, but I thought I'd check it out just in case. If you're reading this, though, then something might have happened.

Love, Finn

P.S. I brought snacks.

Steve looked up from the note, his exasperation clear. "He can't be far. It's been a dry day, so he hasn't gone jumping into any gateways."

Clara blocked him as he tried to walk into the kitchen. "I've spent the past few weeks hoping that even you might be able to get Hugo back, but instead I've watched you flail around, pretending to be in charge, finding the wrong maps, going on Legend Hunts at the petting zoo—"

"I had a map. I saw fur. It was a natural connection to make."

"—and I've been fobbed off by that Council of bloody Twelve time and time again. To what end? My twelve-year-old son has decided he needs to rescue his father all by himself. Now I want you to pick up that phone, or go to your computer, or send up a smoke signal, or do whatever the hell it is you do to contact the Twelve. We have to get Finn back."

Steve sighed. "But you don't even know where he is."

"I know he needs our help."

"He's a young boy, Clara. Young boys have adventures. He'll be back when he gets hungry."

Clara picked up a phone from the table and held it out to him. "Get the Twelve on the line."

"I can't do that, Clara. You know that's not how it works."

"I don't care how it works. Contact them right now."

"If you call them, you invariably get an assistant, a minion, someone like that Assessor. The Twelve don't do conversations. They do rules. They do procedures. They go by the book. And it's a book they've written. And they don't send rescue parties into gateways after their only active Legend Hunter, so they're not likely to send a whole SWAT team over just because Finn has gone walkabout for a few hours."

Clara stared at him with an intensity that made his eyes frazzle. "You don't know, do you?" she said.

"Know what?"

"Finn didn't go to school this morning. They called to say he never showed up."

"I used to do the same when it was double geography."

"And he left here with Emmie."

"Well, I just presume she's out hanging around with..." A ripple of understanding crossed his brow. "...Finn."

As he said this, something caught Steve's eye. The door of the microwave oven, ajar. He opened it and Clara could see a safe tucked inside. Steve turned the dial. *Click.* Turned it the other way. *Click.* And back again. *Clonk.*

He pulled open its door, reached in and held out a newspaper parcel.

"That's a relief," he said. "For a moment, I thought someone had taken all the dangerous stuff."

He unwrapped the paper.

Inside, where there should have been a collection of highly dangerous devices taken from Mr Glad's shop, lay a selection of fruits, pebbles and a cracked water pistol.

Steve uttered a deep, throaty groan, then charged out of the kitchen and up the stairs three at a time. Clara followed him and watched as he threw open Emmie's bedroom door.

"Emmie!" he bellowed as he disappeared inside.

A second later, he was back out again, urgently pushing

past Clara and going straight to another room.

Clara looked into Emmie's bedroom and saw clothes on the floor, schoolbooks on the desk and a bed unmade. But no Emmie.

She followed Steve into the other room. He was leaning over a desk beside a bank of cameras lined up at the window, turning on the computer, punching keys furiously.

"What are you doing?" she asked.

"Contacting the Twelve," he said. "We need to get our kids back."

23

"**D**o you hear something?" Finn asked the others.

They hadn't walked much further in search of clear ground, but he couldn't be sure if that unshakeable crawling on his skin was the strange sensation he'd been feeling or the justified paranoia that they were being watched.

Or both.

They stopped, and the only sounds were the creaks of Finn's and Emmie's armour settling. But, when they walked on again, Finn could sense it clearly now. He knew the others could too. The forest seemed to wake, as if matching their pace, tracking them. There was rustling. Shaking. Scurrying. Behind them. Alongside them. Unseen but present with every step.

Thinking he caught movement in the sliver of sky above them, Finn twisted his head upwards. There was a sound that reminded him of bed sheets flapping on a washing line and the flat roof of cloud appeared to stir for just a moment. Then it was still again.

"Did you see that?" he asked Emmie. "Last time I was on the Infested Side, something came from the sky. It wasn't a nice thing either."

Emmie looked up. "But you desiccated it, Finn, right?"

"Sort of," Finn pointed out. "It didn't work properly. I only half desiccated the Legend. It was horrible."

"Well, at least I have my bag of tricks here," she said, sorting through the contents of her backpack. "Although we only have these pineapple things left."

"Knock-out Boxes," observed Estravon. "Be careful with those."

"I'm going to try the scanner again." As Finn took it from his bag, he looked at Estravon. "Please don't grab it this time."

"I always dreamed of going on a real mission," Estravon sighed. "That dream didn't include pushy twelve-year-olds."

The scanner flickered. Finn gave it a small shake and the map solidified. Finn felt a moment of elation. It was working. His sense of triumph didn't last long.

In the centre of the map, they saw themselves as

red dots and around them it was as if an avalanche of luminescent green was flowing towards them, overtaking them. *Blip. Blip. Blip. Blip.* Unseen Legends at their five o'clock. Three o'clock. Nine o'clock. Almost everywhere o'clock.

"Oh dear," said Emmie.

"And yet still they wait," observed Estravon. "We've managed to walk this far since the cave and we can hear them out there. When we move, they move. When we make noise, they make noise. But we've seen no Legends since. Do you know what the odds against that are? It doesn't matter. Well, it does, but what matters most is that we haven't been attacked since the Shapeshifter and – strange as it is to say this – I don't like that. At all."

"Why don't you just count your blessings?" asked Emmie.

"I did. I came up with a grand total of zero."

Finn was forcing himself to look away from the green dots that were Legends concentrating on the map itself. "The way that bit of the map ends there, just ahead of us, might be where the forest stops."

Estravon looked at it, nodded. "It's possible," he said, "but I'm not sure what it leads to. It could be a cliff. A wall. An acid waterfall. They have those here. Look it up."

"Hold on," said Emmie, staring intently at the scanner. "The Legends are the green dots, right?"

"Yes," confirmed Finn.

"And humans show up as red ones. So we're the three red dots in the middle," she continued.

"Uh-huh," agreed Finn.

"Then how come there are four red dots?"

They each stared at the screen and, sure enough, they saw a clump of three dots, so close together it was hard to distinguish one from the other. And ahead of them, in a clearer area at the very edge, was another red dot.

At which exact point the scanner sparked, causing Finn to drop it. Picking it up gingerly, he immediately confirmed it was lifeless.

In the trees, there were noises, as if the whole forest was craning to see what had just happened.

But Finn, Emmie and Estravon weren't looking behind them. Or around them. They were instead looking into the trees directly ahead of them.

At the silhouette staring back.

T hey dashed towards the figure. The ground tore at their ankles, jabbed at their shins, but their eyes were trained on the same sight ahead.

It was a human. A man, it seemed. And his outline suggested he was in Legend Hunter's armour.

"Dad?"

Finn ran, the legs of his fighting suit bashing against each other. The malfunctioning scanner spilled from his open bag as he dashed into the trees, distracting him so that he lost his footing in the wiry undergrowth and hit the ground.

Emmie passed him, fighting against the weight of the armour on her body.

Finn popped himself up again. Resumed the chase.

Estravon had followed, but jumped back to pick up the dropped scanner. As he did, the forest closed in on him a little. Hesitating, he abandoned the idea of grabbing the

scanner and instead loped after Emmie and Finn, finding them quickly by the sound of clanking metal.

"Something strange is going on back there," he said as he overtook them.

"There he is!" shouted Finn, pointing at the figure moving away from them. "Dad?"

"For crying out loud, don't cry out loud," hissed Estravon.

The figure looked back, then stepped behind the wide girth of a tree and out of view.

It took them maybe twenty seconds to reach the point where the man had stood. Presuming he must have moved further ahead, Finn started running again, until the trees were gone and he had burst into a clearing, a sudden emptiness in the world, where the hard earth was replaced by black, pitted stone.

He kept moving, searching for the figure, steadily realising that his view was no longer obscured by trees, but by a black mist that grew thick around him.

"Finn?" he heard Emmie call, but he had already pushed further into the murk.

Finn had spotted the figure, a dark shape swallowed by the gloom. He had noticed a light too, a deep reddish glow hovering above the ground. But, when Finn reached the spot he thought it might have been, he found nothing and could see nothing.

"Emmie?" he called meekly.

"I'm here," answered Emmie, standing so close it gave him an almighty scare.

"I'm here too," announced Estravon, frightening both of them so that their fighting suits wobbled with shock.

The three stood in the swirling cloud, trying to calm the thump of their hearts.

"Where is he?" asked Emmie.

"I don't know," said Finn, breathless. He couldn't even be sure which way they'd come in or which way was out.

"Was that your dad?" she asked.

"I think so," said Finn, peering into the fog. "I don't know. It had to be."

"Maybe he was part of a rescue party," suggested Emmie.

"Then why did he run away from us?" asked Estravon. "That's hardly the standard approach to being rescued."

Nobody had an answer for that.

They could hardly make out anything more than a few steps ahead. Soil had given way to rock – flat and pockmarked, covered in stones and slabs as if this part of the Infested Side had once been pulverised by the fist of some awesome giant. Which wasn't necessarily out of the question.

"I've never wandered into a trap before," said Estravon, "but I'm sure this is how it would feel."

They moved forward, halting at the sound of a dull *phwoosh* from somewhere away to their right.

Crack.

Silence again.

They walked on, but soon stalled at the sound of another *phwoosh* accompanied by a dim flicker of light in the fog. Then, almost close enough to scorch Finn's left elbow, a *phwoosh* of flame leaped from a small gouge in the ground, and just as quickly dropped and disappeared.

"It's not fog," said Finn. "It's smoke."

"The odds worsen with every step," said Estravon.

They hunched over and carefully examined the bite in the rock from which the flame had jumped. The rock here was frazzled, long ago distorted by fire.

From somewhere deep in the smoke they heard another *phwoosh* and a *crack* a moment later. Then another. Again a muted smudge of flame burned and died before the unnerving *crack* of a rock hitting the ground beside them caused each to jump away.

"I feel like we've walked into a barbecue," Finn said to Emmie. She managed to raise a smile.

Phwoosh. A rock hummed past Finn's ear, hitting the ground right beside them.

"We could use the scanner if you hadn't dropped it," said Estravon, sounding jittery. "Why it wasn't affixed to your fighting suit in the proper manner, I don't know."

"So, you just left it there?" said Emmie, placing a hand over her mouth to stop herself coughing in the throat-scraping smoke.

"I would've picked it up except that I think I'd have lost a limb if I'd done so," said Estravon.

"Shush," said Finn.

There was a new noise, close by, but whatever was making it was invisible in the smoke. It sounded like a whimper.

They swung round to face it. Emmie rummaged through her bag and pulled out something that looked like a green bottle with the fronds of a pineapple attached and waved it in the general direction of the whimpering.

Estravon carefully reached across to the device and turned it the other way round in her hands. "It would help to point it in the right direction," he whispered.

Phwoosh. A purple flame shot up from the rocks between them. Its heat singed the edges of Emmie's skirt. Finn stepped round it as it died away, just about dodging another jet of fire ahead of them. His fighting suit rattled like a string of cans behind a newly-weds' car.

Phwoosh. More flame a little distance away, then a *crack* as another large piece of rock hit the ground near them.

"Any thoughts?" asked Emmie. "Sooner or later the flames are going to burn us or one of those rocks is going to land right on us."

Phwoosh.

"A few thoughts," said Finn. "No good ones, though."

Crack.

"How about we retrace our steps and go back the way we came?" Emmie said.

"Which way was that?" asked Estravon, peering into the thick wall of fog surrounding them. "It's not like we left a trail of breadcrumbs."

"Quiet," said Finn because, at that moment, becoming a walking barbecue was suddenly less of a priority.

He had heard a voice. In the fog. Close.

"Sausages," the voice said. "Sausages."

"What *is* that?" Emmie asked.

"Sausages," the voice said.

"And why is it saying sausages?"

"Sausages," the voice repeated.

"Is it Hugo?" asked Estravon.

"Definitely not," confirmed Finn.

A flame *phwooshed* just behind them.

"Sausages," the voice shouted impatiently.

"I think it just wants sausages," said Finn, leaning into the smoke.

"Of course he does not want sausages!" snapped a second, unseen voice. This one was strained, higher pitched. "He wants your help."

This was followed by a long, pained dog howl cutting through the almost suffocating gloom.

Above, the smoke stirred briefly, accompanied by the same sound of whipping canvas that Finn had heard

in the forest. A wing, it cleared a pocket of air along the ground just long enough for them to see a creature ahead.

It had a wet nose and a long snout. Its meaty muscles occasionally twitched under a sleek dark coat. Its front teeth protruded through a gap in its thin lips. And its tail was trapped beneath a flat rock.

The smoke closed in again.

"It's a dog," said Finn.

"It's not a dog," said Estravon.

"You saw its nose," said Emmie. "It's definitely a dog."

"It might *look* like a dog," said Estravon. "It might howl like a dog. It might roll over and have its tummy tickled like a dog for all I care. But consider this: in the millennia since the canine was domesticated by humans, is there a single recorded instance of a dog talking?"

"Sausages," said the dog.

"Except, I grant you, for the occasional dog who can bark the word sausages."

"*Humans*," said the second voice, still out of view, but strained and uncomfortable as if it were being sat on. "He knows you are humans. He calls you sausages because you smell of sausages. You humans always smell of sausages. Now help us."

Emmie had lifted the pineapple-like device above her head in readiness.

Finn made up his mind. Dog or not, a trap or not, this creature seemed to need their help and he hated to think of a living thing in pain.

"I can't just walk away from a suffering animal," Finn said, stepping forward.

"Yes, you really can," Estravon sighed. Emmie lifted the weapon a little higher.

Just to the left of them, the *phwooosh* of another flame and the *crack* of a rock propelled upwards were close enough to make them all jump a little.

Finn stopped just short of the Legend, able to make out the dog but nothing else. "Where's the other one of you?" he asked.

"You are looking at us," said the second voice. "You just cannot see me."

"Are you invisible?" asked Emmie, arriving alongside Finn.

"No, I am *not* invisible," said the strained voice. "I am trapped under a rock. Look, how about we have a big discussion *after* you free me?"

"How can we trust you?" said Finn.

"Human," said the trapped voice.

"It keeps saying that," said Estravon, "as if it thinks we don't know what we are."

"We will bring you to him," the voice clarified. "We will bring you to the human."

*P*hwoosh. An ignition deep in the smoke, like lightning from a distant storm. *Crack.*

Finn and Emmie looked at each other, eyes widening at this new possibility. Estravon opened his mouth to complain, but the other two had already stepped forward through the murk and cautiously worked their way round the Legend at a safe distance.

It looked like a dog, huge, and tough, even curled up the way it was. At the rear, they saw that its tail was wedged under a large slab of stone that must have been propelled there by one of the flames. The base of the tail, where it met the dog's backside, was just visible: a glimpse of vivid green, a surprising shock of colour in a world so muted.

"It could be a Shapeshifter," Estravon warned.

Finn looked at the large animal. It appeared so vulnerable there, unprotected against attack. Its mouth hung open at the sides, its teeth resting on drooling lips. It seemed to him to lack something he had seen in other Legends: murderous intent.

So, tugged by sympathy he couldn't resist, Finn stepped closer. The dog shifted, tried again to pull its tail from under the rock.

"Ouch," said the tail.

The three of them flinched at that, but Finn worked up the courage to walk round and peer under the large slab. Poking out from the far side was the arrow-shaped head of a snake. Thin. Bright green. Its scaly body led back under the rock until it appeared again on the other side to merge with the furry stump at the dog's backside.

The tail was a snake. The snake a tail. Whichever way around. And it was surprisingly talkative.

"Stop it, you hairy lump," demanded the snake-tail as the dog whimpered and shifted again. "I will not have a scale left if you keep pulling like that."

The dog moved again. The snake-tail complained again.

"You're a dog," said Emmie, "with a talking snake for a tail?"

"If you are just going to point out everything you see, things will get boring very quickly," responded the snake-tail.

Estravon snapped a picture with his camera.

"You saw the human?" queried Finn, suspicious now.

"Yes," responded the snake-tail. "He asked us. To guide you."

"Describe him then."

"He had flesh. Some hair. Metal skin. Sausages. You all smell of sausages."

Emmie wrinkled her nose in derision at that vague description.

Finn squinted at the dog end of the Legend. "We need more if we're to trust you," he said and walked away again, bluffing a bit, half hoping the Legend wouldn't let him go.

"*You!*" the snake-tail shouted. "The human looks like you. Not these other two. You."

Finn considered that, then walked to the rear of the dog and began pulling at the rock. It was too heavy. Emmie helped too, but the rock refused to budge off the snake-tail trapped beneath.

"Fantastic," said Estravon. "You're both actually convinced by that."

Clearly unhappy with circumstances but out of options, Estravon finally came to help. He grabbed the rock firmly to pull hard on it while the other two pushed from underneath. It took another couple of goes, but eventually they forced the heavy stone aside.

The dog part of the Legend immediately whipped its tail forward and began licking and scratching at it with its huge paws. This would have been relatively normal, even for the Infested Side, if the tail hadn't immediately complained very loudly about the whole thing.

"Stop it!" the snake-tail commanded. "You will break the skin."

When the dog did finally cease scratching and licking, and the snake-tail was released to hang back between its legs, Finn, Emmie and Estravon couldn't help but gawp at the sight.

"You should take a step back," said the snake, flicking its forked tongue laconically.

Neither Finn, Emmie nor Estravon took a step back.

"*Now*," insisted the tail.

They stood back and, a moment later, a *phwoooosh* of flame leaped from the spot on which they'd stood, shooting a piece of rock upwards and away. The heat prickled the skin on Finn's face. The threat of burning suddenly seemed a little too real.

"You are in the Fire Spits. If you want to get out of here unharmed, you must follow our trail. We understand this world. We were born of it, share a royal bloodline going back as far as the great Masters of the Seven—"

The dog cocked its leg to pee.

"No splashing!" said the snake-tail, pulling itself up and out of the way. "No splashing!"

There was splashing.

"Every. Single. Time," the snake-tail said forlornly.

"If you know this place so well," said Finn, "how come you ended up trapped like that?"

"We know the *way through*," said the snake-tail. "That is different from knowing where every rock is going to land. We would not even be in here if the other human had not asked us to wait for you."

"Thanks," said Finn.

"Thank us when we get out of here in one uncooked piece," it said sniffily. Then the dog moved off, the snake-tail's eyes trained on the trio of disbelieving humans standing in the smoke as the dog part walked away. "Well, come on then," it said. "Follow me or get roasted. Or squashed."

It didn't seem like much of a choice.

They followed.

Above, there was an ominous *swoosh* in the cloud, the hint of a wing unfurling above the smoke as a ghoulish shadow glided over them.

The dog groaned, barked, growled.

"He wants to know if you are feeling well," the snake-tail said to Finn.

Finn wasn't sure how to respond. He was in a smoke-filled plain on the Infested Side and had the feeling they were being watched from above. "Yes," he said eventually.

"Good. Do mention any changes. Now the human will be at the tower."

"Tower?" exclaimed Finn.

"Yes. He will arrive when the snow on the mountain above it turns completely black. No earlier. No later. You had better hurry," said the tail. "Although I do not see that you have much choice. You have brought a lot of enemies in your wake. They are out there, in the forest, and the only thing they find more attractive than the smell of sausages is cooked sausages."

The Legend walked on until it was enveloped in the smoke.

Finn glanced at Emmie and Estravon and knew they were thinking the same as him. There was no way back. No way out. No way that was safe. They shouldn't even be contemplating the idea of following a strange Legend across a flaming landscape on the Infested Side. But they had no choice.

They followed the Legend.

'The Three Explodings of Niall Blacktongue'
From *The Chronicles of the Sky's Collapse*,
as told by the inhabitants of the Infested Side

"A war is coming," Gantrua told Niall Blacktongue. "My war."

The human had been spared death with a whisper heard only by Gantrua on a scaffold all those years before. What strangled words did he say that day? A promise perhaps. A secret. A betrayal. No one knew. No one wanted to ask because those would be the last words out of their mouths that did not end in "aaarrrgghhhhhh".

Whatever the truth, those words had contained a power that saved Blacktongue's life and seeded a strange bond between the human and the great Fomorian. Gantrua would visit Blacktongue's tower to converse with him, and the rumour of what they talked about would ripple afterwards through the ranks of guards outside.

"There are seven rulers of Legends in this world, and we fight each other more than we fight the humans now," Gantrua said on one such visit. "But there is room for one ruler only."

Blacktongue was quiet. Even when left alone, only two sounds were heard from the tower. One was a murmured mantra during his meditations. The other was the incessant scratching of his nails on the wall, where it was said a mural was growing, from floor to ceiling, formed from the dust and clay pressed by scrawny human fingers.

It was a vision, said the guards. A prophecy of some terrible event yet to happen.

"And there are other enemies," Gantrua continued, the grim light of day throwing out a great shadow of muscle and armour. He picked up a wet, clay-smeared stone from beneath the mural, clasped it in his palm. "There is a resistance growing, a rebellion. It will be crushed."

Gantrua opened his hand. The stone was dust.

The human listened, silent. It was as if that explosion all those years ago was still settling within him. When he had first ignited in the forest, it had appeared accidental, triggered by a spear, a tiny puncture from which a shockwave emerged that destroyed half an army, a forest.

The effect was described as akin to being kicked by every one of a Sleipnir's hooves at the same time, while being shot out of a catapult, pulled backwards by a giant and hit in the face with a mountain.

At least that was what it felt like to those standing half a league away.

"Out there," Gantrua said, motioning behind him, "those lug-headed idiots wonder why I keep you alive. They hear your chanting and ask what possible power such puny words can hold. But I know it's not the words that hold power. It's the opposite. The words keep your true power at bay."

Blacktongue's eye twitched. A truth had been struck upon.

"I know that the energy you let wreak havoc when you first came here is still within you, that it takes all your effort to contain it." He brought his face so close to Blacktongue's that the teeth of his grille pressed against the human's skin. "I will offer you a deal."

Gantrua raised himself again. Blacktongue breathed deeply, evenly, masking the tremor within his lungs.

"I will help you find the boy again," said the Fomorian, "to stop him before he destroys everything.

But, before that, you will do something for me."

Blacktongue paused in his scratching and looked at him.

"You will destroy my enemies," Gantrua told him. "And, when that is done, we will kill the boy. Together."

27

It was a case of so far, so good.

Or, at least, a case of so far, so not as horrific as it could be.

The Legend was guiding Finn, Emmie and Estravon, and neither the dog at the front nor the snake at its tail had eaten them. Or bitten them. Or pawed them or poisoned them. It hadn't delivered them into the jaws of an army of Legends. It had instead carefully led them through what it called the Fire Spits.

"Do not worry about the stones you can hear falling," the snake-tail had told them. "It is the ones you do not hear that will get you."

Sweatier, with their lungs suffering but not scorched, they cleared the smoking earth and entered instead fields of tall hard reeds that jutted from the ground like spears. After the claustrophobia of the Petrified Forest and the gloom of the Fire Pits, this wide stretch of open ground, bathed by grey light, was oddly welcoming.

The Legend made straight for a path of broken reeds, crushed into the sand by what Finn guessed must have been years of passing feet. Or paws. Or claws. Or all of them together.

Either side of the fields were the remains of more giant trees, long dead, half-light reflecting off branches turned to glass. At this remove, there were glimpses of colour in them. Dull emerald, deep brown, a hint of yellow in blotches along their length. They were the colours of nature, apparently long buried in this most unnatural of landscapes. It was as if the Infested Side was a world in decay. A place where colour had given up.

From the depths of the trees came growing sounds of life. A howl, some grunts, the occasional scream. They carried a worrying edge of impatience which put a scamper in Finn's step. While Finn hated to admit it, even just to himself, Estravon was right. Why hadn't the Legends come to attack them yet? What was holding them back?

Finn, Emmie and Estravon followed behind the dog-snake Legend, at a cautious distance, while the snake-tail kept its eyes on Finn even as it bobbed behind the rest of its body.

"What do you think this Legend is?" Emmie asked

Finn as they walked.

"Not sure. A Chimera maybe?" he responded.

"A Chimera?" spluttered the snake-tail as its dog's body stopped and growled. "As if we would be so common. You can hardly move ten paces in this place without bumping into a Chimera. We are not a Chimera. How many goat heads do you see here?"

The Legend turned, like a catwalk model, to show each side. Dog and snake then waited for an answer.

Estravon took another picture.

"None," admitted Finn.

"Precisely."

The Legend walked on again.

"You're a Cerberus," announced Emmie.

The dog bucked a little, growled. "Steady, Cornelius," the snake said to him. "Why must everyone presume we are the Cerberus? Do they see three dog heads? No. Lion paws? Absent. But everyone goes on about the Cerberus. It is always about the Cerberus. We are *not* the Cerberus."

"Sorry."

"We are the Orthrus."

Finn looked blank.

"*The* Orthrus," the snake-tail repeated, clearly

expectant of a positive response.

Finn struggled to recall any mention of such a Legend, but Estravon seemed to have heard of it before. "Aren't you supposed to have two dog heads at the front?" he asked it.

The dog snarled.

"Cornelius says we will do our best to grow another one before we next meet," said the snake-tail.

Orthrus

The Orthrus recommenced its march along the path, the snake-tail grumbling. "A *Chimera*, honestly. Three heads and not a brain between you."

"What's your name?" asked Finn in the hope of

mollifying the Legend. "Is Cornelius like your, erm, front end?"

"We share a body, but we don't share a soul and we don't share a name," said the snake. "Hiss."

"But then what's *your* name?" Finn repeated.

"Hiss."

Finn didn't respond at first, but the penny finally dropped. "Oh, your *name* is Hiss."

"Why would it not be?" Hiss asked, bobbing along behind Cornelius. "It is a family name. What does Hiss mean in your world?"

Emmie shrugged. "It means, well, *hiss*. Something snakes do."

Estravon spoke. "It would be like calling your dog part Bark."

The dog barked.

Hiss tutted. "Well, here the name Hiss means Great Serpent of the Northern Climate Whose Name is Itself a Source of Wondrous Power That Tremors Like a Quake Through the Annals of the Ages— Stop that!"

Cornelius was scratching violently at its backside to rid itself of a buzzing insect.

When the Orthrus moved on again, Hiss grumbled as he swayed behind Cornelius. "You might be trapped in this world, but I am trapped *here*, between these legs. All hopes and dreams at the mercy of his bladder and itches."

Finn and the others once more let a small gap grow, while keeping alert to the sporadic noises from the woods. When they stopped again, Cornelius barked at something in the ground while wagging his tail excitedly. Or rather wagging Hiss, who screamed, "You will make me sick!"

Cornelius stood back from where he had dug a hole and maggot-like creatures poured out of it. The dog shoved in its snout and began to feast noisily.

"He does not even offer you any first," Hiss said to the humans, but their disgusted reaction said it all. "You do not want scaldgrubs? More for Cornelius then. Be thankful he found those. When he is hungry, he can get a little bitey."

Cornelius licked his lips. The rasp was of tongue on sandpaper.

"I have food," Finn said to Emmie and Estravon as he pulled his bag to the front and reached in for his own supplies. He pulled out an apple so blackened and soft it practically disintegrated in his hand. Then an orange: shrivelled and white, almost entirely devoured by mould. His sandwiches looked like they might crawl from the lunchbox and slither away. Each of them had been fresh and tasty when put there only hours previously, but now looked like they'd been left to rot for weeks.

There was only one thing left to try. "I've a packet of crisps," he said. "They're sort of immortal, I think."

He opened the pack, the foil popping as the bag deflated, and pulled out a crunchy, salty sliver and ate it. Sure enough, it was perfect. He shoved some more into his mouth, passing the bag to Emmie while he licked his fingers and picked at the crumbs that littered his chest.

"These taste so good," said Emmie through a mouthful of crisps.

"Well, isn't this great?" said Estravon, his voice heavy with sarcasm. "I'm trapped here with two kids. I'm violating approximately forty-seven separate rules about fraternising with the enemy. And the only food on offer is a choice between fresh maggots or heavily salted snacks. Hardly a balanced diet. At least if you had something sweet I could..."

He relented and took the crisps.

For the first time since before the Fire Spits, Finn felt the charge through his arm again and struggled to hide his discomfort as it ran through his veins and shocked his shoulder. He could see that Hiss had noticed, but said nothing.

Finn diverted attention, asking as calmly as he could, "Why are you helping us?"

"Sausages," said Cornelius.

"I wish he'd stop that," said Estravon. "It sounds like he's reading a menu."

"He means," said Hiss, "that the other human sent word out that, if you ever showed up, there would be a reward for bringing you to him safely."

"What reward?" asked Emmie.

"Sausages," said Cornelius.

"Actual sausages," confirmed Hiss. "Quite a delicacy here."

"But how do we know you're bringing us to the right human?" Estravon asked, picking bits of crisp from between his teeth.

"How many humans can there be wandering around, hiding among the Legends, avoiding capture?" asked Hiss. "Believe me, your very presence has boosted the numbers significantly."

From the massive trees, there came more movement and noise. A *kkrrnch*. A *taheeeeetahee*.

"And those Legends, why don't they come out?" Estravon asked the Orthrus. "They're out there, but they don't show themselves."

"Legend is the human word," said Hiss as Cornelius lapped up some scaldgrubs that were trying to escape up his cheek. "Some of us find it quite offensive, to be honest, just presuming we are all the same like that."

"What do you call yourselves?"

"By our names or by our type," said Hiss, seemingly irked by the need to explain all of this. "And, when we need to describe all of us collectively, we personally prefer a word that you could not pronounce."

"Try us," said Estravon.

"Tell them, Cornelius," said Hiss. The dog swallowed whatever scaldgrubs were in its mouth and let out a long, strangulated sound that seemed to come from deep in its belly, via the spleen and bowel, and which rattled round its jaws for a couple of seconds after it had finished.

"How would you spell that?" said Estravon, searching for his pencil and notepad.

Finn felt that buzz through his arm again, the same one that had held the crystal in Darkmouth. It was like he was grabbing an electric fence, but couldn't let go. "I'm friends with a Legend," he said, in a strained voice, but hoping that talking might distract him from the strange sensation. "Well, sort of. And he never told me any of that."

"You are *friends* with one of us?" said Hiss. "I doubt that."

"Yeah. A Hogboon. Broonie is his name. We got to know him quite well. Maybe he lives around here somewhere."

"You do not know Broonie," said Hiss.

"We do," insisted Emmie. "We even helped him escape back here."

Estravon looked sharply at her and Finn's heart sank that she'd let go of that secret. Estravon took out his notepad and wrote something down.

"Broonie can help us," continued Emmie, undaunted.

"No, he cannot," said Hiss.

"He can," said Finn. "Maybe." The strange feeling in his arm wouldn't leave him, but seemed instead to be spreading across his shoulder blades.

"No," insisted Hiss. "He cannot. There is only one Broonie among the Hogboons here and right now he is not in a position even to help himself."

There was a howl from deep in the forest.

"You never answered my first question," said Estravon. "We've been followed by Legends since we arrived here, but they don't attack us. Why?"

"Perhaps they wish to avoid infection," said Hiss. "Not

so many years ago, a human was brought here and half this world ended up with a very nasty rash."

"That doesn't sound right," said Estravon.

"Trust me, it was not a pleasant place to have an itch."

"No," said Estravon. "I mean, that can't be the reason they don't attack us. We've little armour. We're low on weapons. I didn't spend a year studying Higher-level Tactical Warfare to believe they're just ignoring us. I'd guess it has something to do with the boy, doesn't it?"

They all looked to Finn. As their eyes turned on him, he felt woozy – but not because of their attention. Instead, the strange energy was still vibrating in his arm, pulsing through his shoulder, his neck.

He found it hard to see. The light was dimming, a chill creeping across the Infested World. Away from them, he could make out the ridge of mountains, among which rose a great peak hugged by the carpet of cloud. He could just about focus on its snow-cap, a sliver of darkness eating into it.

Emmie hoovered up the last of the crisps, picking up the crumbs with the tip of her finger. "Are you OK, Finn?" he heard her ask as she turned to him.

His head swam. He opened his mouth to speak. Nothing came out.

"Finn?" she said.

A bolt ran through his chest, down his back.

Then he was gone. Out. Like someone had pressed an off switch in his mind.

28

"**W**ake up, Finn," Emmie was saying. "Finn, come on."

He had already woken. He thought he had anyway. He couldn't be entirely sure.

"That's what happens when you rely solely on crisps for nutrition," he heard Estravon proclaim and Finn knew for certain he was awake.

He jolted upright.

Emmie and Estravon stood over him, either side. She was obviously concerned, biting her lip as she jittered back and forth, unsure quite what to do to help. The Assessor just looked a bit annoyed.

The Orthrus was watching, but Cornelius had nervously backed away a couple of steps while Hiss quietly whispered reassurances to him.

Finn heard the snake-tail say, "We must stay."

Stay for what? thought Finn and it seemed to

kick-start his mind again. Clarity flooded back into his head, normality into his body, vitality into his legs. He sprang to his feet, feeling almost like he didn't have much choice about it.

"Don't do that again, Finn. Please," said Emmie. "What happened?"

"I don't know," answered Finn. "The crystal, I think. When I opened the gateway."

Without even realising it, he was holding the right side of his waist, just above the belt of the fighting suit. Finn had fallen on something sharp and the growing pain of that was only now beginning to nag at him.

"Did you bring any medical equipment in that bag?" asked Estravon, observing Finn. "Or did you think the crisp packet would bandage you up if need be?"

"Stop it," said Emmie.

"Be very careful," warned Estravon. "I am forced by the rules to accompany him, but not you. Don't forget that."

Finn closed his eyes and let the energy relax within the fibres of his body, settle into every blood cell. He felt a calm washing through him, but it was almost instinctive, as if it was his mind's way of fighting back at whatever was trying to take over.

"Do you hear that?" Estravon whispered.

They each listened, Hiss narrowing his eyes as he watched the humans.

"No," said Emmie after a few seconds.

"Exactly. Nothing. It's all gone quiet."

Just saying that seemed to break the spell. Unseen in the world around them, a hubbub grew again steadily, a low murmur.

"Maybe Estravon's right. Maybe we do need real food," Emmie said. "If we find Broonie, he can get some."

"No, he cannot," said Hiss.

"We could at least try," said Emmie, but Cornelius had already moved on again.

Finn's bag felt heavy on his back, his steel trousers dragged at his legs, but he reckoned he had enough energy to go with the Orthrus.

They pushed through thick, hard reeds, which now reached to their shoulders. Estravon resumed his complaints about the damage it was causing to his suit. Then he complained that no one seemed to be listening to his complaints.

Which wasn't true at all. They were just ignoring them.

Finn worked up the strength to walk alongside the

Orthrus. He needed to ask it something. "Why did you look so worried back there, when I fell?"

The snake was hanging low, swaying metronomically. It appeared to be trying to sleep. Without opening his eyes, Hiss spoke. "When we first met, why did you think we were a Shapeshifter?"

"Because we met one at the cave where our gateway opened," answered Finn.

"And Finn killed it," said Emmie excitedly, arriving alongside. "You should've seen him do it. He was merciless."

Cornelius stopped. Hiss looked as intrigued as a snake could. "You killed a Shapeshifter?"

"No," insisted Finn, hurt by the insinuation. "We just trapped it, left it tied up. I feel kind of bad about it, to be honest."

"I don't," said Estravon from behind.

"The Shapeshifter was in a cave, yes?" asked Hiss, eyes open again. "Would it have been the Cave at the End of the World by any chance?"

"Really smelly?" asked Emmie.

"Golden goo and stalactites?" added Finn.

"Stalag*mites*," said Estravon.

Cornelius gave the strangest laugh, a dog's wheeze of

amusement. "What my other half is saying," said Hiss, "is that you put the Skin-Walker out of action. He feeds off new forms, you see. A touch of another creature is all it takes and he can become them."

"I touched it," Finn recalled. "When I thought it was Mrs Bright."

"Then he shows them a vision of themselves," continued Hiss. "He mimics them. Toys with them. It is how he gets his energy. And only then does he kill them. But that is irrelevant for now. What matters is not that you stopped the Shapeshifter, but what you stopped him from *guarding*."

"Which was?" asked Estravon.

"That is the problem with you humans. You do not ever believe the answer could be falling at your small, oddly-shaped feet. What do you think is within those stalagmites that could be worth guarding? Something that could have great power?"

Finn thought about it for a moment. "The stalagmites," he said. "Do they contain crystals?"

"Well done," hissed Hiss, swaying as Cornelius moved forward again. "You disabled the very thing stopping you from getting home, then ran away without even realising it. You really are not the brightest snakes on the head of the Medusa, are you?"

"I told you we should have stayed at that cave," said Estravon, his anger boiling. "Standard rescue procedure dictates you stay with your gateway and await rescue."

"You ran away quicker than any of us," Emmie told him.

"The three of you ran quite a distance too," said Hiss. "Now your biggest problem is not how to get back to those crystals so you can return to the Promised World, but rather who might get there before you. Because, without their guard, there is nothing to stop those crystals from being discovered and plundered."

"Why is it called the Cave at the End of the World?" asked Estravon.

Hiss shrugged, or at least got the closest to shrugging a snake could manage. "No one seems to know. It certainly does not look anything like the actual end of the world and I have been there. Totally different place altogether." Hiss paused and swung towards Finn, asking urgently, "Hold on, are you bleeding?"

Finn looked at his waist, where the band of his fighting suit pushed up over his school sweater. There was a tear through to the skin and it was stained with fresh blood. "It happened when I fell, back when we were eating. I must've scraped it against a stone or something," he said. "I don't think it's too bad."

"I'll be the judge of that," said Estravon. "I'm not having you dying over here, on my watch." He paused. "The paperwork would be *appalling*."

"It's just a scratch," said Finn as Estravon bent to examine it. "OK, a big scratch," he added once he saw a look of concern cross the Assessor's face.

"It's not very deep. And it's not very life-threatening, but it's trickling blood all the same and you could get an infection if you're not careful," Estravon said, straightening up.

"There you go," said Finn, pulling his sweater back over the cut. "I told you it wasn't serious."

Around them, deep in the reeds, came noises. Creeping. Listening. Tracking. Still refusing to show themselves.

"You do not think it is *serious?*" said Hiss. "You are *bleeding*. You might as well waggle your fleshy behind at the creatures in those trees. You have to stop. You will drive them crazy."

"I can't just *stop* bleeding," said Finn.

"At that rate," said Estravon, "his blood will not coagulate until approximately—"

"Shut up," Hiss told him.

227

The Orthrus started back into the forest, quickening its pace all of a sudden. Finn felt the molten lead of panic beginning to pour into his stomach again, that old familiar feeling.

Cornelius growled.

"You are right, we are almost there," Hiss said to him, then spoke to the three humans. "It is just beyond these reeds."

"We're almost at the tower?" asked Finn because the mountain still seemed a distance away, a dark shadow touching the edge of the snow-cap.

"No. We will get there before the snow turns black," said Hiss. "But that is not where we are going right now."

"Where are we going?" asked Finn.

"We are taking a detour," said Hiss. "To get something to stop that bleeding."

"Detour?" said Estravon. "No one said anything about taking any detours."

"The human boy says he knows the Hogboon called Broonie," said Hiss and rose high enough to press his face to Estravon's. "We need help, and Hogboons have ways and means to heal such cuts. So, we are going to see Broonie."

29

There had been dark moments in Darkmouth's past, but its people had never come out to help.

They had not come out to help during the Little Siege of 1783.

They had not come out for the Somewhat Bigger Siege of 1784.

Eighty years ago an ancestor of Finn's, Leonora the Wild, misplaced her house keys and the people of Darkmouth didn't even come out to help find those.

But two of their young were missing, so the inhabitants of the last Blighted Village had come out to help this time. They walked the beaches, combed the fields, poked through the ditches. Clara visited the school, addressing Finn and Emmie's class with Steve, jittery, alongside her, in his fighting suit for some reason that no one really understood.

"If any of you has seen them, please let us know," she said kindly.

The pupils sat in awkward silence, the seriousness of this weighing on them. Or most of them. The Savage twins watched with quiet amusement.

"And if you do know where they are," Finn's mother said, "please let them know they're not in any trouble."

Steve tutted loudly at that. Unable to keep quiet any longer, he stepped forward. "Listen. You're all smart little beggars, right? This is serious stuff, not just a silly game. It's Legend Hunter business. You wouldn't understand, but this is about stopping you all being torn into little meaty chunks ultimately. So, you know, get on your phones or whatever and let's get this sorted soon."

Steve stepped back, apparently satisfied. Clara stared at him in disbelief. Mrs McDaid fought to hide her displeasure. The children gawked.

Class was let out early so pupils could join the long lines scouring the town, heads down, searching for clues. Finn and Emmie's classmates grew as giddy as the adults were gravely serious. The Savage twins were particularly reluctant helpers, taking their place in the line with hands in pockets, joking throughout, even as Mrs McDaid informed them that this was a very serious matter and they should treat it as such.

"Hold on, I think I've found Finn," Conn said to Manus. "No, actually, it's just a worm. It was hard to tell the difference."

"There are so many weeds here, he could be any one of them," Manus said to Conn.

"If I hear another word from either one of you, there'll be a serious punishment for you both. There's nothing funny about Finn's special circumstances," said a passing Mrs McDaid.

The twins sniggered at that. As their teacher walked away, Conn spotted something colourful in the grass, a wristband snagged on a thorn, a vivid splash of primary colours against the green. He drew Manus's attention to it.

"I've seen this before," Conn said. "On the Legend blunder's wrist."

"I guess we need to do something with it," said Manus.

"You're right," agreed Conn. He ground the wristband into the undergrowth with his heel, where it couldn't be seen. Then the twins moved on with the rest of the line.

30

On the Infested Side, the stabbing reeds ended just as suddenly as they'd begun.

Finn followed the Orthrus past them and emerged into a wide rolling expanse of hard scrub, pitted muck and stones. It looked as if the area had been smeared on to the landscape, a rough oval pressed into the glass forest that jutted high on three sides.

At its centre, the ground slumped away into a wide bowl. A thin column of blue smoke rose from a dwelling cut into the earth to touch the uniform cloud pressed low on the world. The odour of a fiery hearth was welcoming above the pervasive putridness of the air.

"Wait here and try not to bleed everywhere," Hiss said to Finn. From the woods came a burble of whispers and muted shrieks. Something seemed to dart across the forest floor to their left. Something else leaped through branches.

Against a world so devoid of colour and warmth, the deep red of Finn's blood had a near extraordinary vibrancy. It trickled through the dirt on his fingers, dribbled down his hand and on to the armour, where it then ran at pace towards the ground. The little splashes of red were like blossoms on the dirt.

"Sorry about the bleeding," Finn said.

"Not exactly your fault, Finn," said Emmie.

Estravon stood at their backs, watching over their heads as the Orthrus trotted towards the dwelling. "Here's the deal," he said. "We get to that tower, we get your father, we get *back* to the cave and all those crystals and then we get out of here. We've been too lucky for too long. About three hours forty-three minutes too long, to be accurate. And that includes a minute of anticipated luck I've added as a statistical margin of error."

Finn sighed. "Could you at least try and be a bit cheery?" he asked. "It's not as if I don't have enough worry in my head as it is."

"For a couple of people who've done very little but collapse and bleed and run into suspiciously helpful two-headed Legends, you're very cocky all of a sudden."

In the glum light, a momentary darkness passed over them.

Finn looked up at the sky and, while he saw nothing, he knew something had been there. *The something with wings*.

Shuddering, he moved towards the hovel in the depression and heard voices. One of them was thin and kind of familiar.

"Take those humans away from us now," said that voice, "or I swear by the blasted nose of Great-uncle Ilfridus, I will bury you in ravenous biteworms."

"It is Broonie this, Broonie that from these humans," said Hiss. "We will delay you for no longer than the beat of a hummingdragon's wing. Just see him, give us some sputumweed for his wound and we will be on our way."

"Out of the question," said the voice.

"You hear that malevolence in the forest?" said Hiss. "They are waiting. Watching. They want the humans."

"Let 'em have 'em."

"Although this is hard to fathom, the soldiers in that forest are afraid of this child. They have heard rumours, a warning that precedes him. Their instinct draws them to him, but so far their biggest fight has been with their own urges to kill him. You do not want them this nervous on your mudstep. And you certainly do not want the boy hanging around."

Finn edged closer, peeking over the top of the roof,

layered with flattened stalks, a column of smoke rising steadily. He could now see the Orthrus talking to a short Legend in rags, wearing a hat that was more holes than material and under which large green ears hung. It was a Hogboon, but Finn could not make out his face.

"Leave us in peace," the Hogboon begged.

"We both know that some of those in the forest right now would not be pleased to realise that in your hovel are bags of scumweavels which, by the letter of the law, were theirs to begin with."

"I found those scumweavels."

"True, but you found them when breaking into their dwellings."

There was a momentary silence, then a sigh. "If Broonie comes out, you promise you'll go?"

"Add some sputumweed to the deal and we will leave. We have to stop the boy's bleeding. I swear on the life of my brother."

Cornelius gave a disgruntled snort.

Finn leaned forward a bit more, sending some dirt falling from the ridge. The Hogboon lifted his gaze so that Finn could see the face under the brim of the tattered hat. His nose was long, his ears longer and his skin a shade of green just a little lighter. There was a certain resemblance to Broonie, but it wasn't him.

The Hogboon called back into the dwelling. "Phlemooka, bring Broonie out to us. Just for a moment."

"Sausage," said Cornelius, nodding at Finn to come down.

Emmie scrambled down ahead. "I think it's cute when he calls you sausage."

"Being considered meat can't be good for anyone's chances of getting out alive," said Estravon, passing him next.

Finn climbed down to join them, leaving a bright smudge of blood behind on the dirt, and came face to face with the Hogboon. The look he got in return was one of deep distrust laced with a certain curiosity.

"Eugh," exclaimed the Hogboon, nose wrinkled in disgust. "I heard about human ears, but to actually see them in the flesh. And those nostrils. Hardly big enough to fit half a toe into."

"I just want to register my opposition to this meeting, in the strongest terms possible," said Estravon as he searched for something in his pocket.

Another Hogboon stood at the door to the hovel. A female, she cradled rags from which Finn could just about see a small green face poking out. A baby Hogboon. And this must be its mother, Finn presumed. She had a face that while utterly strange appeared kindly.

"Whaddya want, ye wartless uglies?" she rasped.

The male Hogboon pointed at Finn, and the mother held the bundle towards him, using a crooked finger to reveal the infant's face. "This is Broonie," she said. "Now get lost."

"Oh, he's so cute," said Emmie, craning for a peek. The baby Hogboon sneezed on her.

Estravon was muttering something about his camera.

"I'm sorry," said Finn, looking from the Hogboon to the Orthrus, "but that's not Broonie. Or it's not the Broonie we know. He's much older than that."

"No, he is not," said the father Hogboon.

"Oh, he is," confirmed Emmie. "I don't know how old you two might be——"

"You impertinent bag of skin," said the mother Hogboon.

"But he was much older. Like you. An adult Hogboon."

Estravon was still muttering. "It must have fallen from my pocket while we lay down..."

"I don't know who ye met," the mother said, "but ye won't find another Broonie this side of the Forest of Woe. Broonie is a unique name."

"She made it up," said the father. "I wasn't that keen meself."

"So, I promise ye that there's only one of him in this world," continued the mother Hogboon, "and ye're looking at him. Now go away."

Estravon began to scramble back up the mound. "My camera," he called down. "Did anyone see it? I only borrowed it from the office. I have to give it back. Otherwise there'll be no end of forms to—"

A screech carried through the air and everyone looked towards the forest. When they turned back, the mother and baby Hogboon had retreated inside.

"You're a portent of disaster," continued the father, "and we could do without any disaster so early in the evening. It ruins the appetite."

Another howl from the woods, the growing sound of a forest ready to burst.

The Hogboon disappeared back into his hovel, slamming the rickety door behind him.

"The sputumweed!" Hiss cried to the closing door. He then rose at Cornelius's rear to meet Finn's eyeline. "Next time you claim to know a Legend, try and make sure they are a little older than larvae."

"But I do know Broonie. And, if that was him, then..."

"Where's Estravon gone?" asked Emmie, looking back up the mound.

Estravon was nowhere to be seen. His mutterings had stopped. Instead, the sounds of the forest were almost on top of them now, gleeful suddenly.

"Something's not right," said Emmie.

Cornelius whined.

"We need to go to the tower *now*," said Hiss. "The snow will be black soon. We have little time."

"We can't just leave Estravon behind," said Finn.

They heard an angry shout. It sounded like Estravon. From the raised ground edging behind the hovel, an object came tumbling high through the air and embedded itself at their feet. Finn picked it up. It was a pen. A silver ballpoint. Where ink should be, there was blood.

"Estravon, are you OK?" Finn called.

In the sky, a dark shape crossed swiftly over them, low, a screech piercing the thin cloud. Both Cornelius and Hiss watched it pass.

Hiss sighed as if pressed into doing something he didn't want to.

"Right, we will go and find the tall human. You two short ones stay here. Do not move under any circumstances. And while we are gone, boy, please *stop* bleeding."

The Orthrus bounded away, clearing the mound with

an almost unbroken stride.

From the forest on either side, the noise rose another notch so that the whoops and howls were almost deafening.

Finn felt a trickle of blood run down his leg and pool along the rim of his armour at the ankle, where it dripped to the ground. He smeared at it with the back of his hand. Felt the soil beneath his feet weaken a little, as if it had been stirred.

At the Hogboon's hovel, windows were being shuttered. One by one.

"What do we do?" Finn asked Emmie.

"We could use some of these devices to fight," she said, rummaging through her bag.

"My dad's taught me about setting up a defensive perimeter to hold out against attack," suggested Finn. "We could try that."

The ground trembled again, soil bubbling at the small red splodges of crimson where Finn's blood had dripped.

"Or we could run?" said Emmie.

"Running sounds good," said Finn.

They ran.

31

In the forest behind them, the noise built to a crescendo. Howls. Shrieks. Screeches. Shouts. One long, ululating *yekeyekeyekeyekeyekeyeke* that cut through everything and echoed through the frozen woods.

Noise, frenzy, tumult, hunger.

Meanwhile, Finn's and Emmie's armour made a chorus of clanks and creaks and a dozen other sounds that were simply guaranteed to alert any Legend to their whereabouts.

"I know this isn't what you want to hear," said Emmie, getting breathless under the weight of jolting steel, "but do you think you might actually—"

"I really *can't* just stop bleeding on demand!"

He felt his waist, looked again at the blood on his hand. Behind him, the *blot, blot, blot* of blood on soil.

They put some distance between themselves and the frenzy, or at least it sounded like that as they found

themselves slowing in the dense, fossilised forest and heard only their own panting for the stale air. They crouched down by the wide sleek trunk of a tall tree, the two halves of their shared fighting suit knocking against it as they caught their breath.

"I actually like this place," said Emmie.

Finn snorted a laugh through his heaving breaths, before realising she wasn't joking.

"It beats hanging around at home," she grinned, "or sitting in the car, waiting for everyone else to get things done."

"Maybe we need to swap dads," said Finn, then wished he hadn't. "I don't mean I want to leave my dad here or anything."

"I think that's pretty clear. You jumped into a gateway to come and rescue him."

"To be honest, it sucked us into it."

"You teamed up with a Legend to go on a quest across the Infested Side."

"Yeah, but I'm still worried the Orthrus is just bringing us somewhere so they can do terrible things to us," said Finn.

"You've defeated Legends."

"Kind of run away from them mostly," admitted Finn.

"And all to save the last Legend Hunter."

"And get people killed."

"Oh, are you worried about Estravon? He's probably boring a couple of Legends to death with rules right now." She thrust her chin upwards, pursed her lips and spoke in Estravon's unimpressed tones. "Actually, by order of the Twelve, your talons are contrary to rule 47-slash-Q of the Proper Use of Talons in Battle Laws."

"I will have to report you," Finn added, doing his own impression of the Assessor. "Your talons will be replaced with the appropriate ones."

"And then—"

"But only then—"

"—will we proceed with the fighting."

A sound in the forest cut off the silliness, as if the soil was turning. Finn fell quiet again. "I hope Mam's OK."

"Listen, we'll be back home soon," said Emmie, refusing to let him dwell on it. "I'm sure of it. We'll be bored stiff in Mrs McDaid's geography class before you know it, and we'll hardly be able to believe we were ever here."

Finn inhaled deeply. "I just need to get my dad back."

"You will, Finn."

"All of this is my fault. I'm a walking disaster. I can't even bleed properly."

"It really isn't your fault," Emmie insisted. "Why do you keep saying that? Why do you keep blaming yourself?"

"He said I'd find him. He told me I would. I have to get him home. Or else it'll all be my fault."

"You're blaming yourself for something you haven't even failed at yet."

Somewhere, the sound of stirring soil was growing, very slowly. It filled the silence between Finn and Emmie.

"If I get my dad back, I'll have proved myself. I'll have done it and will have earned my Legend Hunter name," said Finn, looking down at the shreds of what must once have been trees and branches and buds and life, but which were now just the crunchy carpet of a dying world. "If I do this, I think I'll have the right to leave the Legend Hunter stuff behind. To do whatever I want with my life. No one could call me a coward for giving it up. Not after this. I'd have proved that and could *choose* what I want to do. They'd have to let me. I could be a vet, like I've always wanted. Do you see what I mean?"

"You'd miss it really," said Emmie. "I'll miss it if I have to stop. This just feels so, I don't know, *right* to me."

"At least you have a choice in how you feel," said Finn.

The noise came louder, closer. An approaching churning through the undergrowth. "I don't think it's safe here at all," he said. "We need to go."

"Which way?" asked Emmie. "This forest is pretty dense."

Finn quickly pulled his now-saggy backpack round to the front, wincing as it brushed against the still-seeping cut at his waist, and fished out the radio. "I'll try and call Dad again." But there wasn't so much as a crackle from it, just a gentle white noise. "Must be blocked by the trees," he said.

The growing noise in the forest sounded like roots stretching, awakening.

"You don't *really* like it here, do you?" Finn asked Emmie.

"I actually do," she said, with whispered enthusiasm. "It sort of grows on you or something. Do you not feel it?"

"Not really," he said, but didn't have any more time to dwell on the subject. He noticed something else, a wriggle beneath the soles of his boots. "What about that? Did you feel that?" he said.

"Nah."

The soil felt loose beneath him, as if shifting away. As Finn stood up, he thought he saw something move in the trees ahead of them.

"Did you see *that?*" he whispered to Emmie.

"Yeah," she said. A creature burst from the forest. Tall. Wolf-like but on two legs. Hair grew on welts, which in turn grew on bumps. It crashed straight into their path, howling. Even in the blur of its arrival, Finn recognised it immediately as a Grendel. He had read about it. Seen the drawings. A creature terminally annoyed. Never happy. Always looking for a fight.

It had found one.

They turned to run.

Another Grendel appeared ahead of them, pink tongue lolling through grinding teeth, ears pricked at the top of its head. Its nose glistened at the end of its snarling snout. It stalked calmly from the trees as if it had been waiting for them, lips curling in anticipation.

Finn and Emmie stopped, trapped between the two Legends.

Emmie yanked her bag forward and pulled the pineapple device from it. She turned it hurriedly, trying to find an obvious trigger or switch. She found clasps on either side, bound at a split running through the centre of the device. She sprang them open and the pineapple fronds gently unfurled.

"What does it do?" she wondered, fretful.

The pineapple started to hiss, as if pressure was building within it and desperate to burst out.

"I've no idea and I wouldn't hold it any longer to find out," answered Finn. Grabbing the device from her, he threw it to the ground between them and the approaching Grendels.

Then Finn and Emmie ran in the opposite direction. The Legends hurdled the device to get to them. As they did, the pineapple weapon spluttered a faint wisp of powder from the thin line at its centre, then burst open with a violent *phaamp* – spraying a geyser of foam straight upwards into the Grendels' trajectory.

The Legends froze mid-leap, hanging for a moment in that pose before dropping either side. They thudded to the ground with their teeth bared, claws out, like toppled statues.

Finn and Emmie had paused too as they turned to

watch, but a nearby noise shook them alert again and they ran, bags jolting on their backs, crashing across the ground in whatever direction seemed easiest to cross.

"This way," they both said at the same time and ran in different directions.

Finn realised what had happened and skidded to a stop just as another Grendel emerged from the thick growth, crashing between himself and Emmie, cutting them off from each other. When it steadied itself, it was facing Finn.

It stretched a wicked grin to fully display its jaws – and, for the first time, Finn felt woozy, whether from fear or the blood still seeping gently from his cut, he couldn't be sure. The ground was uneven beneath him. The Legend crept towards him slowly, as if sizing him up.

There was a wolf whistle. The Legend turned to face it. "Over here, you fleapit!" shouted Emmie's voice from among the dead wood.

The creature turned towards it, ears pricked, pinhole eyes fixed on something. It took a moment for Finn to see a dull glint of armour, just an edge of it, crouched behind a wide tree.

"No!" he shouted. "Ignore her – come here!"

But it kept on moving towards where Emmie was hiding behind the glassy bark.

"Emmie!" he shouted. "Emmie, it's coming! Be careful."

Another Grendel emerged from the trees, and the two creatures closed in on her in a pincer movement. Then they stopped and Finn could see one of the Legends clawing at the armour. The top half of the fighting suit fell to the ground, empty and loose.

A pineapple-shape rolled slowly from its open neck.

The Legends' brows furrowed. Then their eyes widened in realisation.

Phaamp.

Two more frozen Legends tipped over with surprised looks stuck on their faces.

Finn found himself smiling widely. A grin that made cheeks ache that had had little practice in recent weeks. "Emmie!" he hissed as loudly as he could without actually shouting. "That was fantastic."

There was no response. He searched the trees for her. "Emmie. Come out, Emmie. They're gone. It's only me."

There was no sign of her.

He looked around to see which way she might have gone. Splashes of colour caught his eye. Pages and glossy pictures, utterly out of place here. It was one of Emmie's schoolbooks, open on the dark forest floor.

History Now.

Just ahead was another, shiny pages snagged on the undergrowth.

Improve Your English 4.

Books littered the way, making a paper trail for Finn to follow. *Let's Do Maths!* Then a copybook, Emmie's work scribbled through it, idle doodles in the margins. The red pen of a correction mark, Mrs McDaid's writing. A tick. *V. good.*

The trail of books ended at a large clearing, blasted stumps littering the ground as if the roof of the forest had been blown clean off.

From the further edges of the ring of trees, Legends were pouring in, flooding towards the middle. And it took Finn a moment to see why.

Emmie was trapped at the centre, pressed up against a blasted stump.

Helpless. Surrounded by Legends.

And, for the first time since Finn had met her, she looked very, very afraid.

32

Finn watched as Emmie jumped on to the wide tree stump and rummaged through her schoolbag, then tipped it over in the hope that a last device would fall out. But she shook out only pencils and sharpenings, bits of food and wrappings, the incongruous materials of a whole other world, a whole other life.

The Legends crowded in towards her, screaming through mouths rimmed with teeth, through heads rimmed with mouths, through necks rimmed with heads.

"Emmie!"

Finn stepped into the clearing. How odd she suddenly looked to him. Her school uniform exposed again, her bag covered in rough graffiti and doodles, all these normal things in a world on the far side of normality.

She caught sight of him. "Finn! Help, Finn!"

Above the clearing, there was a swirl in the cloud. The stirrings of a whirlpool.

A screech, incoming, stabbing through the world, shredding the sky.

Finn saw a serpent, wings folded along a coiled body, its fangs long curved needles in a mouth open to a grotesque width. Plummeting fast. Its body straightened and fully spread, its wings resembled umbrellas wrecked in the wind.

It banked, levelled off, zeroed in on its target.

Serpent

The Legends heard it too, then reacted to the sight of it with a new urgency, picking up speed as they ran towards Emmie.

She was the only one who didn't see it. Her focus was entirely on the Legends that surrounded her, snapping, howling, fighting to be the first to get to her.

She threw her empty schoolbag at an onrushing Legend.

It ate it.

"Finn!" she called again, distress making her voice hoarse.

"Emmie!" Finn jolted forward. Helpless. Powerless.

Claws raised, teeth bared, the Legends surged at Emmie.

But the flying serpent got to her first.

33

Emmie was gone so quickly, lifted and taken as if she weighed nothing. The serpent's flight was unchecked as it snatched her in its teeth in one swift movement. The Legends on the ground had no time to react. By the time Finn called her name again, she was already halfway across the sky. "Emmie!"

His voice fell uselessly short.

She disappeared fast. At first, she was a kicking, flailing figure in the jaws of the flying serpent, its long teeth curving round her. Then she was in the clouds.

Gone.

"Emmie," Finn repeated. But there was no shout this time, just a croaked exclamation of shock and heartbreak.

After which, he hardly breathed, just stared, paralysed. When his lungs finally jolted into action again, a sensation surged through him that was as powerful as any he'd experienced in this place. Any place.

Anger. Determination. A deep desire for revenge.

It was fuelled by the energy building within him again. The crackle through his arm. A surge in his chest. A force he could barely contain. Which he could not control.

Finn picked up a sharp, petrified branch and used it to quickly hack at another until it snapped off. With one in each hand, he advanced from the treeline, wielding his improvised swords. Anger had taken over, shoving his cowardice into a corner of his mind.

Swinging one blade, pointing the other, he summoned every training session, every minute of practice into this moment. Recalled every move he had learned, every punch and kick.

"You took Emmie!" he shouted at the Legends. "You. Took. Emmie."

He was going to carve his way through them. Going to wreak his revenge on them. Going to take all of them on.

Their attention was now fixed firmly on him. An array of Legends of such terrifying variety he couldn't even focus on them.

"Come on!" he screamed.

A dozen Legends faced him.

"Come on!"

Maybe a couple of dozen. Snarling, ruthless.

Actually, more like fifty, he realised.

They had all turned towards him.

Possibly a hundred Legends, now that he could see them better.

Moving straight for him.

He thought of all those moves he'd tried but failed to do. All those training sessions with his father that had ended in disappointment. Every punch he'd missed. Every kick that had gone awry.

He knew exactly what he needed to do.

Finn ran away.

34

Blood still dripped from Finn, weakness fighting with his adrenalin and beginning to take over his body.

In response to each step he took, the ground seemed to shift again, making his movements uncertain, as if the earth was grabbing at him. Behind him was the renewed *splot*, *splot*, *splot* of dripping blood.

He felt the energy travelling through his body. He recognised it so well already. The same energy as when he had passed out before. The same force that had been building in him since touching the crystal in the Darkmouth cave. It was even more powerful now. Threatening to become overwhelming.

His vision blanked out for a moment, a brief darkness. But his legs ignored that and kept him moving, crashing across the ground, pinballing off the trees, stumbling over the solid tendrils and roots in his path.

On his back, his schoolbag bounced. Below his waist, the legs of his fighting suit clattered.

The Legends were gaining on him. Whatever caution or fear had held them back before seemed to have gone. Maybe they were attracted by the blood. Maybe they were angry at having lost Emmie. But they wanted him now and they would have him.

To his right, Finn saw the mountains, sloping sharply up from the edge of the forest, the cloud rising with them as if they were tucked snug beneath a blanket. At the peak of the tallest, the snow was darkening with the fading light.

Finn swerved awkwardly in that direction and the forest floor dropped away sharply below him.

He lost his footing immediately and fell, sliding on his back for a few metres before clipping a branch and being thrown into a tumble that sent him across hard roots and sharp scrub. He rolled to a halt and lay there askew, looking at the Infested Side from the wrong angle, one leg caught in a briar wrapped round his calf.

He had tumbled into another clearing, just short of a tree stump with bark of slick glass, its edges singed from some ancient catastrophe. Yet again, he noticed colours in it. Like oil in water. A hint of some beauty that must have existed once upon a time, even here.

Through his whole body, another shock of electricity. It felt now like he might convulse, and he had the urge to tear the remainder of the fighting suit from his body for relief from the burning sensation running through him.

The feeling subsided, and he pushed his back up against the trunk and tried to free himself from the briar gripping his leg.

Coming down the slope towards him, through the towering trees, were the hoots and howls of the chasing Legends.

Finn pulled unsuccessfully at the briar, which had dug into the leather between the scratched and dented steel of his armour.

Legends poured into the clearing. Huge, small, wide, thin, hairy, scaly, teeth, fangs, hooves, claws. So many types he could hardly register them. Only that they were falling over themselves as they piled in towards their quarry.

And Finn felt a strange calm, deep within him, that came from realising the chase was over. But it was not the calm of knowing he couldn't escape them now. There was something else. Though he didn't know how or why, he felt a growing sense that in this world, at this moment, the power lay with him.

For the first time in his life, he *wanted* the Legends to attack.

Except they didn't. Instead, they stopped. Completely. Suddenly. A silence settling across their ranks as they paused at the treeline.

They were watching something. It wasn't Finn.

Between him and the Legends, it was as if the soil writhed. Dry, hard earth bubbled where Finn's blood stained the ground. The soil squirmed at each drop, running along a trail from bloodstain to bloodstain until it reached him.

Finn kicked out, tried again to free himself and to get up. As he did so, the earth beneath him gave way a little. He wriggled to untangle himself, but every time he pulled away, the briar seemed to tighten further, digging into his leg, wrapping round the ankle armour.

The Legends crept a little closer, careful in their step, but watchful as much as ravenous.

Finn sank a few centimetres into the soil. The dry earth crumbled at his foot, drawing his boot into the dirt. He grabbed at the tree trunk, his palm sliding along the smooth bark as the soil pulled him down.

His legs were now fully submerged in the devouring

earth. Boiling soil squirmed up his waist, towards his chest.

It was then that Finn realised what was happening.

The ground itself was eating him. He was being dragged into its belly.

The soil sucked him in further until it was at his neck, then spilled into his mouth so he had to spit it out, straining to keep his face above ground.

He fought, spat, scraped at the soil.

But it was no use. The hungry earth had him.

Finn's last vision was of the howling mouths of the Legends. Crowding over him. Watching. Waiting to pick at the bones.

And then there was nothing.

No light. No air.

Only darkness.

35

Finn's life did not flash before his eyes.

No prophecy burned in his mind.

He did not think of his mother. Or his father. Or Emmie. Or anyone.

He did not think of Darkmouth, of the house, of the safe cocoon of his bedroom.

Instead, he thought of only one thing. That his finger was a bit tingly.

Then he thought his veins felt somewhat zingy. His arms tremulous. That something was cascading through his body.

It started in the hand that had held the crystal and Finn knew it would end in something utterly terrible.

He felt the anger and grief over losing Emmie. His guilt over losing his father. The despair at being lost on the Infested Side. The fear of losing his life here, in the stomach of this alien world.

It should have weakened him. Instead, it mixed with whatever energy that crystal had given him and the result was the unmistakable welling of that feeling he had never truly known before.

Power.

Finn knew in that moment that he would use it.

He ordered the energy to convulse through his body, to ripple in a wave up his arm, into his torso. The atoms in his body became sticks of dynamite. His veins a fizzing fuse along which fires ran until—

36

Finn's mind was taken apart a million different ways and put back together in not entirely the right order.

He did not know where he began or ended. He was everything. Everywhere. At once. His thoughts floating embers, gently settling on a burning dream.

That was *kind of* how it felt anyway. Finn had never exploded before, so he really didn't have much to compare it with.

37

The energy rushed out from him, in a great wave, blasting in every direction.

At the centre of it all, where the ground had swallowed him, Finn's body was intact. More or less. When the explosion of energy ended, he lay where he was a moment longer while his neurons reassembled themselves. It felt like he was still snagged on a dream. Half awake. Half alive. Around him fell a fine rain of dirt and pebbles.

He had blown a crater in the earth, open to the bleak but welcome approach of the Infested Side night.

His breaths coming shallow and fast, he opened his mouth to say something, but couldn't quite recall how to speak. He told his left arm to push himself up, but his right leg moved instead. Finn stayed where he was. The soil was still now. The forest quiet.

Eventually, carefully, he ordered his right big toe to

waggle. His left ear responded.

So, he waited some more and, when he was sure he could wriggle his fingers without his nose twitching instead, he found the co-ordination to stand.

The crater was as high as his waist. The world around him had been flattened. In a wide radius outwards from where he had been buried, scrub and trees were either shattered or pushed aside, trunks leaning at an angle so that their roots peeked out from under them.

But the soil was still. Dead again.

I did this, he thought. *Did I really do this?*

A surviving Legend, a small thing like a ferret crossed with a tiny unicorn, picked itself up, saw him, squealed and bolted away.

A high-pitched crackle rang in Finn's ears, obscuring the hard splattering of falling soil and the low moans of injured Legends trying to crawl away.

He patted his waist. The cut was no longer sore.

The world felt white-hot. Finn felt white-hot.

His armour *was* white-hot.

He tore at his legs, shook it free, not even needing to pull it down over his boots because it came away in his hand. Smoking squares of metal and melted leather dropped in bits into the crater. Looking down, he was relieved to find that his trousers were more or less holding together. The further down his body he looked, the less damage there was. The epicentre of whatever happened seemed to have been his right arm and chest, where his jumper and shirt had been fried and he was suddenly regretful that he'd worn a cat T-shirt as a vest. The poor animal in the picture looked quite distressed, with a burnt and still smoking hole where each eye used to be.

Yet his skin was surprisingly cool. There were no burns. Instead, the cut at his waist had stopped bleeding, closed over almost completely. And, when his probing fingers found a ridge on his skin, he pulled the T-shirt aside to see a single jagged scar running from his right shoulder to the dead centre of his chest. Despite being fresh, it appeared faded and long healed over.

In the crater behind him lay the watch Estravon had given him, its straps torn, its mechanical insides blasted out. Beside it was his schoolbag. Its straps had evaporated, but the rest of it was whole and discarded as if he'd just walked in from school and thrown it down there.

The force had come mostly from his front, outwards.

He had *exploded*. He had become a weapon, a strange force in this very strange world. He didn't understand it and, if he ever did meet his father, Emmie, Estravon, anyone ever again, he wasn't sure he'd be able to explain either.

What have I just done? he wondered. *How did I do it?*

It was clear to him that whatever had been building inside him since he'd been frazzled by the red crystal back in Darkmouth had finally reached boiling point – as if the crystal had started a fire inside him that had kept growing until it burst out of his skin.

And, when it had, he had become powerful in a way he had never felt before.

An intermittent crackle sounded in his ears – like an after-echo.

Around him was a ring of fallen Legends, those few who were able to still scrambling away in various states of distress. They made for the forest, where the trees had been decimated. Finn watched them until they were all gone.

Which was when he saw what he'd been looking for.

In the gap in the trees ahead, a hole punched open by the force of the explosion. And, through it, a rising of the land, the beginnings of a climb towards the mountains that ate up the sky. And, on that slope, a glimpse of stone. High. White. Rounded.

A tower.

The crackling sound was insistent in his head.

Sqwuak. Chhikk.

He put a hand on the edge of the crater, levered himself out of it. Squinted at the tower again and, above it, at the almost completely blackened snow of the mountains. The light would soon be gone. He needed to move quickly.

Sqwuak in Finn's ears. *Sqwekk.*

The noise was coming from inside the crater. He jumped back in.

Squerk. Chesssk.

It was inside his bag. Finn picked it up and pulled out the radio. Its plastic casing warm, its antenna bent a little, but otherwise undamaged, protected beneath him when he had exploded upwards.

Squelck. Clikk.

"—*Fin*nnn*nn*nnn—" said his father's voice.

38

"I'm so close, Dad!" Finn shouted into the radio, "I can see the tower. I can see it. I'm going to be there really soon. Wait for me, please. Wait."

His father's reply was a little clearer this time, but distortion still wracked the signal, his father's words broken, very few of them coming through clearly.

"—**Cave**—"

And even those were being flung across the airwaves, stretched out, looped.

"—**T**ow**WWW**wwer—"

"I can see it. I can see the tower. I'm on my way now."

Finn held the radio tight, volume up. It was a lifeline he didn't want to let go of. Excitement, relief, joy coursed through him. The tower was a gleaming beacon on the mountain slope. Ivory white, Finn saw it as a piercing promise of hope.

"...**ti**me..."

The sounds stopped, the signal silenced again. Why were his father's messages always too short, Finn wondered? He wanted to *talk* to him, not just hear him.

The straps of the bag being burnt through, he made a decision to leave it behind, which he felt bad about because his mam had only bought it for him a short while ago, and his schoolbooks were in there too. His mam had spent an afternoon wrapping them in clear plastic for him, sticking his name on each one. It was so unfair on her, he thought. Plus, he'd get into so much trouble at school.

But he had to leave them all behind. They'd only be a burden. So, he took the radio from his bag and clipped it to the waistband of his trousers. He then tested the last drops of water in the bottle before deciding it was safe to swig them.

Just before he put the bag down for good, he spotted the old red notebook buried near the bottom. The edges of its pages were a little crisp and had yellowed another couple of shades, but it was otherwise undamaged. He shoved it into his back pocket.

Finn took one last glance at the remnants of his fighting suit in the crater, steam rising as they cooled. That armour had taken him ages to make. Hours of

stitching metal on metal, carefully matching the padding to the right seams, adjusting where it pinched, trying it on to see if it fitted, and then being told by his parents to add an extra panel or two so that he could grow into it.

And it still hadn't been particularly good.

His heart sank at the thought of going through all that again. At least, for the first time, he felt genuine confidence there would *be* a next time.

He thought of his mam, and what she might be doing now, how annoyed she'd be, how worried, furious, desperate.

He thought of Emmie. He shivered with the horrible guilt that he couldn't save her. He had brought her to the Infested Side and now she was gone, taken by a ghastly serpent and flown off to a fate he couldn't bear to imagine. He had to fight the urge to let the possibilities cripple him. He couldn't allow himself to think the worst. He'd done enough of that.

No. He refused to let that thought in. He had to hope she was still out there somewhere.

He thought too of the missing Estravon, the bloody pen a sign that something awful had put an end to his note-taking. Cornelius and Hiss were gone too, maybe off to save Estravon, but more likely deciding the risk was no longer worth the sausages.

And he thought of his father and how close he was to finding him. That was all that was left to do now.

Finn had come to the Infested Side and he had survived. He had destroyed. He had found his way to where he needed to be. He had shed his armour and his bag. He had, in one extraordinary moment, shed his weakness. And even in this state – dishevelled, torn, scarred, filthy, lost – he felt new. He felt strong.

The light was fading, a shadow crossing the mountains, the snow gone black on the great peaks above him. Finn was running out of time. He needed to get to the tower. Alone, but knowing that wouldn't be for much longer.

His father was near.

He would know the way home.

It was time for this journey to end.

'The Purge'
From *The Chronicles of the Sky's Collapse*,
as told by the inhabitants of the Infested Side

TWELVE YEARS AGO

For an eternity, Legend had fought Legend, brother had fought quarter-sister, heads had fought tails.

Until what would become known as the Purge, there were seven rulers of the ancient lands, Gantrua among them. They had long been so focused on destroying each other that the war with the humans was lost before it was even fought.

Gantrua realised this madness must end.

He summoned six Wolpertingers before him as messengers, addressing them in the crackling heat of the great hall of fires within his castle. "Each of you will go to a ruler with a letter appealing to their sense of honour and pride."

He then leaned closer to where the Legends waited patiently while heat singed their feathers. "But, because appealing to their honour and pride will not work, the letter also offers a bribe of a hundred crystals each."

Of the six Wolpertingers dispatched by Gantrua, only one returned. Or, rather, its bones came back with a note skewered to a rib.

The invitation was accepted.

So, a summit took place on an island where the seven arsenic rivers met, a place too open to allow ambushes. Each of Gantrua's six rivals arrived as the first half-glimpses of grey light broke through the darkness.

The Rulers of the Ancient Lands were, in no particular order:

- **Jotnar the Most Savage Spiller of Blood, a northern giant.**
- **Tblahfeewfmklwejh the Unspeakable whose form remains too horrible to describe even now.**
- **The Grand Griffin Destroyer of the West.**
- **The Grander Griffin Destroyer of the East.**
- **A creature of the southern wilderness, Yowie.**
- **The Last Gorgon.**

As a show of trust, each was asked to leave their army behind. Each of them brought one anyway.

However, when the six leaders arrived at the centre of the island, they did not find Gantrua there. They did not find his army. Instead, they were greeted by a puny, hooded figure seated at a long table.

The six great leaders of the Infested Side approached the table together, enraged, demanding to know why Gantrua had sent an assistant, an ambassador, an underling.

The figure ignored their rantings, instead murmuring some kind of incantation, a stream of words spilling from him.

Eventually, Jotnar the Most Savage Spiller of Blood lost his patience and snapped the figure's hood back.

It revealed the human, Niall Blacktongue, his eyes closed and his lips moving. Six armies raised their weapons at once, pointed them at one target.

The human ceased his chanting and, when he opened his eyes, the rulers saw they were flooded with raging whirlpools of red.

Niall Blacktongue ignited.

The explosion tore across the island, blasted the arsenic rivers, pulverised every scrap of land for leagues in every direction.

When the dust and glass finally settled, the seven lands had been united under one all-conquering ruler.

Only the human at the centre of it survived the explosion. More or less survived it anyhow. His skin was torn, his mind fragmented, and he was once again forced to retreat to his cell until some version of normality returned to him.

After this, the alliance between Blacktongue and Gantrua deepened. The superlative ruler sought the human's counsel, convened with him privately on matters of strategy, even let him leave the tower to travel with him.

And the human broke his chanting only to speak of the prophecy about the boy, and this vision rippled ever outwards from the tower, reached the ears of every Legend that had them. And those who heard it had three questions:

"What did the human tell Gantrua that allows him such an influence?"

"Will another explosion come?"

And, most importantly, "How far away should we stand when that happens?"

39

Finn felt a surprising sense of freedom, having almost forgotten what it was like to run without wearing what felt like a ton of cutlery over his body.

Shorn of the fighting suit, every step was worth two. The top of the tower was a beacon; the blips and whistles of the radio a signal that he was closer. He moved quickly, unsure why the explosion seemed to have energised rather than exhausted him.

Sqwerrk went the radio.

"Dad," he said into it. "I'm on my way. Wait for me."

But, in contrast to this lightness he felt about his body, his mind was still weighed down by guilt. The guilt he felt about bringing Emmie into this world and the guilt he felt about being unable to rescue her after she had saved him.

Gone.

His only friend.

Vanished, before he could do anything to save her.

He slowed his pace from the effort of shutting out the terrible consequences of her capture by the serpent.

Sprlerk said the radio.

"I'm nearly there, Dad!"

He ordered his legs to get moving again.

Finn distracted himself from the loss of Emmie by thinking of his earliest memories.

There was a hazy remembrance of his father going out to get a Chinese takeaway and coming back with a huge gash down the back of his jacket and a desiccated Legend in the same bag as the rice.

There was the day his father left the door to the Long Hall open and Finn's mother went utterly berserk when she found her toddler frolicking in a box of old grenades.

There was a terrifying view of a face so angry that Finn immediately burst into tears and hid behind his mother. He always believed this to be his only real memory of his great-grandfather, Gerald the Disappointed.

But the memory Finn thought of most as he crossed the dying landscape of the Infested Side was a rainy afternoon in the house when he was no older than two. To amuse his bored son, his father had put his helmet over Finn's head, a piece of armour so oversized and heavy that Finn wobbled off, unsteady and blind, to crash straight into a wall.

His father then spent what seemed to be hours banging a sword off Finn's protected head, each gentle strike sending a tremor through the metal until Finn's head rang. He remembered giggling through every blow, demanding more every time his father hit him with the ancient weapon until he eventually felt sick and started to cry.

It took him a few years to realise his childhood wasn't like everybody else's.

Anyway, as Finn now worked his way through a shattered forest and stabbing reeds on the wrong side of parallel worlds, he thought of that afternoon because until he had released that explosive energy it was the last time he'd felt so protected, invincible, certain he couldn't be hurt, and he needed to hold fast to that feeling because otherwise he was just a twelve-year-old boy, lost on the Infested Side, whose friend Emmie had been taken by a Legend so that it could...

He stopped again. Tightness coiled in his throat. The corners of his eyes watered.

He forced himself to go on, reached for the remembered sense of invincibility from that day with his father, embraced the newfound experience of power from the explosion.

He had wanted to run from his destiny before, but right now he felt drawn towards it. It was an unfamiliar sensation, this lack of fear. *I'll find Dad*, he thought. *I'll find Emmie. And I'll...*

What?

He had a sense that the energy was gone from his body now – he wasn't going to be exploding again. So, what would he do next time? Hit the Legends with a stick?

Stop it, Finn. Just keep going.

Squirp burped the radio.

"I see it, Dad. I see the tower."

Bleeekhkh.

The ground rose so that the trees clawed higher above him. He scrambled up, the shape of the tower lost briefly in a copse of ancient woodland until the ground levelled off and the trees thinned out to reveal the wide barren plain on which the column stood like an immense craggy claw.

Grey clung to the sky, reluctant to slip fully into darkness, but in that light it was impossible to make out any figures at the tower.

Skwerch.

"Dad."

A voice squalled through the static, recognisable as his father's even though the words were a mishmash of echoes and distortion. "—ttttthhh*hh***HHH**HH *EEeEEE*eeEEeeER**RR** **R**R*Rrrrr***YYY***rrr—*"

Finn had no idea what that meant. "I'll see you soon," he responded.

So focused was he on getting to the tower, he didn't notice the steep drop where the clearing met the trees. Not until he fell forward down it.

He had to pump his legs like piston engines and wheel his arms to keep upright, but the momentum sent him crashing to the ground.

The soil didn't try and eat him this time, but, when he jumped to his feet, he saw that he was standing in a wide shadow. Looking up, he saw the tower, white and tapering, at the centre of a vast and almost perfect circle of flat, cleared land.

He still had the radio in one hand, his knuckles white with the grip.

Splerrch the radio said.

"Dad? I'm here."

Squerck. "**F**ii*iiiinn*nnnnn*nn**n**n," said his father's voice.

He ran towards the tower, covering the ground at breakneck pace, the shadow widening around him. He shouted, knowing it was a dangerous thing to do, but not caring right now.

"Dad! Dad! I'm here."

Chwwwerrrpp.

He reached the tower, fat and yellowed at its base, a wall of bleached stone pieces crushed under the weight of the layers that stretched above them.

Skkwiiirrrkkk.

His father's voice drifted again across the radio. Distant, echoing, unclear. **"I**t's— **time**—"

But there was no sign of him yet.

"Dad?"

Finn skirted the curve of the tower, doing almost a full lap that brought him to a heavy iron door only just taller than himself. He pushed at it, but it was heavy and seemed rusted from age. So, he stood at the doorway, one hand pressed on the uneven wall, trying to calm the doubts intruding on his mind.

Skkweeeelk.

A pale powder clung to his hand and, as he clapped it clean, he saw a shape in the wall.

Skleeerk.

It was a bone. Thin and wedged into place.

He stepped back, looked round it and then it dawned on him. The entire tower wall was made of bones.

Some were solid, or cracking, and many had been crushed into dust along the tower's base. But, as Finn followed the tower's rise towards the sky, he saw them clearly. Small bones. Large ones. Of every shape and form. Leg bones. Wing bones. Claws. Spinal columns. A skull staring at him through four eye sockets.

He jumped back, whimpered. "Dad?"

Squalkk. His father's voice came back. So faint that Finn needed to press the radio to his ear to make out the words. But, for a few moments, he heard them, distant but clear.

"—wr*ong time*, Fin*n*— the wr*ong* time— go back— the cave—"

The words faded into white noise, and the white noise gave way to nothing but deep, ominous silence.

What did his dad mean, *the wrong time?*

The only sound in the world seemed to be Finn's breathing. The only other sound in his head was of hope collapsing.

The wrong time.

He was dizzy, his mind spinning. Was this why the

notebook had been filled with dates? Was this what the red crystal had done?

The wrong time.

He thought about the Hogboon baby, Broonie. The one whose parents insisted was the *only* Broonie. Because it wasn't a common Hogboon name, they said. But maybe there was another reason.

The wrong time.

A terrible possibility had formed in Finn's mind.

What if the gateway he'd made from the Darkmouth crystal had brought him to the right place, but the wrong time?

But time travel wasn't possible, Finn told himself. He gazed around. He was standing in a *world* that wasn't possible.

And he was more and more certain now that he was standing in the *past*.

The thought of it paralysed him, left him gulping for breath. He slumped against the wall, dragged his back down it until he was sitting with head in hands. The new reality felt heavier than a thousand fighting suits.

Except that a sound began to intrude on his anguish. Grinding. Ripping. A world being torn where it shouldn't be. The noise grew and grew until it so filled the world that Finn blocked his ears for fear they might shatter.

And it was right at that moment that a gateway crashed into the Infested Side and a ghost stepped out of it.

The sparkling light of the portal was a golden colour mixed with a swirl of blood. It was a fierce intrusion on the Infested Side, hanging in its air like an unwanted guest until eventually, and without warning, it imploded shut.

By then, a hooded figure had stepped from it. A cowl pulled tight. The glint of armour on the legs of his fighting suit. Head bowed, but eyes trained on Finn. Then it removed its hood.

"Granddad?" burbled Finn.

"Well, that confirms who *you* are," said Niall Blacktongue.

Finn stood, slowly, eyes fixed on the new arrival, mouth agape at the sight of him. He had seen his grandfather before, on the Infested Side, riding alongside the Legend they called Gantrua in the moments before his father disappeared. But this was not the same man. He was not

that scarred, half-destroyed figure.

No, this man was far younger. He was, Finn figured, the Niall Blacktongue of the portrait.

"But the painting..." Finn started, while his brain tried to catch up with what his eyes were seeing. "You were... I wasn't even born."

As crazy as it seemed, this was the Niall Blacktongue of a portrait completed just before he disappeared. The Niall Blacktongue that had stared at the clues for so long, waiting for someone to find them. This was the Niall Blacktongue of thirty-five years ago.

Here. Now.

"You're supposed to be—" Finn started.

"Please don't say anything about my future," said his grandfather, raising a hand to silence him.

"—dead," said Finn.

Niall groaned in disappointment at hearing that. "Stand still." He walked towards Finn, pausing when the boy backed towards the bone wall. "I need to be sure. It has happened, hasn't it? You have ignited? All that torn clothing isn't just how you dress in your era, I presume."

He loomed in closer and sniffed. He appeared satisfied but nervous. He twitched, though. Wincing as if in pain before steadying himself. "Don't worry, you're done for now. One crystal causes one ignition. Unless, of course, you can control them, build them up and use them when you need to. Trust me, I know."

As he turned away, Finn saw the line of a scar running down his grandfather's neck, disappearing under the collar of his fighting suit. It looked like the one Finn had across his chest.

"I came to find my dad," said Finn, not quite sure what to say now that everything had been turned on its head. And inside out. And backwards. "Your son. Hugo. Have you seen him?"

"You have to understand, I've just left Hugo," his grandfather said, pointing to the air he'd just walked through, "behind that part of the world right there. That boy is my son. I have no other."

"But that would mean," said Finn, trying to piece the parts together, "you've come through a gateway from the last time you were ever seen in Dark—"

"No more future, please," pleaded his grandfather, animated but not particularly angry.

Finn was struggling to make any sense of this.

"I heard my dad," he said. "On the radio. But he's not here."

Niall bent to inspect the radio attached to Finn's belt.

Finn saw now that he was tense, urgent. As if desperate to get something done, but trying to conceal it. "Did you have that radio on you when you first used a blood crystal?" Niall asked.

"A blood crystal?"

"Yes, yes, a crystal with red dust on it," his grandfather said impatiently.

Finn nodded. "Yes, Dad spoke to me when the gateway opened."

"And, when you ignited, this radio was on you then too?"

"It was in my bag, on my back."

"And what kind of gateway did your father travel through?"

"A gold one. Just normal," answered Finn as if any gateway could be described as normal.

"The crystals from Darkmouth's caves are unique," said Finn's grandfather. "They push through from the Infested Side at the point where the two places join. The leak creates the dust. The dust changes the crystals, makes them open gateways not just between worlds, but also across time. And, when you were attached to that radio while opening a gateway, somehow the physical radio came back to *this* time, while its frequency stayed rooted in your time. Something to do with dimensional resonances, I'd guess. They can be tricky. Get it?"

Finn did not get it. At all.

Niall saw this, sighed. "The crystal must have turned that radio into a time machine of sorts, picking up Hugo's signal across a short distance, but a great gap in time. So, he could be right beside us. He might even be standing in this very spot. But I'm afraid your father is no more in this time than you are in his. So, no. He's not here."

Finn looked blank, not quite able to react any other way. He *felt* blank. He was never going to find his father and had travelled all this way not even knowing that. There was also this new craziness of a grandfather who actually looked younger than Finn's own father. He couldn't hide how adrift he felt, as if the whole Infested Side had been pulled from beneath his feet. He tried to speak and only managed to mutter something that didn't really sound like a word at all.

"Listen, all this time-travel stuff, well, it gives you a headache," said his grandfather. "So, please, don't worry about that. All you need to know is that he's there, we are here and that you're going to be safe."

Safe? wondered Finn. He did not feel safe.

Niall appeared to be finding it difficult to hold eye

contact. A twitch in his shoulders gave Finn the idea he was trying very hard to control an overwhelming edginess. *What's he so stressed about?* Then his grandfather refocused on him, his urgency mixed with discomfort.

"Now I am very sorry to have to do this." Niall Blacktongue pulled a weapon from his cloak. "But I must. For all our futures."

He pointed it at Finn and pulled the trigger.

41

Many years away, yet just a step through a gateway, the sun had dropped from the Darkmouth sky. It was late enough that even the hardiest felt it necessary to wind down the search for the night.

People had looked in the laneways, peered in the yards, but had found nothing and, as the dark drew in, torch beams danced across the stony coastline and through the darker alleys, but the hunt was scaled down as people went home to eat, to rest, to put their own children to bed.

Clara stood at the door of what was left of her surgery. The smashed windows boarded up. Cement hardening in the mixer where it stood beside a diagonal stack of bricks. Warning signs scattered across the front of the building, plastic sheeting flapping over the hole bashed through the wall. Half a door left behind. The sign above it punched out in a couple of places, so that Darkmouth

Dental now simply read *Dark— Dent—*

She had looked. And looked. And shouted Finn's name. And looked again.

She took out her phone and, not for the first time, called Finn.

As it had done each time before, Finn's number went straight to his answerphone message. A few words he stumbled over ("Uh, this is, erm, Finn, leave an, I mean, a message") until rounded off by his audible search for the hash key ("Hold on, wrong button").

"If you're there, Finn," Clara said, "please come home. Please. We've searched and searched, and we know Emmie is with you somewhere. Steve and the Council and the lot of them are useless. I'm better off doing it all myself, to be honest." She realised she was venting. "Anyway, you're not in trouble. So, come on home. I miss you so—"

She was cut off by the long beep of time running out. She pressed the phone against her forehead, let the anguish burn in her.

"I didn't go to your house," said a voice.

She looked up. Saw a man she half knew. Maybe she'd pulled his teeth once. Or filled in a cavity. "Excuse me, I don't—"

"That night. I didn't go there. Maurice Noble is my name. I knew Hugo. Know him, I mean, sorry. Anyway, I met your boy, and the girl too, a couple of days ago. They called at Mrs Bright's next door. Not sure why. So, I feel a duty, you know, to two of our own. I'll keep searching. I won't let a bit of darkness stop me either. Anyway, look after yourself now."

Mrs Bright's neighbour moved off again, not sure if he'd said the right thing. Behind him, Clara slowly began to walk in the other direction, back towards home.

Under the moon's light, and the pinpricks of stars, Maurice Noble kept his head down. It was the habit of a lifetime of living in Darkmouth. He looked at the ground for any sign of those poor children, until he veered down along the seafront, and the rocky shore, where the surf splashed at his shoes.

Away from him, up where the town finally gave way to the thrust of crooked cliffs, high on a verge, he thought he saw someone lit by the moonshine. A man, perhaps, with lank black hair hanging down to a heavy coat. It was as if he had simply materialised there.

Maurice even thought he might recognise him as a face he'd known over the years in Darkmouth.

But that man had been gone since the recent invasion.

His shop a charred shell. Presumed dead.

Maurice raised a hand in greeting. There was no wave in return.

"Is that you, Glad?" Maurice called out, but, when he squinted again, the figure was gone, or more or less anyway, replaced by a drifting shadow of something that may or may not have been there.

42

Finn's arms ached where the rope from Niall Blacktongue's weapon had wrapped them tight to his body. One hand was wedged at the base of his back, the other was jammed at an awkward angle towards his shoulder blades.

His back hurt because he was sitting against the rough bone wall inside the tower, pins and needles fizzling through his left leg as he tried to move without toppling over.

"Sorry," his grandfather had said after shooting a rope at him.

"Sorry," as he'd pushed him through the heavy tower door.

"Sorry," as he'd dropped Finn against the wall.

"If you're really sorry, then let me go," Finn said, trying to kick, but, thanks to the rope, just flopping a bit like a stranded dolphin.

"I can't," his grandfather told him. "It took me so long to find you."

Finn examined his grandfather, his thick blob of hair, his complexion almost as fresh as it was the day he'd had his portrait painted. He looked like Finn's father. Not as muscular, but stronger than Finn had expected him to be. He couldn't decide what was really going on here, was disconcerted by how, even through his anxiety, there was a certain tenderness about his grandfather. As well as what seemed like an undercurrent of fear.

Fear of *Finn*.

What could I do to him? thought Finn. *I can't even scratch my nose.*

But it was there, the fear, alongside the strange gentleness. It was in complete contrast to the blasted, scarred skin of the very same man that Finn had seen at the head of an army of Legends just a few weeks ago. Or many years in the future. Whichever it was. Thinking about it scrambled Finn's mind.

Finn sat up against the wall as best he could, where the shards of bone prodded and scratched at him. Niall faced him from the far curve of the tower's interior. His breathing was uneven at times and he closed his eyes as

if trying to tame it. Finn didn't like the look of that. He didn't like the look of anything in here.

"Are you going to hand me over to the Legends?" Finn asked.

"No!" insisted Niall, indignant, shaking his head as he fumbled under his heavy cloak, as though searching for something. "This tower is made from the bodies of every Legend ever imprisoned here. Hundreds of years of the dead, piled higher and higher. The Legends don't really like coming to this place. Too many ghosts. We're not here to become new ones."

"But you talked to the Legends. You got Cornelius and Hiss, the Orthrus, to guide us here. I mean, that must have been you, right?" Finn thought back to Hiss telling them that the human who had given him his instructions had looked like Finn.

He'd thought it was his father. He'd been very wrong.

"Well, yes, it was," said Niall. "But it doesn't matter that I talked to the Legends. It's what I talked to them *about* that's important."

"What did you talk to them about?"

His grandfather removed a small metal cylinder from beneath his cloak. "You."

Finn felt dizzy. "Why?" he asked.

"Because you will be there at the end of everything."

Finn felt even dizzier.

He'd tried to dismiss the prophecy so many times, tried not to think about it, but now his grandfather had come to the Infested Side just to find Finn and his head was spinning with the idea that actually he really *was* important in all of this.

Important in a way that made his grandfather afraid of him.

He shuddered, tried to concentrate on the moment, to take stock. He recognised the cylinder Niall was carrying as a Desiccator canister. This situation was not developing in a particularly cheery manner.

Finn pushed his legs out, tried to back his way up the wall, but couldn't get his balance. "What are you going to do with that? Are you going to desiccate me?"

"I'm going to save you," said Niall as if it was the most obvious thing in the world. "I'm going to save everybody."

Finn didn't understand. He was tied up on the Infested Side. How was this being *saved*?

Placing the canister on the floor, his grandfather gave it a little tap with his finger and immediately an arrow wobbled into action on the cylinder, starting a climb from zero towards a 100 scratched at the top.

"Thirty-two years," Niall said, walking to a grate high in the door and peering out at the grim landscape beyond.

Finn shifted against the wall, moved his back along the spiking bones.

"That's how far back in time you've travelled," Niall went on, returning to Finn. "The blood crystals in Darkmouth are unique, as far as I know. They seem to grow at the join between our two worlds, almost as if pushed through from this, the Infested Side."

He crouched down, facing Finn. "If you just pluck a crystal and open a gateway, as you must have done, it will always bring you back thirty-two years from the day you do it. Why? I don't honestly know. But here's the stranger thing – it's all about the dust. It seems to be created by the effort of growing the crystals in the fracture between here and there. And if you fiddle with that dust, mess with the quantities and all that, then you can use it to travel many years into the past or..."

Niall reached for Finn, causing him to flinch. He showed an empty palm as a gesture that he meant no harm and lifted the red notebook that was sticking from the pocket of Finn's blackened school trousers.

"...you can travel to the future."

He stood up to flick through the notebook. On the

floor, the cylinder's gauge reached 20. Finn had seen a Legend desiccated on the Infested Side before, when Steve had shot a flying serpent as it attacked Broonie. The result had been a flailing, horrible mess. Finn did not want to become one of those. He moved again up the wall, an infinitesimal amount, hoping Niall couldn't see what he was doing.

"Have you travelled in time too?" he asked Niall, to distract him.

"To meet you? Yes. I've come forward three years, give or take," his grandfather said, not looking up from the notebook, but grimacing just a touch, due to some unseen discomfort. "You travelled back from your time. I travelled forward from mine to intercept you. The mathematics are all here, in this notebook," he said, shaking his head. "I've only just left this behind in Darkmouth, but to you it must be a relic, ancient history. Do you know what these are?" He showed Finn what looked like scribbled equations.

"Calculations?" asked Finn, feeling the rope dig into his wrists.

"Yes," said Niall. "See this graph here? It's how much dust needs to be on the crystal to take you to a particular year. They're just ordinary crystals underneath, but once the dust interacts with them it changes everything."

Finn peered at it, trying to understand, and even through the spidery scrawl of Niall's handwriting got a sense of what it meant. "But this notebook is also so much more," said Niall, still leafing through the journal. "It's also a diary, in maths and diagrams and whatnot, of my search for you."

Finn winced again at a pain that seemed to very briefly pass through him. He began to realise it must be energy, from whatever crystal Niall had used to open his gateway, crackling through him just as it had done before the explosion.

That made Finn wriggle more against the bone wall.

The gauge crept past 40. Finn felt nerves prickle his skin. He did not want the device to reach 100.

"You need to know why I'm doing this. You need to know it's for the right reason," said his grandfather.

"Doing what?"

Niall took a breath. Released it slowly. The cylinder's gauge wobbled past 50.

"I rediscovered that cave. 'The Cave at the Beginning of the World' it was called centuries ago, because every day, as the first light of morning touched the crystals, a gateway would open, quite naturally, on its own."

The Cave at the Beginning of the World, Finn thought. *Linked to the Cave at the End of the World.*

"So, I learned to control the crystals. Sometimes I cleaned them of their dust. Sometimes I caked them in it. And then I opened gateways to see where they would take me. They always brought me to the Infested Side. But not always to the same *time*. After each journey, I recorded the results. That's how I was able to build that graph, make those calculations, travel to this exact point in time."

Finn's shoulders tensed, he ground his teeth, let the energy pass.

"Anyway," continued Niall, "I survived those journeys to the Infested Side the same way you did. Igniting when the energy inside me from using the crystal built up to the point where I couldn't hold it any more. Destroying when necessary. I kept travelling back in time, forward in time. I travelled as far as the crystals would take me. But here's the thing: there was a dead end. It would only take me as far as one particular day. One specific moment. A day in the future where something terrible happens. A catastrophe more destructive than anything I had seen before. And I saw you there. I saw you tearing the sky apart."

Niall dropped his hand by his side, the notebook flapping open in his loose grip. He looked at Finn. "I was in the future, on the Infested Side, yet I could see Darkmouth beneath a great sea of fire, engulfing the town we'd protected for generations. Spreading out across the entire world. And at its centre was you. You," he repeated as if bemused by that idea. "You were at the end of the world. You will *be* the end of the world. *Both* worlds."

Finn had stopped squirming. Almost stopped breathing. The silence in the tower was as thick as the stench that pervaded the whole of the Infested Side, but Finn's head was loud with confusion and fear and the prophecy ringing like an alarm in his head. He didn't want to believe it. It sounded impossible. Then again, he'd exploded once already today. Impossible was losing all meaning.

"I..." Finn swallowed, his mouth dry. "...destroy the world?"

"*Worlds* technically. But yes, I'm afraid so."

Finn swallowed again. "So, what are you going to do with me?"

"Ask yourself: what would you do if you saw that? What would you do to stop it? Ah, you're only a boy. I don't expect you to have the answers." Niall cocked his head a little, fingered the notebook with both hands. "I couldn't just travel to any point in time, wander into Darkmouth and stop you. Remember, the crystals only lead to the Infested Side. But then, on one trip here, by pure luck I saw a man and a girl and you."

Finn had a flashback to the figure they'd chased into the Fire Spits. "That was you we saw in the forest."

Niall looked at the canister. It was past 80 now and moving steadily upwards. He seemed patient, deliberately so, as if scared he would lose control.

"I had found you, here of all places," Niall continued. "But I still needed to isolate the right moment to intercept you. If you had used a blood crystal to come through, I knew you'd be in danger of exploding as soon as I touched you. So, I moved back and forth, tracking down a point *after* you'd ignited, but before the Legends could realise you were now powerless and capture you."

He stood at the high narrow grate in the tower's

door. Finn shifted awkwardly at the wall where he was stranded.

"Keeping the Legends away was easy enough," Niall continued. "I spread rumours about how dangerous you were and they believed me because, well, they saw my power at first hand. Finding the Orthrus to guide you was easy too because it belongs to those in this world who want peace, just like I do."

Finn rubbed his back against the bones of the wall, felt their sharpness against his ropes. Time was running out. He needed to get out of here. Somehow. And then he had a thought.

"Maybe we can get to my dad, using crystals here and ones in Darkmouth. Or something," he added, because he really didn't know how it worked. "If we find him, he'll know what to do, how to fix everything."

His grandfather opened the notebook, flipped through it until he found the place he wanted. Then he held it so close to Finn's nose that he had to back away from it to focus. It was a page Finn had seen before, covered in numbers and squiggles and intersecting circles.

"See that? That's one way we could find your dad. One way to cross from here and *now* to here and *then*. You open a gateway from here to the Darkmouth of *your* time, then, without stepping through, you immediately use a crystal to open another gateway right next to it. The two portals stuck together essentially make a tunnel that links this Infested Side now to Darkmouth in the future, and then loops back into the Infested Side of the future."

Niall saw the blank look on Finn's face. "It's complicated. But it could work. All three places and times would be connected. You would just open a door from this Infested Side, through Darkmouth and into where Hugo is stuck. He could step right through and go home if he wanted."

"So, we can do it?"

"No." Niall moved his thumb and revealed a doodle of a skull and crossbones. "Well, you could, but only if you want to kill everyone in Darkmouth. Attaching one portal to another is very, very messy. It would almost certainly rip apart the fabric of space and time, leave a gaping hole between Darkmouth and the Infested Side. And it would not be so easy to just zip it up again."

Finn's heart sank.

The arrow on the Desiccator device stopped moving, pressing the gauge's ceiling a touch past 100. It began to whistle, like a kettle coming to the boil. Instead of attending to it, Niall put the notebook in the torn pocket of Finn's shirt, tapping it to make sure it was in fully. He smelled of harsh soap, but there was something else beneath it. Something rotten.

Despite that, Finn felt a flash of hope: *As long as I have the notebook, if I can get back to the cave, I can get home,* he thought. *I only need to add dust to a crystal according to those calculations and then—*

"No," said Niall, and for a second Finn worried that he could read his thoughts. "I'm afraid your father will have to find his own way back. Just like I did. And, in the end, I just had to do it the old-fashioned way."

He rolled his sleeve to the elbow. With each turn of the material, a new scar was revealed, progressively more fresh – some slices, some gouges, one oozing still. And, around them, red powder stained the rucked skin. He kept rolling up his sleeve until he reached a fresh wound, into which was clumsily stitched a red crystal, bloodied, protruding from the skin.

Finn recoiled, feeling ill, the stench of half-healed flesh wafting at him. "You attached them to yourself," he gasped. "You're crazy."

"This is the last crystal," said Niall, a heavy sadness dragging at his words. "In case I was lost here, I blocked off the cave in Darkmouth before I left. Removed all evidence of it apart from a few hidden clues. You found the map in the painting, I presume?"

Finn didn't have the stomach to even answer. He kept fidgeting against the wall, searching for the sharp bones at his back.

"I'm sorry you're so uncomfortable," said Niall. "It will be over soon."

From his cloak, he pulled the long barrel of a rudimentary Desiccator. He picked up the cylinder and began to screw it to its underside. "Desiccator fluid needs time to work properly here, otherwise it's, well, not pleasant. It's ready now. But you have to understand that whatever they call me in your time – a disgrace, a traitor, whatever – one thing I am not is a killer."

"You can't desiccate me. You might as well kill me."

"No. I'll bring you back to Darkmouth. You'll be one of so many desiccations, but you'll be safe. Darkmouth will be safe. You'll be alive, just not quite as you know it now."

"But I've done nothing wrong," said Finn, panic lifting his voice an octave.

"Not yet."

"I can change it. Whatever happened, I can stop it."

317

Niall lifted the Desiccator to his shoulder and pointed it at Finn. "I'm so very, very sorry."

With a *snap* at Finn's back, the sharp bone he had been using to saw at the rope finally cut through. Before his grandfather had time to pull the trigger on the Desiccator, Finn had bolted up the staircase.

43

Finn went two steps at a time, hands pushing against the narrowing walls, round and round, round again, dizziness in his head, fire in his lungs.

Behind him, Niall's boots scraped a steady, unhurried rhythm on the stairs. His voice floated from below. "It will be OK. Please."

It would not be OK. Finn knew that. He wasn't quite sure how he was going to change it, though.

The tower seemed never-ending as Finn raced up, bouncing against walls, crashing shoulder against bone. The steps were irregular, carved as they were from a solid mass of the dead, so that he slipped a couple of times, scrambling back to his feet to flee further up towards wherever it would lead him.

The scratch of his grandfather's boots echoed from down the stairwell as Finn pushed himself up, *willed* himself up further, even as his legs burned from the effort.

The steps ended suddenly as the tower opened up into another narrower room. Finn sprinted round the curve in the hope that it would lead on to another staircase, but there was no gap in the wall of wedged bones. They were less weathered now, more fully formed, and included the empty, uncaring eyes of a skull that looked far too human for Finn's liking.

He had reached the top of the tower.

"There is no other way," Niall's voice said, with a sadness as heavy as his approaching steps.

Dim light trickled into the room through a high, simple window punched out of the bones. Finn dug a foot in a narrow crevice in the wall and hoisted himself up. Carefully, he swung round until he was sitting on a window ledge jagged with finger bones, wings, claws, and facing back into the room.

When Niall Blacktongue eventually arrived, his mantra came first, a murmured stream of words. Then the barrel of the Desiccator held straight out. Then Niall himself, cloak dragging on the steps, almost dutiful in his approach.

Finn reached out of the window to the exterior wall and found a firm grip to carefully pull himself up so that his feet were on the ledge and the rest of him in the frigid air outside the tower. He had hoped to find its roof, but there wasn't one. Instead, the tower tapered for another few metres to the top, and from the bare ledge there was no way to get to it safely.

That was Finn's first mistake. His second was to look down.

Through shreds of cloud, the tower plunged away beneath him. There was nothing between him and the ground but a horrible chasm of empty air. The trees were terribly small below. The hint of a breeze sent a shudder through his body and he gripped on tight, so that it didn't even bother him that he was pressing a cheek against a dead-eyed and freezing-cold skull. It felt like he was clinging on to the edge of the world.

In the room, Niall was urging him to come back in. "You must be careful," he said. "I don't want you to fall."

Finn's knuckles were white against the tower wall. He felt panic rushing through him, looked for the energy to ignite, but couldn't find any sign that he could light that fuse.

"There's no way down or up," said his grandfather. "Come back in."

"I'll only come in if you promise you won't hurt me!" Finn shouted, his face pressed hard against the prickling bones.

"It won't hurt," said Niall, which was not exactly the answer Finn needed.

Finn worked up the courage to quickly glance down the wall again. His grandfather was right: there was no way down other than to fall. The climb up was far too perilous. There was no way out of this but back inside.

He looked for a firm hold, something to lever him back through the window, but instead his eye caught sight of something far below. The sight so utterly baffled him that it briefly distracted him from the desperation of his situation.

It was a dog. A basset hound.

"Yappy?" muttered Finn.

As if hearing him, the dog looked up and, even at this height, Finn could see its great drooping eyes, its body sagging between a dumpy front and stumpy rear. There was no doubt it was Mrs Bright's pet snuffling its way across the scrub, cocking a leg to pee, as if it was taking just another journey between Darkmouth lamp-posts.

Finn felt his fingers loosen their grip on the wall, forcing him to concentrate again on the matter of his survival. His grandfather was at the window now, leaning into the void, reaching out a hand. "Take it," he ordered. Finn didn't want to, but he had nowhere else to go.

It was death or desiccation.

Out of options, Finn took his grandfather's hand and allowed himself to be carefully manoeuvred back down on to the ledge, where he again sat facing Niall Blacktongue, who was pointing the Desiccator straight at him.

But there was someone else in the room.

"Dog," said Finn.

"Yes, I saw that below." Niall's finger tightened on the trigger. "But I really have to desiccate you now. I'm so sorry."

"No," said Finn, insistent, his eyes motioning beyond his grandfather's shoulder. "There's a dog behind you."

Niall turned his head a little and was greeted by the sight of a muscular canine and the vibrant green snake-tail of a pretty fierce-looking Orthrus.

"Sausages," said Cornelius and swiped at Niall with a great paw.

44

With the reactions and strength of a true Legend Hunter, Niall blocked the blow, but the force was still enough to send him reeling across the room. The blood crystal in his arm was dislodged and bounced across the floor.

Mouth wide, fangs bared, Hiss lunged at him from the rear. Niall rolled away from his bite at the last possible moment.

Reaching the entrance to the stairwell, Niall jumped to his feet, getting hold of his Desiccator.

"Don't let him shoot!" Finn warned as he backed against the far wall. Cornelius clawed the weapon from Niall's hand and it spun against the ceiling to land on its long muzzle. It fired.

A blast of blue shot through its barrel, splintering the weapon while spreading a desiccating wave across the room. It quickly chewed up the pulverised bone of the

floor as it pooled towards the wall, towards the crystal.

"No!" Niall tried to reach for it, but it was too late. The desiccating wave swallowed the crystal, and it gulped and shrank to a mere grain of sand. "I'm lost," he said, before belatedly realising the danger of the spreading wave and springing back towards the stairs, his cloak riding high behind him.

Far heavier, Cornelius laboured to leap and grip the tower wall with his paws while Hiss screamed at him, "Higher! Higher!"

Finn jumped for the window ledge, pulling himself up as a long, rippling *whoooop* sucked the bones into rock and the Desiccator wave bit a wound out of the tower beneath him. It crumpled the wall, opening up a great hole on to the outside. Finn dropped to the yawning edge, saving himself only by grabbing desperately at a protruding leg bone as a large white ball of desiccated tower rolled past him and plunged into the gloom below.

He clung on, feet dangling into nothing, the ground far below him. The leg bone he was holding creaked alarmingly.

Niall's face appeared across the new chasm in the tower. He reached out for his grandson.

Finn jolted downwards, away from him, his weight

straining the bone's hold in the wall, and he found himself hanging even further out into emptiness. The sweat on his palms greasing his grip. His flailing legs searching for a hold. Unable to let go to reach for his grandfather's hand.

The bone bent. Finn swung his legs. Swung them again. Higher. Gaining momentum. Getting closer to the open edge of the tower. *One more go*, he willed himself. *One more go*.

He swung his legs again and knew immediately it would be enough to reach safety.

The bone snapped.

The ground spun into view, then the trees, then the face of his grandfather. It was a moment when everything seemed to hold in place, as if he could stay where he was, stop the world, climb up.

But, when he grabbed at the air, there was nothing to hold on to.

Finn fell.

45

The air rushed in Finn's ears, the wall blurred past. The tower of bleached bones was stained by Finn's flailing, falling shadow. But then a larger shadow appeared, deep black, and consumed his. It spread, quickly sharpening, finding shape, swooping down on him, enveloping him in immense spiked wings.

What Finn saw first was that it was a great flying serpent. The same flying serpent, or at least the same species, that had flown off with Emmie.

What he saw next were the serpent's teeth. The Legend used them to pluck him from the air and, almost immediately, he was flopping, helpless and trapped, in the curved spindles of its jaws.

A second ago he'd been falling towards certain death. Now an enormous flying monster had caught him in its mouth to carry him to a completely different certain death.

It was a mixed blessing.

Heart racing, Finn fought instinctively, pounded at the creature, trying to make it let him go. But it wasn't biting him yet, nor was it crushing him. Finn had the bizarre thought that it may even have caught him in such a way that he was being *protected* by its teeth. He saw the ground racing past as the creature flew away from the tower.

There was a jolt and the creature dropped as it was hit by something from above. Its teeth tightened round Finn's body and again he felt awful vulnerability mixed with the horrible sensation of his stomach going one way and his body the other.

Finn leaned out from between the teeth, craned his head to look up, trying to see what was going on.

A cloak dropped into view, wrapping round the serpent's head.

The creature went into a tailspin, while Finn flailed in its jaws, and Niall Blacktongue, having apparently jumped from the tower to wrestle it mid-air, shouted, "We have to stop it! Before it's too late."

Finn had only a moment to appreciate just how crazed his grandfather was. He braced himself as they crashed to the ground, winced at the thudding impact as the serpent slid violently across the scrub and briars. When they finally skidded to a stop, Finn was still held tight and puncture-free in the serpent's jaws, its damp breath heaving about him.

But Niall was gone, flung away across the ground, where he lay face down, stunned.

The serpent beat its wings again, pushing itself away across the ground, Finn still in its mouth. Finn saw his grandfather look up, push himself to his feet and watch. Even as the distance grew greater between them, the look on his grandfather's face was clear. It was of crushing loss.

Then Niall dropped his head, appearing to breathe deeply, seek calm.

Finding its strength, the serpent gained speed across the ground, rose into the sky just before almost scraping the scalp of the only witness to the whole fight: an ancient, eyeless woman, sitting alone on the edge of the forest.

The serpent passed within a metre of her, beating its mighty leather wings as it passed, Finn still hanging upside down from its jaws. She gasped in bewilderment, and her single tooth shook free and dropped to the ground at her feet.

On the other side of the clearing, where the damaged

tower of the dead stood, an army of Legends burst from the trees.

Finn's last sight of his grandfather was of him fleeing across the dead earth.

46

Those who couldn't search Darkmouth brought lasagne. There had been a lot of lasagne in the hours since the children had gone missing. Plates of lasagne. Trays of lasagne. Overcooked lasagne. Undercooked lasagne. Vegetarian lasagne. Frozen lasagne. Fresh lasagne. Lots and lots of lasagne, and every portion a sincere sign of pasta-layered support for Clara.

She shut the door on another generous donation of dinner, left it on the hall table with the rest and stood motionless for a short while as, not for the first time, the gravity of events took hold of her. It had only been a matter of hours, but Finn's disappearance had knocked away all the faith and optimism she'd held for Hugo's return.

They were both gone, and it was the first time she'd allowed hopelessness to seep into her thoughts.

Clara shook her head, to wake herself from that dark

daydream, and dragged her resolve back to the surface. Strength was needed, she thought. Focus. Belief.

She began the long journey to the library, past the paintings, the generations lined up one after another. This wasn't her family, but the one she had brought her son into. She ignored their stares, resisted the urge to curse the vicious Gerald the Disappointed or throw a plate of lasagne at Niall Blacktongue and his poisoned legacy.

The Long Hall, like so much of the house, was still a mess, half buried under the detritus of the search for the map. She almost tripped on a tin box covered in switches, an egg whisk at the end of it, which lay propped up by the library door.

Inside, Steve was at the desk. His mood had been unwaveringly intense in the hours since he realised Emmie was missing too, utterly focused but edged with an anger he could barely contain. Clara wasn't entirely sure if he was angry with himself, with Emmie, with everyone, or with something else unmentioned.

In the last few hours, they had co-ordinated the search effort, stayed in contact with the remaining volunteers, occasionally leaving to drive to town, get updates and suggest to the temporary sergeant that he might want to leave his station for once because it was unlikely the kids were going to pop out of a desk drawer.

Clara had grudgingly accepted Steve's presence in the house because the library was better equipped than the spare bedroom at his rented house. Steve in return had grudgingly accepted her hand in the search because he had also spent a great deal of time in whispered conversation with the Council of Twelve, glued to the computer monitor yet frequently animated in his reactions to whoever he was talking with.

"I have this under control," Clara heard Steve insist to an unseen figure on the screen.

"Is a rescue team on its way?" she asked as he abruptly ended the conversation.

"You know how it is. Rules. Regulations. All that," he said, clearly irked by something else, although not enough that he didn't wince at Clara's suggestion for where she wanted to shove those rules and regulations.

At one point, looking over his shoulder, she saw a one-line query from the Twelve on the screen. "Please advise on your current situational awareness of the location of official Assessor."

"What does that mean?" she asked.

"It means, do we know where Estravon is?"

Steve typed a response. "Have established a blue force tracking situation in order to fully establish the critical information and carry out all appropriate action as necessary, in accordance with established protocols 96 and 176c."

"What does *that* mean?" asked Clara.

"'No.'"

He leaned back, hands behind his head, feet up on the adjacent chair. "Normally, I'd reckon Estravon was just off somewhere polishing his shoes, but it's a bit of a coincidence, don't you think?"

"Are you saying Finn and Emmie are with that office joker?"

"Maybe, although it doesn't seem right," said Steve. "Emmie would never let that happen."

"And Finn would?"

"No. Well, it's possible. Look, let's be honest, he's not the most strong-willed of boys."

"Be very careful what you say next because I'm standing beside a large..." Clara threw a glance at the giant Reanimator in the centre of the library, still surrounded by balls of Legends. "...device thingy that is rigged to desiccate any living being in this room."

Steve sighed. "Look, Clara, all I'm saying is that

training Emmie was just a duty, a tradition really. I presumed she'd be part of a new generation, the sort that would be happy as a Half-Hunter, without the massive psychological damage that comes from growing up in a town like this."

"Massive psychological damage?" spluttered Clara.

"Don't pretend it's not true," he said. "Legend Hunters are not a balanced lot. Trust me. I had an uncle who was literally called Dave the Unbalanced, and it wasn't because he kept falling over. Well, not only because of that."

"Get to the point of your insult so I can get on with kicking you out of my house."

"I'm just saying that Finn is clearly different. All that *actual* Legend Hunting has left him a bit vulnerable. He's a lovely kid, don't get me wrong, but he's a little more reserved than other kids his age and somewhat easy to manipulate. I'm sure you'd acknowledge that yourself."

Clara kicked the empty chair away from under Steve's feet, causing him to wobble and desperately grab on to the table to stay upright. She stared at him. "I'll acknowledge nothing to a man who doesn't know anything about my family other than what he spied down a long-lens camera, and so little about this house that he's hardly capable of walking to the bathroom without taking a wrong turn into the broom cupboard. By the way, I've noticed you're getting very comfortable in here for someone who's only passing through."

"That still remains to be decided," he said, swivelling the chair back towards the desk.

Clara swung the chair back round so she could glare at him properly. "No. It really does not."

The computer went *ping*.

After establishing that he could safely manoeuvre the chair to face the computer, Steve did so. On the screen, a little icon of a phone flashed green, begging to be pressed.

"I have to take this call," he said, looking at Clara in a way that clearly demanded privacy.

"Then take it," she said, not moving.

"I'm prohibited while you're—"

Clara grabbed the mouse and answered the call.

As Steve complained, a person appeared on the screen. A woman, half in shadow, in what seemed to be an office somewhere. Behind her, a faded poster of a screaming Legend bursting through a wall above the lines *Always Be Vigilant. Always Be Valiant.*

Steve fell silent immediately.

Clara stared into the screen. "Right," she said. "I've lived by your rules long enough. I haven't been on a family holiday for twelve years. I told my parents Hugo was a management consultant for the first year we were together and prayed they asked no follow-up questions because even now I have no idea what a management consultant does. And, most importantly, I let you lot have my son. Now you owe me. You will help me get him back."

"Clara," said the woman, friendly, warm, but still largely hidden in shadow. "It is so lovely to finally meet you, even if it is across a screen."

Clara said nothing, a bit taken aback at this kindness. The woman continued. "I can assure you there are a great many Half-Hunters on the way to Darkmouth as we speak. They'll be with you very soon and I know every one of them is eager to get involved, almost as eager as Steven there."

Steve was sporting a sullen look of embarrassment.

"Help is on its way?" asked Clara, her aggression waning.

"If I could be there myself, I would," said the woman.

"I'm sorry, I didn't get your name," said Clara.

Steve slid up to the keyboard. "Thank you for your assistance and please pass on our gratitude to the Council of Twelve." His teeth were so gritted the words escaped like air from a punctured tyre. "Over and out."

He ended the call, then sat isolated in his own thoughts.

"Now *that's* how you get things done," said Clara.

At the back of the room, a section of shelves rattled, a gust of wind perhaps from the door to the street hidden behind. Steve stood up from his chair and walked towards it, stopping to pick up a map on the way and examine it.

"Was that one of the Council of Twelve?" Clara asked.

"An assistant to them. And she was sitting at the desk Hugo is supposed to occupy if he ever gets back."

"Which he will, as we've just found out."

"You asked for help, Clara," Steve said, "but you may not like what's coming."

"What do you—?" Clara didn't get to finish that thought because, as Steve went to pull at the rattling section of shelves, it swung open.

Emmie stood in the gap behind it. Ragged. Pale. Not smelling nearly as nice as Steve was used to. But very much alive.

"No shouting at me, please," she said to her dad

wearily. She held up a tray and looked at Finn's mother. "I hope you don't mind that I ate some of this lasagne, Clara. I'm starving."

Finn kept pounding at the serpent. Shouted demands. Pleaded. He even grew angry and lobbed a few empty threats at it. "I exploded down there. I will do it again. Don't make me. You'll regret it."

At that, the creature swivelled a black oval eye and observed him for a few seconds until its lids blinked wetly and it fixed its eyes on the horizon once more. As if it understood fully that it was dealing with a mere boy, stumbling from one crisis to another. That look was enough to shut Finn up for a little while.

"What did you do with Emmie?" he asked.

The creature didn't even turn round for that one, but simply flew on, gaining height until they entered the clouds and Finn could see nothing but a thick bleak soup, and, with his clothes so shredded, he felt the deep chill in every part of his body. Fear added a few extra shudders. He wondered if this was where the Legend lived. If this was where its nest might be. If this was where it would feed him to its chicks or whatever monstrosities it bred. He couldn't imagine.

Well, he could, but he didn't want to.

The serpent rose further, until it punctured the layer of cloud and Finn was greeted by something he had never anticipated. Beauty. Colour. Clear air. A sky rich in blues, streaked by deep oranges and reds, and light crisper than he'd ever seen before.

It was stunning. An entire sky hidden from the world below the cloud, cut off from it by that murky border.

And then the serpent dropped again, gliding back into the fog, emerging once more above the landscape of the Infested Side. Yet the beauty did not dissipate altogether. Instead, Finn could see far beyond the forest to a great shimmering waterfall carved into the horizon way beyond, a long ridge over which a foaming torrent fell, then branched into wide rivers, each of them a glorious yellow that lit up even the darkening world. The rivers ribboned, gleaming, into the beyond.

It was strange to suddenly be silenced by the beauty of this world of monsters. Especially at this height, from this crazy angle, wedged between long thin fangs that looked like they could slice Finn open as easily as an envelope.

The Legend's wings swept into motion, rocking the sky and Finn's stomach. Its dank breath heated his waist, while his legs dangled out one side and his head and shoulders the other, both exposed to the whistling cold of the Infested Side. Finn really wished his sweater hadn't been reduced to rags.

This felt like the end, as if he was being brought somewhere terrible. *A nest for sure*, he decided, *filled with snapping baby serpents eager for their next meal.* Flopping upside down, he was a helpless dragon snack.

"Let me go!" he said. Then he looked down and thought twice about that request. "Put me down!" he said instead, slapping at the serpent again, worrying what would happen if it tightened its grip, and fearing what would happen if it let go.

After a while – Finn couldn't be sure if it was two minutes or twenty – the serpent arced a little, then plummeted suddenly, straight down, arrowing through the sky. Finn felt his guts lurch towards his throat, then his feet, before bobbing about between the two.

It was only as they sped towards the ground that Finn recognised the destination rushing up at him. He could see a clearing in the trees and a fat hump of rock getting bigger and bigger until a dark entrance was visible.

They were right back where he had started.

The serpent was returning him to the Cave at the End of the World.

48

The serpent arrested its plummet at the last possible moment, a turning of its wings stopping it almost dead a few centimetres off the ground. It opened its jaws, rolling Finn helplessly from them so that he hit the earth hard, grunting at the shock.

He tried to jump straight up, not keen on being eaten by any carnivorous soil, but only made it as far as his knees – he remained on all fours for a long moment while the travel sickness passed. During this time, the serpent settled on to the ground beside him with a grace that belied its huge size, raised itself on its belly as it stretched its wings before folding them along its sinuous, powerful back.

Then it waited, as yet showing no apparent interest in eating him.

Eventually, Finn found the strength to stand. The serpent looked beyond him, then dropped its slender

head, and Finn backed away, before understanding that it was motioning him towards the dark of the cave.

He looked at the entrance, then back at the serpent for confirmation, before carefully walking forward. He paused at the mouth of the cave and listened. All was quiet. There was no squealing. No fury. He peered in. Even in the half-dark, he could see the outline of a creature – a large mass of bottle-green fur on the ground. It was the Skin-Walker, lying at a horrid angle, limbs trapped in the wire they had fired at it.

It wasn't moving. It wasn't breathing. It was clearly dead.

The relief Finn felt immediately gave way to a deep guilt at having been responsible for killing this Shapeshifter. No matter what it had done to him, or attempted to do to him, it had been a living Legend, simply doing what it had been born to do.

He turned back to the serpent out there in the dusk. "Is that why you want me to go in there?" he asked. "I didn't mean to kill it."

The serpent motioned towards the cave again. Finn squinted and saw a scrap of paper tucked under one of the fallen Legend's claws. He reached down and carefully pulled it clear.

The serpent watched, impassive, as if passing no judgement on him. Instead, it spread its wings, raised its slender neck and lifted itself off the ground. It swooped so low Finn was forced to duck, before it picked up height and disappeared back into the sky above the surrounding trees and out of view.

"Hold on, why did you leave me here?" he shouted after the departing shape. "Why did you save me?" It did not return, and Finn was left with only guilt and confusion for company.

Except he was not alone. This became clear when Estravon burst from the nearby trees and tried to kill him.

"**E**stravon!" said Finn. "You're alive."

"Don't say another word," Estravon snarled, producing a razor-sharp branch from behind his back and holding it high. "I'm on to you."

Finn stepped back, then kept stepping back when it became apparent that Estravon was going to keep coming at him. One arm of his suit jacket had been torn off and his trouser legs were frayed. He had only one shoe on. There were spatters of blood on his pink shirt and his green tie was severed at the collar. He looked half crazed.

"What are you talking about?" asked Finn, still backing away.

Estravon swung the blade at Finn, forcing him to duck and dodge, to scrabble round a rock to avoid another swing of the improvised weapon.

"You heard me," said Estravon, coming after him still. "I won't make the same mistake twice."

Estravon threw the branch at him, and Finn sidestepped just quickly enough for it to skim past his ear and ricochet off a large stone behind him. "Hey, that could have hurt!"

"Don't. Say. Another. Word," ordered Estravon. "Show yourself fully so we can make a proper fight of this."

He then delivered a throaty yell, spun and kicked out with a finesse and force that surprised Finn, but not enough that he didn't drop to the ground and roll out of the way before stumbling back on to his feet, privately thanking all those hours his father had cajoled him into training.

"Did you get a bang on the head, Estravon?" Then Finn figured it out. "Hold on, you think I'm—"

Estravon swung at him again, this time with his bare hands. "Stand still, you shapeshifting freak. And no changing."

"Wait," begged Finn, hands out, putting some distance between them. "I'm me. The dead thing inside the cave is the one that pretended to be me."

"Oh yeah, I'm not falling for that trick again. Show yourself, hairball."

Finn realised he needed to do something devastating to stop this assault, something that would stun Estravon completely.

"Snuggles!" he shouted.

Estravon paused, fists clenched. "What did you say?"

"Snuggles! Snuggles! That's what you say in your sleep. Snuggles. 'Come here, Snuggles.'"

Estravon looked at him, face reddening. "You couldn't possibly know that."

"Emmie heard you. She told me. Snuggles!"

"Stop that."

"OK," said Finn.

"Promise me."

"I promise. No more mention of your toy Snuggles."

"If you ever tell anyone about that, I'll make sure it contravenes at least seventeen separate rules and half a dozen subregulations."

"Fine."

"And Snuggles was not a cuddly toy. He was my first cat." Estravon choked up a tiny bit. "I loved that cat." He backed towards the cave, carefully reversing over the rubble at its mouth, and peeked inside, where he could see the body of the Shapeshifter, twisted in a final despairing pose.

"How did you get here?" Finn asked.

"The Orthrus," said Estravon, climbing back out. "When I was attacked by those Legends, it scooped me up, outran the attackers and dropped me here. Then it turned and ran off again. It didn't explain anything, although that snake-tail wasn't happy. It kept complaining that I was digging my heels into its spleen. How am I supposed to know where a snake keeps its spleen?"

"I blew up," Finn said.

"I was doing just fine, as it happened," said Estravon blithely. "Enjoying the fight in a surprising way, getting to live out something I've only ever read about, or the rules about anyway. And it's amazing what kind of damage you can do when armed only with a pen. Hold on a second, you blew up?"

"Yep."

"Like, *bang* blew up?"

"Well, kind of."

Estravon scanned him, had a look at the top of Finn's head and inspected his charred clothes, peering at the ruined kitty on his T-shirt. "You do look a little crispy around the edges." He sniffed deeply. "And, oddly, you smell a bit like sausages."

"It happened after Emmie was taken by a serpent."

"Taken? Is she—?"

"Before I got to the tower of bones," continued Finn.

"Tower? Of bones?"

"Yeah, where Niall Blacktongue found me."

"Niall *Blacktongue*?"

"Yeah, when I realised that the blood crystal had brought us back in time."

"Back in where now?" spluttered Estravon.

"Back in time. Thirty-two years, more or less," confirmed Finn.

"Because of the red crystals?" Estravon was getting increasingly exasperated.

"Yeah. Well, the red dust on the crystals," clarified Finn. "My granddad said they're only found in Darkmouth for some reason."

"And Hugo's here too?"

"No," said Finn. "He's on the Infested Side, but in the future. The present. Whichever it is."

Estravon just stared at him for a few seconds, as if all that information was dropping into his brain like coins in a slot.

"Right," he said eventually. "Let's for a moment presume that all of what you say is true: that we came back in time, Emmie's missing, you exploded, Hugo's not here, but your ghost granddad is, and we're trapped in the past without a red crystal to get us home. In that case, there's only one question that really matters right now.

Why are you smiling?"

Finn was indeed smiling. He couldn't help it. There was a strange delight welling within him, an exhilaration not just at having survived all he'd been through, but also at having figured something out.

"For a start," Finn said, "the same giant flying lizard thing that grabbed Emmie grabbed me. Or at least it looked pretty similar. So, if I'm still alive, then maybe she is."

"I haven't seen her," said Estravon cautiously, as if to dampen Finn's enthusiasm just a bit, in case he got his hopes up too much.

"I think she might even have gone home, through that cave."

Estravon still looked unconvinced.

"No, don't shake your head," said Finn. "You see, I saw Yappy in this world."

"Yappy?"

"Yeah."

"The dog?"

"A real dog. Mrs Bright's dog. No snakes for a tail or anything. It was at the tower after I got there. And I think it might have got there because a gateway opened in the cave, and I think Emmie went the other way."

"What makes you so sure?" asked Estravon warily.

Finn handed him the torn page. "Because I found this inside the cave." On it was a pencil drawing of a cross-eyed Minotaur with knotted horns, the same one Emmie had drawn for him in school.

Estravon glanced back at the cave as he pondered Finn's theory, then let out a long, weary sigh. "But there's something else, isn't there?"

"Yep," said Finn, grinning widely now. "I'm delighted to see you."

"Why?" Estravon was suspicious.

"Because you're still wearing your suit jacket, or most of it anyway, and that means you should have something tucked just inside it."

Estravon patted his jacket, felt the package in his breast pocket. Reaching in, he pulled out the clear bag with its red and white dust, the remnants of the two crystals brought through from Darkmouth.

"That," said Finn with a wide grin, "is our way home."

50

A short while passed before the Orthrus dropped out of the sky, delivered to the cave by the serpent. Cornelius skidded to a halt while Hiss screamed at him to take it easy. Cornelius did not take it easy.

After delivering them, the serpent pulled high again above the ground, circled the area and then landed behind the bickering Orthrus. It shook its wings, stirring the dust, before settling into a pose that was almost statuesque.

"If it was not for all those scaldgrubs you eat, we would not be such a heavy cargo," Hiss said.

Cornelius growled at him.

Hiss's voice rose, insulted. "I am certainly not a hairless twig, you flatulent lump."

Finn watched all of this from the mouth of the cave, his head in the light, his body in shade. "You saved Emmie

too, didn't you?" he said to the serpent. "You brought her here."

The serpent lowered its head in what Finn presumed was a nod. Its large eyes burned with silent intelligence. Then it snapped at the bickering Cornelius and Hiss in a way that made it clear to everyone – not least the Orthrus – that the serpent was very much in charge. As if embarrassed, the dog whined, while the snake-tail slunk low at the rear.

From within the cave came a muffled exclamation of frustration from Estravon. "Come on, you blasted thing."

"Did she get home?" asked Finn, ignoring the shout.

"It would appear so," said Hiss, now shaking dust from his scales, glancing at the serpent as if for approval to continue. Finn felt like exploding again, but with delight this time. She wasn't dead. She hadn't been eaten, gnawed, fed to any giant chicks.

"She was carried here just in time for the opening of a gateway," Hiss said. "They have started opening again only recently after many years' quiet. They have been opening from the human side of the world. Our, erm, flying friend managed to get here before it was too late. It helped, of course, that you had seen fit to slay the cave's protector as soon as you arrived in this land."

"I didn't mean to," said Finn sincerely.

From inside the cave, an increasingly furious Estravon could be heard shouting, "If this thing doesn't come out, I'm going to clobber it."

"We saved you both, but we should be honest and say that we did not know if we should," explained Hiss. "Not at first anyway. We met the human and agreed to help guide you to him, to see if what he had told us about you was true. We could have killed you. And we would have if necessary." He turned to the serpent again, as if for permission to continue. "But the decision was made to let you live. To help you leave."

"By who?"

Hiss twisted to look at the serpent.

"The serpent made that decision?" said Finn.

"Yes."

"And you must do what it says?"

"Yes."

"So, the serpent is your master?"

Cornelius gave a strangled howl.

"Mistress actually," clarified Hiss. "And she is a Quetzalcóatl. No mere serpent."

Finn remembered the swishes in the cloud, the shadows that had occasionally fallen over them on their journey.

"She was following us after we arrived here."

"No," said Hiss. "It was not always her. There are others like her. Others with us."

"I swear I am going to smash you to pieces!" yelled Estravon from the cave.

Hiss looked again to the serpent, checking for any sign of disapproval. The creature did not respond in any way and that seemed a cue to continue.

"The human thought a few sausages were enough to manipulate us," said Hiss. "We are not so easily manipulated. In reality, we were the ones manipulating the human."

Cornelius barked.

"Yes," said Hiss, "some sausages would have been nice too."

"But why save us?" Finn asked.

Behind the Orthrus, the Legend rose. As it spread its wings and focused on Finn, he suddenly saw compassion and peacefulness glow in its eyes.

Hiss appeared to enter a trance. "Many of us are tired of endless war with the humans," he explained, the tenor of his voice different, as if the words were not his. "We only want our own world now. A peaceful world. A change is coming. You must return. You must tell them."

Hiss snapped out of the trance, flickered his tongue rapidly while shaking his arrow-shaped head. "I hate it when she does that," he said. "We have a link. Telepathic. Just me and her. Not the mutt at the front. It gives me a frightful headache. Another burden placed on me in this life."

The serpent settled again, leaving Finn somewhat gobsmacked, unsure how to respond.

"Ah, does the dragon speak?" said Estravon, who had been watching the exchange from the front of the cave, where he was rubbing hands that looked red and raw. He answered his own question. "Of course it speaks. The trees probably have a few words if you push the right branch. Now did Finn tell you his plan? No? Well, all I'll say is that you Legends, or whatever you call yourselves, had better not go dying in the next few decades or it's not going to be a great plan."

Estravon went back into the cave, but popped his head out again to complete a thought. "Oh, and you might want to think twice about relying on that boy there. He is a walking, talking, clanking disaster. Everything he touches results in catastrophe."

He disappeared again, resuming his loud struggle with whatever it was he was loudly struggling with.

Finn ignored him. He had been through enough now that he was just going to go with the plan he'd concocted. Even if all the other ones had failed.

"How long do you live for?" he asked Cornelius and Hiss.

Cornelius growled.

"That is a delicate matter," said Hiss.

"Sorry, I didn't mean to ask a personal question."

"It is not that," explained Hiss. "If he dies, then I am stuck where he drops. If I die, he must drag around my poor lifeless body for the rest of his pitiful life. And, trust me, getting a mate when you have a corpse stuck to your backside is not as easy as it might sound."

Cornelius whined.

"It is tough enough as it is in our condition frankly," added Hiss. "Why do you ask?"

"Because we don't come from here," explained Finn.

"That is hardly news," said Hiss.

"What I mean is that we don't come from this *time*. The gateway that opens from my world into this one also opens from my present to the past. Or your present to the future. What I mean is that I come from *your* future. My grandfather comes from the past." Finn blew out his cheeks. "It gives me a headache even trying to explain it."

"You should try having two headaches simultaneously," said Hiss. Cornelius groaned in agreement.

"The point is," said Finn, "I need you to find my father. But it won't be for a long, long time. Thirty-two years from now."

"Minus just over two weeks," Estravon interjected from the cave.

"Minus just over two weeks," confirmed Finn. "But, when he comes through in the future, you need to be ready to save him and tell him."

Hiss appeared to zone out for a moment, then snap back into focus. He glanced at the Quetzalcóatl. "She says you will need to be more specific than that."

"I can't," said Finn. "No, wait, I can. It's just after the invasion, when Manticores cross over from here to my world."

"We are often invading your world," said Hiss.

"No, not in my time. There's only one invasion then because the gateways have closed. Darkmouth is the only Blighted Village left in my world. My father will come through after this one invasion, years after the gateways stop opening everywhere else."

The serpent blew a great hot breath from its snout, stretched its wings.

"All I ask is that, if you find him, you rescue him and

help him come here. To this cave. Just over two weeks after the invasion. It might be the only chance he has. Please."

Cornelius shook his head forlornly.

"*That* is your plan?" asked Hiss.

"Yep," said Finn cheerily.

"I am sure you could concoct a worse plan, but I am struggling to think how."

"Actually, I think it's a very good one," said Finn.

"What makes you so confident?" said Hiss.

"Because it's already worked." He waited while that sank in with either end of the Orthrus. But it didn't seem to, so he explained. "All that time I thought Dad was on my radio telling us to go to the tower, he was warning us to stay away from it. Because he knew who was there. He knew what could happen. And he knew all of that because you told him. You *will* tell him."

"But..." said Hiss. "If..."

Cornelius moaned.

They each looked at the serpent. After a few seconds of contemplation, it bowed its head.

"It would seem you have an agreement," said Hiss.

From the cave came a triumphant cry. Estravon emerged, a crumbling stalagmite in one hand and a crystal held aloft in the other. "Got it!"

51

Finn carefully worked the crystal into the bag, turning it slowly, checking to see if the coating of red dust stuck.

Estravon was examining the calculations and ratios written in Niall Blacktongue's notebook. Finn had explained what these calculations meant – or rather his best guesses based on everything his grandfather had said in the tower. Estravon fancied his chances of putting his Advanced Gateway Chemistry studies to good use. Both knew it was a gamble as to whether they'd get the right amount of dust on to the crystal to open a time-travelling gateway back to Darkmouth.

"Little more," Estravon suggested. "Don't miss any spots."

"There are strange things in with this dust," said Finn, looking closely at small brown particles mixed with the sparkling white and red of the pulverised crystals. "Maybe

it's a unique chemical compound created by the joining of two worlds."

Estravon peered into the bag. "No," he said, "that's my sandwich. Well, the crumbs left over from it. It was the only bag I had." He caught Finn's eye. "Don't give me that look. I'd spent the night in my car. It wasn't like I could put a roast chicken in the oven."

Finn returned to coating the crystal. "It better not have any effect on the gateway."

"Oh, you mean worse than blowing open the very fabric of time and space itself based on some dodgy calculations in your grandfather's notebook?" said Estravon. "Anyway, if a gateway opens naturally when the sun hits the cave in Darkmouth, then why don't we just wait for that to happen?"

"The Legends will be coming to find us here. Do you want to wait a minute longer on the Infested Side?"

"That's the first thing you've said that makes any sense," said Estravon. "Let's get a move on." He peered into the bag as Finn continued to dip and turn the crystal. "But I'd be lying if I said it hasn't been an extraordinary experience here. Apart from the sickness, the attacks, the violence, the inadvertent time travel, your father not being here at all, your rogue grandfather turning up instead, death stalking our every step and, most worryingly, the repeated rule-breaking, it's been... invigorating, to say the least."

Finn pulled the crystal from the bag and together they examined it.

The serpent circled in the sky, watching for signs of approaching Legends. It was joined by a second Quetzalcóatl, before each banked away to keep watch from separate pieces of sky. Cornelius and Hiss patrolled the edge of the clearing, their presence obvious only from the bickering that broke out on the occasions when Cornelius wanted to cock a leg and mark his territory.

Estravon flicked through the notebook, still examining Niall's calculations. "That's almost enough dust now, I'd say." He thumbed through a couple of other pages. "Your grandfather was such a wasted talent. This is incredible work on the crystals. There'll be great interest in his findings. It should be possible, subject to agreement by the Twelve, to use his research to adapt a Darkmouth crystal, punch through to the Infested Side and grab your father if he's still waiting there."

Finn said nothing, returning the crystal to the bag to add a little more dust. But his silence wasn't just down to concentration. Estravon seemed to sense that. "You're up to something," he said.

"I'm not," said Finn, focusing on the crystal.

"Don't lie to me," Estravon said. "I just gave you good news about how we might look for your father and you didn't bat an eyelid. You just keep on covering that crystal, which at this stage is dustier than a Half-Hunter's fighting suit. Let's confirm this. The plan is to use this dusted crystal to get home and then, after the appropriate criteria have been satisfied, we will clean a Darkmouth crystal of all dust and use it to get to your father. So, repeat after me. That. Is. The. Plan."

Finn did not repeat after him.

"You've got some other dumb notion in your head, I can sense it," said Estravon.

Finn took the crystal from the bag, and stared at it. "We're going to need another crystal," he said.

"No, we're not. Not unless this one doesn't work or

you want to use a second one to do something incredibly stupid."

"When I was at the tower with my grandfather—"

"Ah, so you've selected the stupid option."

"—he told me what happens when you open two gateways together."

"He wrote about it too. Look, it's clear as day." Estravon held up the notebook and its drawing of intersecting circles and a skull and crossbones. "See that? That's maths language for 'it'll be a disaster so don't be an idiot'."

"We can use this dust to open one gateway to our time…" Finn began to explain.

"You *never* mess with maths," said Estravon through a pinched mouth.

"…and we can *then* use a normal crystal from this cave to open a second gateway straight from Darkmouth to my dad's time on the Infested Side." Finn was trying to get the idea right in his mind, to see it clearly, simply. But he knew he must sound desperate. Which he was. "The way my grandfather explained it, it's kind of possible to have, like, two gateways at once which hopefully will be linked. Like a loop."

"Kind of?" said Estravon, incredulous. "*Hopefully?*"

"It should be easy," Finn concluded, trying to convince

himself as much as Estravon.

"Oh yes," said Estravon, losing his composure, "we *could* do that when we get home, after a while, subject to full approval from the Twelve. But we *cannot* do it on the whim of some crazed, famously incompetent twelve-year-old."

Away from them, Cornelius barked and disappeared into the trees. Finn noticed that the serpents weren't anywhere to be seen either.

"I've told them to bring my dad to this cave, in the future," said Finn, holding the red-dusted crystal and moving towards a stalagmite at the cave's entrance, which he proceeded to kick at. "I promised him I'd be there. The longer he stays there, the more chance something awful will..." He couldn't bring himself to finish the sentence.

"You've promised him nothing yet," Estravon said forcefully. "You're still thirty-two years away, more or less, from even getting that message delivered."

Finn kept kicking at the stalagmite, hardly scratching it.

Outside the cave, they heard Cornelius barking urgently. Estravon used that distraction as a chance to rush at Finn and twist his arm expertly behind his back so that he was forced to open his hand and release his hold on the crystal he had covered in dust.

They could hear Hiss shouting something.

"Give it back!" demanded Finn. "Give me that crystal."

"I'm just about OK with trying this dust trick to get us home to our place," said Estravon, releasing Finn's arm and taking a couple of steps further into the cave, "but I am *not* keen on live experiments with the very fabric of space-time."

"Why can't you just *forget* the rules for five minutes?" Finn pleaded.

"I have, as it happens, but only because there are no rules to deal with the craziness of this idea."

The Orthrus burst from the treeline, skidding to a halt at the cave. Hiss lifted himself up from behind. "We have visitors. They are not happy."

At the same time, the two serpents appeared high above them. A third joined them and together they banked and dived towards something unseen in the forest. Finn snatched at Estravon, trying to grab the crystal back, but the Assessor retreated further into the cave.

"You have no idea of the consequences of all of this," he told Finn. "You can't just mix a crystal from one world with dust from another and then throw a whole other crystal on top of that. After you've just exploded.

Especially after you've just exploded."

Outside, in the forest, bare trees suddenly darkened with life and there was a wave of noise. Of screaming. Of crashing. Of trees being smashed to smithereens. The serpents swooped low ahead of the wave of Legends, blowing a fierce blast of heat in their path.

Finn looked at the edge of the snarling forest, then back to Estravon. But he had gone deeper into the cave. Finn followed, the fear filling his head less to do with the attacking hordes and more to do with the thought of losing that crystal. Panting, he dodged between stalagmites, avoided the dripping goo, stumbled over a rock and finally caught up with Estravon in the chamber where they had first arrived on the Infested Side.

"I can't let you do this," said Estravon, holding his small torch in one hand, the crystal in the other. "There still need to be rules. Everything collapses without rules."

"We can't leave my father behind. He would never leave me behind. Never. I'll do everything I can to find him."

"And I will help you." Estravon dropped the crystal to the ground, placed his foot over it. "But I have to stop you from destroying the world first."

"No," Finn begged, panic in his throat, his breath

quickening. He knew that if they waited for the Twelve to approve a rescue mission from Darkmouth it could take weeks, and every second his father was on the Infested Side was a risk.

"Please don't come any closer," said Estravon, tipping the crystal with his heel.

But Finn did, pushed forward by an instinct to protect the crystal and its dust. He heard the crack before he realised Estravon had stood on it, then saw him press hard, the full weight of his leg on the crystal. When he pulled away, the dust and crystal were smears on the floor of the cave.

There was noise pouring into Finn's head. The head-rush of his own shock. The mayhem of the Legends reaching the cave.

"You've just killed my dad," said Finn, awake to the sound of violence filling the cave. "You've killed all of us!"

52

A creature crashed into the chamber, a blur of teeth, hair and claws under Estravon's torchlight, a gnashing fury scrambling to get them.

It reached Finn first, and he somehow dodged its charge so that it smashed against a stalagmite behind him. As the Legend stood again, Finn recognised it as a Grendel, standing over him with wolf snout, thick fur hanging over burning eyes. It looked very, very annoyed.

Then a pen arrowed across the torchlight, embedding itself in what might have been an ear. Or another eye. Finn couldn't be sure. Either way, the Legend howled.

"Let's go!" shouted Estravon.

But there was nowhere to go. Only rock behind them. The sound of oncoming Legends ahead of them.

"We *could* have got out of here if you hadn't squashed the crystal," said Finn.

Estravon's torch swung again, its beam reflecting off the claws of the recovered Legend. Finn raised his arms to protect himself. Then he heard biting. But it wasn't coming from the Grendel.

When Estravon's light finally caught up with the frenzy, it illuminated Hiss's fangs, rounded and sharp and biting down hard on the waist of the attacking Legend. There was a whimper from the Grendel, a spasm, and then it collapsed amid the debris of smashed stalagmites.

"Oh, the relief of finally getting to bite something," said Hiss, stretching out. "I really needed to let that venom out."

Without explanation, Finn grabbed the torch from Estravon's hand and turned it off so they were in near total darkness.

"Not again. What are you—?" started Estravon.

"Wait," interrupted Finn.

In the silence was a noise. A wrenching. A groaning. It was as if the air around them was being cleaved open, torn roughly. It was low at first, but grew quickly.

And in the darkness was something even deeper, a small well of crimson, getting bigger, boring through the wall between worlds.

Finn and Estravon looked at each other and both said

the only thing they needed to.

"Get down!"

They hit the ground just as the red gateway burst into the cave, a terrifying, vibrant scar looming above them, gorging on the air, bloated coils of energy writhing at its edges.

Emmie's head popped through from the other side.

"Hi, Finn!" she said. "Nice kitty T-shirt."

F rom the ground, Finn raised a hand and waved at Emmie.

She disappeared again suddenly, as if dragged back into her world by something malevolent.

"Emmie!" called Finn.

Steve appeared in her place, head first, helmet on, Desiccator in hand, stepping through the gateway while still looking back into the world he was leaving behind. "You've been on the Infested Side once already," he told the unseen Emmie. "That's enough for one day."

Steve turned to Finn. His dark visor could not mask his deep irritation. "Right. You two. Let's go. Now."

Estravon jumped up, his ragged trouser ends flapping in the glimmering light. "Protocol suggests..." Another Legend arrived in the chamber and the Orthrus jumped straight for it, the two disappearing with a terrific crash behind some large stalagmites. "Actually, I've no idea

what protocol suggests other than I get the hell out of here right now."

Estravon made for the gateway, where Steve grabbed him and pulled him through.

Finn remained, hesitant even as behind him a fight raged, illuminated by the streaming gateway.

"Don't make me drag you in here," Steve growled.

Finn felt paralysed. If he stepped back into Darkmouth, he would see his mother again, but he'd lose his father.

"This is the second time I've stood at a gateway telling you to hurry up," said Steve. "And it's the last time. So hurry up."

If Finn stayed, there was nothing left for him here but probable death. Or, at best, an unhinged grandfather.

He turned towards the cave just as Cornelius and Hiss managed to subdue another invading Grendel. "Do not be a dumb animal!" Hiss shouted at him.

Finn stepped towards the gateway, but stopped mid-stride.

"What are you waiting for?" demanded Steve, hand held out.

On the ground under the felled Grendel, amid the ruins of a stalagmite, the deep red light of the gateway danced off a clear crystal.

Finn dropped to the cave floor, beside the filthy bulk of the Legend's body, and tried to grab the crystal – but it was wedged underneath the stricken Grendel's ribcage, which rose and fell, with each hot, stinking breath.

"Whatever you're thinking—" Steve started to say. His words were drowned out by a shrill call of defiance from the flying serpents, who were at the entrance to the cave now, facing the howls and onslaughts of attacking Legends.

Finn waited for a breath from the comatose Grendel to lift its ribcage and free the crystal. After what seemed an eternity, it breathed deep and Finn pulled hard. The crystal came away so easily he dropped on to his backside and had to force himself back up again.

"I'm ready!" he shouted at Steve and strode towards the gateway. Then he hesitated in front of it, the portal a grinding whirlpool of bloodshot energy, tendrils crawling and diving at the edges.

"Ready for what?" asked Steve.

Finn had made up his mind. Every one of his decisions so far had been disastrous, to some extent or other, but he was finally giving in to that, going with it. Because it was still better than making no decision.

He couldn't bring a crystal through without attaching

it to his flesh. But he didn't *need* to bring it through. A gateway home was open. He had a clear crystal.

In the notebook was that drawing of two gateways. Of the skull and crossbones. It was an obvious warning.

But he needed to get his father back. His father had *told* him he would.

Finn held the crystal up.

"Whatever you're going to do," said Steve, "don't do it."

Finn did it.

He held the crystal to the very edge of the red gateway. It stuck without effort.

"That was a really stupid thing to do," blurted Steve, "and now you're on your own." He disappeared back into Darkmouth.

But Finn could not follow. The crystal had stuck to the red gateway and Finn was stuck to it in turn. Just as when he had activated the blood crystal the first time.

He had no time to panic. He knew what was about to happen, so he tensed for the dark power of the crystal, got ready to allow the energy in, to accept the pain and let it infuse him.

More Legends had broken their way into the chamber, arriving with the snap of stalagmites, the crash of rock.

The cave was being overrun.

Just in time, the crystal decided it was the right moment to release Finn. With a painful jolt of electricity, he was flung away from the crystal and into the red gateway.

54

Time occupied every corner of Finn's mind. Or his mind occupied every corner of time. Maybe both. Or neither.

He heard a distant sound of thunder.

Then Finn was through, stumbling backwards on to the floor of the Darkmouth cave, with its gravel and pebbles and general lack of goo. All of it shimmering in the grinding red light of the gateway.

And he felt OK. Physically anyway.

Mentally was another story. Because here he was in Darkmouth, which meant the double portal hadn't worked. He hadn't looped through to his father's time on the Infested Side.

A familiar feeling of failure threatened to crush him, like the rock roof of the cave collapsing.

Emmie was facing him, Steve too, with his visor now open. Estravon was beside him, still frayed about the

edges. Each of them stared.

"I couldn't find my dad," choked Finn. "He wasn't there. He was—"

But they weren't looking at him.

They were looking at something behind him.

"Just when you think things are getting a little better..." said Estravon.

Slowly, Finn turned round. And saw a hole in the world. Not a gateway, with its pulsating edges, but a large clean wound in the fabric between Darkmouth and the Infested Side. As if each was of the same world, separated only by an open window.

But the cave no longer led to another cave. Instead, the view of the Infested Side was of rock, soil, craters torn from the ground and filled with the crushed stems of stalagmites. It was where the cave *used to be*, but had since been torn apart, destroyed. It was of wide-open space imposed on the land, the glass trees of the forest crushed into sand. It was a view of flat sky above.

And it was a view of war.

The sky was filled with Quetzalcóatl fighting Quetzalcóatl. Some had wings marked with blood-red stripes, and they dived at enemy serpents. In squadrons. As individuals. Biting. Wrestling. The scene was one of pandemonium and noise and a smell so vile it poured thickly through the window Finn had opened.

A felled serpent spiralled down from on high. They watched it fall, wings tattered, slender neck pushed back by the wind, until it hit the ground with a sickening thud.

And, diving out of its way, they saw a single Orthrus, its coat grey with age but the green of its snake-tail as vivid as it had been when Finn had seen it only minutes before.

Yet Finn knew instantly that this was the Infested Side of now. And the Orthrus was thirty-two years older than when he had last seen him.

Cornelius and Hiss slowed, their movements stiff, as if to confirm what Finn was thinking. Then they sat down and noticed the hole, saw the humans watching them, but almost immediately looked away. Up. Towards the battle in the sky.

Finn followed their gaze, trying to find some order in the chaos, to find what it was they were looking at.

A glint caught his eye.

"There!" he said, pointing at a lone serpent darting through the tumultuous sky. On its back, they could see the flash of a blade. A glimmer of armour. A human clinging on against the force of the dive.

Even at that distance, it was clear that his fighting suit was riven with scars and gashes; his skin filthy; a beard grimy and wild.

But only one thing mattered to Finn. He had found his father.

'Hugo's Rescue'
From *The Chronicles of the Sky's Collapse,*
as told by the inhabitants of the Infested Side

SIX WEEKS AND TWO DAYS AGO

Humans live such short lives it's a wonder we haven't been able to just wait until they all died off before taking over an empty Promised World. Then again, there always seem to be new ones to replace the old ones. They're like a nasty rash that no amount of scratching will clear.

Niall Blacktongue had a son, who in turn had a son of his own. And, when word came that both of these humans had appeared through a gateway near the Forest of Woe, Blacktongue rode alongside Gantrua and a great army to intercept them.

Some of that army found the Hogboon first. His name was Broonie and he had been sent by Gantrua to the Promised World to deliver a crystal. He was not expected to return.

One of the Fomorian soldiers picked him up to interrogate him.

"How did you get back? Did you collaborate with the humans?"

"Ercckhkkkk," replied Broonie. "Krcchaccchh."

The Fomorian soldier realised he should stop holding him by the throat.

"I escaped," Broonie eventually spluttered when he could talk again. "I swear, by the gnarled mole on my father's ear, I killed many humans to get here."

Seeing that the Fomorian soldiers crowding round him still had their suspicions, the Hogboon decided to take a bolder approach. Broonie raised himself up as tall as he could. It was not very tall, but it would have to do. He spoke with his deepest, most authoritative voice – which was not at all deep, or authoritative, but would also have to do.

"I am an agent of Gantrua, the ruler of these worlds," he announced, "and should any harm come to me you will find yourself in the Coronium mines for all of eternity. Or, at the very least, forever."

The Fomorians were a little taken aback by this and glanced at each other, unsure how seriously to take the threat.

Broonie felt confident. "You had better heed my words, underling."

The Fomorian soldier's fist landed squarely on the top of Broonie's head. They did not believe his threat.

The soldier picked him up and carried him in one

hand, bringing him towards the open gateway and the humans he had just abandoned.

There they merged again with the great army bearing down on the human Legend Hunter, Hugo the Great.

At the head of that army rode two figures. The huge and terrifying Gantrua and the frail but determined Niall Blacktongue.

Blacktongue is said to have stared at the son he had not seen for many darkenings and prepared to ignite, to release his one final blast of power.

Except there was a maelstrom in the clouds. A Quetzalcóatl dived from the sky. Two more followed behind it. Then more – so many they were impossible to count, until the sky above was dark with serpents.

Dive-bombing. Biting. Scattering the battalions.

And, when they left, the human called Hugo was gone too.

Gantrua cursed the skies, a great rage that thundered through the ground.

As he did that, another serpent returned, grabbed Broonie from his Fomorian captor and flew him away too.

Gantrua raged even louder.

From the Darkmouth cave, Finn watched his father come swooping towards them on the back of the flying serpent, bent low, clinging to its neck as it pierced through the battle. Finn's breath was shallow, the aftershock of the crystal's energy subsumed by the urgency gripping him.

"Come on, Dad!"

Finn stood at the great open wound in the world, the crunching red light of the gateway strobing beside it. Darkmouth on one side. The Infested Side on the other. The view to the chaos of that world hung there, as if it were a TV screen. He had caused this, but the consequences of what he had done would have to wait. He just needed his dad back now.

He stepped forward. "Dad!"

Steve put a hand on Finn's shoulder to hold him back.

"Your dad's going to make it," said Emmie.

Then another Quetzalcóatl hit the serpent Hugo rode, careening into its underbelly and sending it into a spin. Colliding with the flank of another creature, it briefly righted itself, but not in time to arrest its dive.

Hugo's serpent crashed to the ground, chin and neck first, skidding along its belly and gouging through the dirt until it halted suddenly, sending Hugo tumbling forward through the air.

"Dad!"

Hugo absorbed the fall, rolling expertly before pouncing to his feet and breaking into a run.

He had about fifty metres to go.

"Wow," said Emmie.

"I need to learn that," admitted Steve.

"This is incredible," said an astonished Estravon. "And so, so bad."

At an angle to Hugo, Cornelius was gaining too, aiming straight for the open wound. Finn's father kept running. There was a sudden and great smash of bodies between him and the portal as two wrestling Quetzalcóatls hit the ground. Their collision threw up a plume of dirt and glass about them, tearing a scar in the ground before they rose again, still grappling and biting at each other.

Hugo burst through the dust without breaking his pace.

"Nearly there, Dad!" Finn yelled again, though he had no idea if his father could hear him above the noise. "Nearly there!"

His father stopped dead.

He was so close Finn reckoned he could have stretched out his hands, his fingers parting the frigid air of the Infested Side, and touched him.

Steve pointed his Desiccator at Hugo. "Get in now or I'll turn you into a tennis ball and bring you home myself."

Hugo ignored him and waited instead for the Orthrus to arrive. Cornelius loped up, panting. His eyelids hung heavy and his mouth drooped to one side. Finn had seen the Orthrus only hours before and yet so many years had evidently passed.

"Cornelius!" shouted Finn.

"Hiss!" said Emmie.

Hiss lifted his head to their height, nodded in the direction of the battle being fought above them. "All this because of you," he said. "Yet you are still a child after so many years."

Hugo took hold of Cornelius's jowls like he would an

old family dog. "Thank you," he said. "Both of you."

"What is it with you lot?" Steve asked, deeply impatient. "Maybe your whole family should just move over there and start a petting zoo."

Then Hiss said something Finn couldn't hear and his father frowned. "I can't take him," he said.

"You must, Hugo," Hiss answered.

"He has no place in Darkmouth," Hugo insisted.

"He will be killed if he stays here," said Hiss, and Cornelius turned and galloped off before Hugo had another chance to complain about the matter. Whatever it was.

"Who are you talking about?" asked Estravon. He was taking notes again.

"Can we just get moving here?" asked Steve. "We've got two doors wide open to the Infested Side, which means one of two things is going to happen. Either something comes out. Or we get sucked in. Or both things happen and then we're all toast."

A large rock thudded to the ground beside Hugo, shocking him into action again. He darted the last few metres against the background of battle and catastrophe, of Quetzalcóatls blackening the sky.

At the window between the Infested Side and Darkmouth, he took one last look behind him, at the battle still being fought, as if he should not be abandoning it.

"What are you waiting for?" Steve asked.

Hugo looked at Finn, the grinding light of the red gateway mirrored in his eyes. It seemed to be all it took to make his mind up.

Finn's father stepped into Darkmouth.

He looked as if he had been through hell. Twice. But beneath the dirt and the damage and the bird's nest of a beard, Finn could see the strength of his father as bright as any gateway. Hugo placed two hands on Finn's shoulders, gripped him hard.

"Did you blow this hole open?" his father asked him.

"Only to help you, Dad."

His father shook his head slowly, stared at him. "You collaborated with the Legends too? Got involved in a war that could have terrible consequences?"

Finn nodded, eyes dropping now as he considered what he'd done. "Yeah, I suppose."

"And came up with some ridiculous, thirty-two-year-long plan to carry a message to me to meet here."

"I wasn't sure what else to—"

His father broke into a grin, squeezed Finn's shoulders so tightly it hurt. "See, didn't I always say we'd make a great Legend Hunter out of you some day?"

A tsunami of relief burst through Finn. His dad was home. He was here. And, almost as good, he wasn't telling him off about blowing open a huge hole between the worlds.

"Now say thanks to the nice Orthrus, Finn," his father said.

Finn looked through the great hole into the Infested Side to see that Cornelius and Hiss had returned. Finn noticed now that round Cornelius's neck was a chain. A dog tag hung from it, tarnished and scuffed, but with its words still just about visible. *My name is Yappy. If you find me, you can keep me.*

"Thank you," Finn said.

But Cornelius and Hiss were distracted by something on their side, just out of view, as if hiding in the folds of an open curtain.

"I'm not going," Finn heard a voice say. Reedy, nasal, indignant. "I swear by the callused gums of my uncle Emphra."

"You are not staying here," insisted Hiss. And, with that, Cornelius snarled, darted out of sight and returned, dragging a cranky Hogboon by its ragged collar. He had familiar gnarled green skin, wide ears and wider nostrils.

"Broonie!" Finn said.

"Unfortunately," said Broonie.

Emmie turned to Estravon. "I *told* you we knew a Legend."

"I wouldn't boast about that," said Estravon, making a note.

"We are *not* taking *him*," insisted Steve.

Cornelius snapped at Broonie, who jumped in through the open wound and into the cave, back into Darkmouth.

"No choice," said Hiss.

"That goes against every rule written," declared Estravon. "And every rule not yet written."

"It looks like he'll have to stay," said Hugo. Then, seeing the look on Estravon's face, said, "And you must be the one the Legends came to know as the Great Screecher."

"I am Estravon Oakbound, Assessor to the Subcommittee—"

Hugo cut him off. "So, why is this other gateway open?"

Emmie stepped forward. "We opened it to rescue Finn. With a crystal that grew in this cave. I showed my dad how to do it. Told him to wear gloves too so he wouldn't get frazzled like Finn did. I've been to the Infested Side. And back again. It was brilliant."

"Well, *she* has not changed," said Hiss.

Cornelius was becoming jumpy. Serpents were still fighting, the shrieks of aggression and pain cutting through the air so loudly they were echoing in the cave of another world. Hiss looked skyward, then towards the forest. "Others are coming. We must go and fight. We will defend this place for as long as possible, but you must find a way to close that window."

The Orthrus turned to go, but as it did Emmie remembered something.

"Cornelius," she called out and put her hand into the pocket of her fighting suit. "This is for you." Emmie flung a dozen half-mushed and very raw sausages through the hole.

"Sausages!" Cornelius barked joyfully, grabbing them, gobbling them and, with Hiss once again complaining about being wagged from side-to-side in delight, bolting away until they had merged with the battle.

57

There were six of them in the Darkmouth cave, five humans of various degrees of dishevellment, plus one stranded, sullen Hogboon.

They stood facing a cranking gateway to the Infested Side of the past and a gaping hole to a fierce battle taking place right now in that same world.

Finn's head hurt. He wasn't sure if it was the crystal, travelling through the gateway or the very thought of the situation they were in.

"This really is not ideal," said Estravon.

In the tight space, Finn was pressed close to his father. He couldn't yet believe he was there, that he'd managed to get him back. He didn't care about the damage done. Not yet anyway. He had him back. Darkmouth had its Legend Hunter again.

And there was something else on his mind. Finn's eyes began to sting and a tear ran down his cheek.

"Ah, come on, Finn, there's no need to cry," said his father.

"No, Dad. It's not that. It's the smell," he said, burbling a laugh through his discomfort. "I'm sorry, but you really stink. Sort of like old socks left in a plastic bag or something."

His father bristled. "Well, I can see you haven't changed that much since becoming the saviour of the world."

"It's more like cheese dipped in bleach," said Estravon.

"That smell saved me, as it happens," said Hugo. "I've spent over two weeks in the mountains, hiding among Legends called the Nuppeppō. It's the only place even the most warlike Legends will never venture. Their stench is—"

"Like a full nappy left in the sun?" suggested Estravon.

"Anyway, that's why we smell a bit."

"*We* smell?" exclaimed Broonie. "You lot hardly smell as sweet as swamp roses yourselves."

"Look, I hate to interrupt—" Steve said.

Finn felt a shudder through his arm. The one he had held the crystal with. His father seemed to notice it.

"The serpents swooped down for me. And Broonie," his father said. "They protected us, hid us with the resistance over there."

"I was resisting nobody," Broonie insisted. "I was just trying to get home and now look where I am."

"Listen to me!" snapped Steve. Finally, the others paid him attention. Through the open hole to the Infested Side, they could sense the ground shake. Beneath the fight in the air, the trees were darkening, the gaps between them filling with Legends – Manticores, Fomorians, Wolpertingers – scrabbling over the ground, leaping through the petrified branches.

"They're coming straight for us," said Emmie, pushing in between the others to get a look at the window between worlds.

"Go to the car," her father instructed her.

"But—"

"I'm telling you to go to the car." Steve held out the car keys. "Now." Emmie took the keys and backed towards the cave's exit before finally turning to run.

"You know, I once had a finger chopped off and replaced with a crystal," remarked Broonie. "That now turns out to have been one of my happier days."

Steve reached down to pick up another Desiccator and handed it to Hugo. "I brought you a welcome home gift."

Through the open wound, the rush of Legends grew.

They were clear of the trees now, a great mass pouring towards them.

"What about a Desiccator for me?" Finn asked.

"That *was* for you," said Steve. "But the plan has changed since, you know, you ripped the world in two just to get *him*."

The red gateway to the Infested Side's past also began to pulse and groan. "Lord help us if anything comes through this gateway too," muttered Estravon.

Something did come through.

Then another something.

And the Legends did not stop coming.

T he blue shock of a Desiccator net almost scraped Finn's ear as it *fzzzzed* from Steve's weapon to hit the first screaming Grendel to come out of the red gateway.

With a stifled *whooop*, the Legend shrank into a ball of skin and fur. It hadn't even hit the ground when the next one came through. Steve fired and it too froze, shrank, cracked against the stone floor of the cave.

"Hugo, cover this red gateway!" Steve shouted.

"No, it's better if *you* cover the red gateway," said Hugo.

The crown of another stooping Grendel emerged through the red gateway. They both shot it.

Whooop.

Through the wound, they could see a squadron of Quetzalcóatls diving at the approaching army, sending a clump of Manticores scattering. But there were too many

to stop. Legends filled their view now, and they had almost reached the gaping hole and the way into Darkmouth.

A Grendel came through the red gateway. *Fzzz. Whooop.*

"Get out, Finn," his father said, but, as Finn began to back away, he felt the fizzing of the energy seeping through his body. It felt stronger and more immediate than the first time. It felt raw and raging.

A Manticore reached the great hole into the cave, the first of its kind to leave the battle there. Hugo pulled his trigger and the Desiccator net crossed the threshold between worlds, mutating immediately into a lumpen shape so that, when it caught the Legend, it left it a grotesque, writhing figure. Two Wolpertingers following behind stepped straight past it to clamber into the cave.

They were now under attack from two places. The Infested Side of the past, the Infested Side of the present. One world. Two eras. Too many Legends.

"Everyone back," said Hugo.

"Everybody out," said Steve.

"Get into the cave. Get out of the cave," complained Broonie as he turned to go. "I hate this place. Again."

He scurried through the passageway, Estravon following right behind him.

Finn hesitated. A thought was burrowing into his mind. A way to end this. A way to end everything. He wasn't holding a weapon, but the energy building within told him he could become one.

"What are you waiting for?" his father asked sternly. "You've done your bit. Now go."

Finn did what he was told this time, bumping through the passageway without stopping to inspect the scrapes and bruises he was collecting on the way. Reaching the wide light of the cave opening, he heard the relentless fizz of Desiccators echoing from behind him.

The shooting stopped, so Finn paused at the entrance and listened. Estravon and Broonie were already there, feet on the debris, ready to climb free.

"Maybe it's over already," Finn said.

A Wolpertinger bolted from the cave, springing out of the passage at them until suddenly changing direction mid-jump as Estravon reacted with a high kick to its chest. The Legend leaped up again, only to be hit by a glowing blue Desiccator net and shrunk. Behind it stood Steve, weapon raised, thick blue smoke rising from its barrel.

Finn's dad arrived next, his already battered armour sparking off the rock wall as he broke free, shooting behind him as he ran.

Fzzz. Whooop. Fzzz. Whooop.

But still they came. Legends squeezing through behind them, pouring in from two worlds, the rock around them crumbling under the pressure and crush of invading creatures.

Finn felt the bomb ticking down inside him. Felt its power. His power. He held it in check, prevented it from igniting, because he'd kill everyone around him if he was to explode here.

Then he *realised* he was preventing it. That he had control. It was a match ready to spark, but only when he struck it. He was certain he could ignite when he needed to and destroy the Legends.

If only everyone else could get free of the blast first.

"Lure them to the beach," Steve said. "Trust me."

His father grabbed Finn, pulled him over the rockfall that had once blocked up the cave, that had kept its crystals untouched by daylight and Darkmouth safe from their gateways.

Hugo was still firing as he hurried Finn on.

Fzzz. Whooop. Fzzz. Whooop.

They scrambled away from the mouth of the cave, the brightness of the day flooding Finn's vision. It should have been so welcome, after so long in that awful, hellish place beyond, but he had no time to really appreciate it.

The saltiness in Darkmouth's air, the warmth in the breeze, the smooth, shifting pebbles of the beach, the gently crashing waves and the large black van parked awkwardly almost right against the cave entrance, seaweed clinging to its wheels, its rear doors open and Emmie crouched inside with a very large pineapple-shaped object wedged into a long, improvised weapon propped on her shoulder, which seemed to be made out of a drainpipe.

Finn hadn't expected that bit.

"Seeing as I made it back alive, my dad's finally letting me have a go with Mr Glad's stuff," Emmie announced. "But you should probably get out of the way, Finn."

His father grabbed him again, half dragging him to the far side of the van, where Estravon was already hiding, peering round the bumper with jaw wide open. Broonie was there too, loudly complaining about the whole thing. But he wasn't complaining loudly enough to be heard over the sound of desiccations.

Steve was last to abandon the cave. "Not yet, Emmie," he shouted as he scurried to the van. "Not yet!"

He dashed over to the rest of them, sliding over the pebbles along the side of the van until safely behind it.

"Now!" Steve and Hugo shouted together.

Emmie pulled the trigger.

She was thrown back as the pineapple shot from the

pipe and spun in a swift, brief arc over the short distance to the cave. Landing half buried in the stones, its fronds slid open, like the petals of a flower. The Fomorians, Manticores and Wolpertingers spilling on to the beach hesitated for a moment, arms and paws and claws raised, expecting an explosion.

It didn't happen.

They looked towards her with grins of deep malice.

She looked back, mouth screwed up in sudden concern.

Then the missile burst, a white foam showering the cave entrance and freezing a dozen Legends mid-grin. They tipped over where they stood, a couple of huge Fomorians leaning against each other like drunken statues.

"Brilliant!" said Emmie.

A hush settled over the beach, broken only by the sound of a frozen Manticore sliding down the stones towards the lapping tide. The sparkling seawater smacked at the shore of the narrow beach under the cliffs.

Waiting at the front end of the van, Finn couldn't help but look around. The light of the day was brilliant. A seagull somewhere squawked as seagulls do. The grass waved gently on the clifftop above them, with its crumbling Look-out Post and water-safety ring.

Then Finn's eye caught what he thought was a figure on the cliff. A tall man. Familiar. Appearing as if from nothing, in a silent, agonised stretch.

"Is that Mr—?" he began.

But he had no time to finish his observation because two things happened to distract his attention. One was the sight of new Legends pouring violently out from the cave.

The other was the loudness of the ticking inside him, so clear that Finn was amazed the rest of the beach couldn't hear it.

He was ready to ignite. He needed to. It would be the only way to end this.

"Fall back!" his father was yelling.

In Finn's eyes, the scene on the beach seemed to be unfolding in slow motion: Legends falling over themselves to get from the cave, piling forward through the Desiccator fire, knocking aside newly desiccated Legends before they even hit the ground.

Emmie scrambling from the van, falling on all fours on to the beach in an effort to get away as the Legends reached the vehicle, hitting it so hard it rocked back.

Broonie running as hard as his spindly legs would take him, while the gangly Estravon loped alongside him.

His father grabbing Finn to move him to safety. Desiccators on rapid fire until...

...*fzzzzpt.*

"This canister is dry," his father said. "Retreat."

But the words sounded distant, or like they were being spoken underwater. They were drowned out by the compulsion Finn felt to step in the wrong direction, to go back to the cave. Years of fear overridden by the flames rising inside him.

Steve's Desiccator was the next to run dry, the Half-Hunter pressing the trigger again and again. Nothing but a *fzzzpt* and cursing. A lot of cursing.

A Manticore pounced and Hugo swung the Desiccator like a club, swatting it away, but releasing his grip on Finn.

"I have to stop them," Finn heard himself mutter.

"Retreat," his father was saying, swinging his Desiccator once more.

"I have to..." Finn stepped forward, pushing his father's hand away. He ran. Back towards the cave. Into the seething mass of invading Legends.

60

He could hear Emmie shouting. "Finn!"

A few things went through his mind once he had separated from the rest of them, but really they all boiled down to a wrestle between bravery and his suddenly rediscovered desire to run away.

But there was nowhere for Finn to run. The Legends were crowding round him, so close he could feel the heat off their bodies, the staleness of their breath. Some were whooping, shrill in their delight. Around them, other Legends swarmed onwards, heading towards the others where they stood further up the beach.

Emmie's voice was receding. "Finn!"

He could just about make out a gap up the beach, towards the headland, where his father, Emmie, Broonie, Steve and Estravon must be. Surrounded now. He heard his father's grunts and yells as he fought Legends off by hand. Saw the ripples of kerfuffle. Then his view was

blocked by the Legends crowding round him, savouring their moment of triumph, deciding what to do with him, perhaps how to dispatch him or who should have the honour of doing it.

"Finn!" Emmie's voice was further away still.

Finn let the energy build within him. Was everyone far away enough to be safe? He couldn't be sure. He had no choice anyway. Whatever the consequences, he needed to use his power, to destroy what he could so that he could save the others. Save Darkmouth.

He let the energy build. Let it spark within him. Prepared to let the fire run free.

"Finn!"

Hang on. That wasn't Emmie calling him.

"Finn!"

It was his mother's voice, coming from somewhere above him. He shut down the energy, dampened its spark, craned to see through the crush of Legends. He spotted her on the edge of the cliff, eyes wide in fear, her shout cutting through even the tumult of so many Legends.

She wasn't alone.

His mother placed her fingers in her mouth and delivered a whistle so ear-splitting it caused the entire beach – Legend and human – to turn and see what was happening.

They were greeted by the sight of Clara – an ordinary woman, a civilian, with no weapon – but there were so many others joining her. Each in a fighting suit of different colours. Different styles. Different materials. Too big. Too small. Dusty. Some looking rusty. Some looked like they hadn't been used for generations.

But each figure held a weapon of some shape or form. They were Half-Hunters and there must have been a hundred of them crowding on to the cliff.

Clara stepped right to the edge, mouth tight with determination. "Get away from my son."

The Half-Hunters opened fire.

61

Finn was so awed by what happened next, it took him a moment to realise he should get out of the way.

The noise of the firing Desiccators was extraordinary, as if every storm on the planet had converged on Darkmouth with the sole intent of unleashing every lightning strike in the world.

Added to that was the soft *whooop, whooop, whooop* of each Legend as it was struck and shrunk, a shuffling rhythm beneath the harsh drumming of Desiccator fire.

And the light. It was almost blinding in its blueness. Fat, spreading nets raining from above, some merging to form a mass as bright as the sun above, blinding any Legends in their path, stunning them before they were even hit.

Whooop. Whooop. Whooop.

Still the creatures came, from each timeframe of the Infested Side, piling out from the cave and on to the stones.

Whooop. Whooop. Whooop. Whooop. Whooop.

The sound from the cliff was of Half-Hunters unleashing entire lives of frustration, of finally getting their moment to live out their destinies. Finn dashed to the cave entrance, hiding behind a curling lip of stone and watching the Legends arrive and hardly an instant later become giant hailstones splashing on the shore's edge. They began to pile up there, so that newly arrived Legends were helplessly sliding across the mounting rubble of desiccated comrades.

Whooop. Whooop. Whooop. Splash. Splash. Splash.

The Legends kept coming, struggling now even to leave the cave. The barrage continued, unrelenting, catastrophic. Desiccations rolling back into the gap in the cliff, washing about in the surf.

An old man on a bicycle appeared on the path along the cliff edge, cycling towards the Half-Hunters. The firing stopped, a sudden and deep silence punctured only by the whistled tune the man left hanging in the air as he became aware of what he had stumbled into. At which point, he stopped, turned his bike clumsily, climbed back on to the saddle and cycled away in the direction he'd come from, mumbling curses as he went.

Everyone resumed shooting.

At that point, Finn realised he wanted this to end. He wanted the invasion, the mass desiccations, the unbearable noise, to stop now.

More than that, he wanted the spasm spreading through his arm to go away. He wanted the energy to dissipate, to flow from him gently. But he knew that wouldn't be possible. The destruction was simmering inside him. It would not be long reaching boiling point.

Then everything around him stopped.

The shooting.

The noise.

The light.

The fury.

The desiccations.

The invasions.

But not the electricity in his arm. It was spreading through his shoulder into his chest.

The beach was quiet, except for the cry of gulls high above, the gentle splash of waves, and the clatter of a ball of desiccated Legend rolling down the high, wide pile at the cave's mouth and splashing into the sea.

Along the clifftop, a pall of blue smoke cohered over the barrels of weapons. Excitement lit the eyes of the Half-Hunters as one by one they flipped open their visors, removed their helmets and soaked up the scene, this great moment in their lives.

Clara started to rush along the cliff path, but Hugo raised a hand, a gesture that told her, "not yet". This wasn't over. It was a battlefield and the battle wasn't necessarily won.

All Finn could concentrate on now was the rush in his ears. The bubbling well of energy rising within his hand, his arm, his chest. Impatient.

From out of sight along the clifftop, there was sudden shouting. A figure appeared on its edge, wearing a full fighting suit except for a kilt and metal sporran. He had a sword in each hand and a beard you could lose a Legend in.

"A'm Douglas o' the Isle o' Teeth and a'm here to defend this Blighted Village o' Darkmouth!" he yelled. "Have a'missed anything?"

62

Back up the beach, away from the cave, crouching tight against the cliff, Emmie finally pulled her hand away from her eyes to see if the silence meant the fight really was over.

"That was far too close for comfort," said Estravon, standing up cautiously to survey the carpet of desiccated Legends littering the stones. Emmie had seen a lot in the past couple of days, but that had scared her in a way that left her breathless. At her ribs, she felt a prodding.

"Can you get off me now?"

It was Broonie, wedged beneath her where she had protected him from the hungry aim of the Half-Hunters.

She stood aside, letting him push himself up while shaking his head and dusting down his rags. Emmie sniffed at the stench the Hogboon still carried with him from the Infested Side.

"Why don't you hold your nose?" he asked her. "Your

disgust isn't quite obvious enough."

Hugo was already out on the beach, holding up a hand towards Clara, a wave that doubled as a greeting and a warning to stay on the cliff, in case there were any Legends still lurking in the cave.

Impatient Half-Hunters were making their way down towards them, and the first to reach them raised their Desiccators at the sight of Broonie. He shrank down to protect himself, but Emmie placed herself between him and the barrels.

"Don't you dare," she scowled. "Or you'll regret it."

"Don't look at me," said Steve as they turned to him for support. "I'm only her father. She doesn't listen to me."

He stood forward and aimed a series of hand signals at the Half-Hunters, ending with a closed fist that suggested they wait. Finn's father walked straight past him, grabbing a fresh Desiccator from a Half-Hunter as he did.

He carried the coldness of a soldier still on duty. Warmth and reunions could wait until the mission was done or, perhaps, when all these Half-Hunters weren't watching him. They were crowding on the beach now, high-fiving and tossing desiccated Legends between each other like beach balls, adrenalin fuelling their excitement.

"Are you really alive?" one asked Hugo.

"This would be a pretty good trick if I wasn't," Finn's dad replied, not breaking stride.

"Will you be filing a 114-dash-P form for this?" a Half-Hunter asked Estravon.

"You bet," Estravon answered, pulling the shredded lapels of his suit together and sticking his chin out. "And maybe even a 23-slash-K. After all, you only live once."

They reached the entrance to the cave. There, half buried by the balls of Legends, was a rough black metal sphere. "My van," said Steve glumly. "That'll never iron out."

There was no sign of Finn. Neither was there a sparkle of light, no whirling of a gateway, but there was a dim glow suggesting that if one way to the Infested Side had closed, the other had not. So, they didn't go in. More importantly, nothing came out.

"He didn't get desiccated, did he?" Emmie asked, sorting through the carnage in search of something that might look less than Legendary.

"No, I saw him go in here," said Hugo and began to enter the cave.

Steve, Estravon, Emmie and most of the Half-Hunters

started to follow after him. It only took Hugo to glance over his shoulder for them to know he wanted to do this alone. So they stopped, waited.

Emmie stared after Hugo as he moved further into the cave, rubble-strewn from the invasion, roots dangling through the shredded ceiling, its passageway forced wider by the violence.

Hugo reached the chamber they had fled from. The red gateway was gone, having seemingly exhausted itself during the battle. But the hole between worlds was still open. Unmoving. Unchanged. A fixed blast with its edges uneven and soft, a torn fabric with its stitches pulled and loose.

Grim daylight and rank air seeped in from an Infested Side that was relatively quiet now, the view filled only with the fallen Legends of both Gantrua's army and the resistance. Nothing moved. All life had been swept away by battle, or lost in the invasion of Darkmouth. There were no flying serpents. No snarling Orthruses. No ranks of attacking Legends. No Cornelius and Hiss. Just an abandoned tunnel to the Infested Side, waiting to be exploited.

There was a noise.

From the darkest corner of the chamber, stumbling a

little as he emerged, stepped Finn. Half in grey light, half in darkness.

"You OK?" Hugo asked him.

"Dad..." started Finn.

"I'm sorry, son," said another voice.

Niall Blacktongue pushed Finn forward by the arm.

Finn's father – Niall's son – raised his Desiccator. "Don't take another step," he told him.

"I am coming home, Hugo, and you must let me," Niall said.

"Why should I do that?" demanded Hugo.

"Because it's time I finished what I started."

'The Leaving of Niall Blacktongue'
From *The Chronicles of the Sky's Collapse*,
as told by the inhabitants of the Infested Side

YESTERDAY

After his son had been rescued by the serpents and flown away from him, Blacktongue retired once again to his tower. His mantra recommenced, an incessant stream of words.

Outside, ranks of guards once more circled his prison. Maybe for his protection. Maybe for theirs. No one was quite sure.

Eventually, Gantrua arrived, pushing through those soldiers too slow to step aside or leap away. Trom and Cryf followed him, marching in step, heads up and snarling at any of the Fomorians sniggering at them.

Inside the tower, Blacktongue looked up from where he sat, silenced his mantra and allowed the full intent of Gantrua's sinister grin to fill the room.

"Come with me," the great Fomorian said.

Together they climbed the stairwell, Gantrua grinding the bone to dust as he pressed ahead. Behind him, Blacktongue climbed even slower than he had thirty-two years before when he had followed his grandson up those very stairs. A boy it had taken so long to see again. But one he had thought of every day since.

They reached the room at the top of the tower, the bone melted and set, its walls still mutilated from when his weapon had detonated so long ago. One section still open to the void. They stood at the edge, but did not look down.

High above them, the sky was filling with Quetzalcóatls, all travelling in one direction.

"We have found them," Gantrua said. "Your son and the traitors who sheltered him."

Blacktongue remained silent but for the deep, even wheeze of his breathing.

"An army will meet them. You will lead it." Gantrua turned, the teeth gleaming on the grille at his mouth. They looked freshly sharpened. "And you will destroy them all."

He left Blacktongue where he stood, his long sword scraping the steps as he left the tower, but his presence was still imprinted in the atmosphere. The human eventually left the room too, pulling his hood up so that no Fomorian could divine his emotions as he walked from the tower for the last time.

Trom and Cryf stepped into the building and stood in the flicker of the candlelight, observing the mural painted in clays on the bone.

Rising up the wall, in a sweep of the tower's curved interior, the image was rough yet vivid.

Niall had drawn a sky that went from a blue deeper than any in the Infested Side had ever seen to its familiar grey, hovering above a dirty landscape that melded into a land of unimaginable green.

"That's not good," said Trom.

"I think it's all right," said Cryf. "Nice colours and all."

"That's not what I meant."

"Oh."

The mural contained a human, a boy, in clear anguish high in the sky. The dead centre of a cataclysm at the breaking of two worlds.

63

N iall Blacktongue pushed Finn forward in the cave, the creak of his body almost audible, a thin film of dust on his tattered cloak from where he had left one world for another.

He held a short sword to Finn's neck, its point pressing against his skin. Finn stayed as steady as he could. The energy had such a hold on him he feared even flinching would cause it to ignite.

That, of course, would stop his grandfather. It wouldn't kill Finn. He hoped. It hadn't last time anyway.

But it *would* kill his dad, who was creeping forward with the Desiccator trained at his own father's forehead. Through clenched teeth, he spat venom at Niall. "If you hurt Finn—"

"You can't desiccate me, son," Finn's grandfather rasped, unsteady, as if regretful. "It would mean desiccating both of us, and untangling that mess would not be easy.

Do you remember, when you were very small, I desiccated a Wolpertinger and Hippogriff in the same shot?"

"Stop talking," Hugo told him.

"Of course you don't remember," he said sadly. "You used the feathery, leathery thing as a football. You were so, so young."

A voice called in from outside the cave. It was Steve and they could hear the faint sound of his steps crunching at the entrance. "Is everything OK in there?"

"Stay outside!" Hugo shouted back. "Do not let anyone in."

Sword still held at Finn's neck, Niall edged them both forward another step so that the frigid air of the Infested Side raised goosebumps on Finn's skin, triggering a shiver he struggled to suppress.

"Let him go," Hugo demanded. The anger was building in him like the energy was bubbling inside Finn. Neither could be contained much longer.

"You have to understand," said Niall.

"I understand clearly," said Hugo.

"You don't. You didn't see what I saw. The end of this family, this town. The end of everything."

Finn breathed deep, searched for clarity to calm the welling catastrophe within him. He had tried not to engage with his grandfather's vision, with the prophecy, the idea that he really would do something terrible if he wasn't stopped. Now it loomed within him, casting a shadow.

What if I really am going to destroy everything?

Energy pulsed and bubbled in his veins.

"There must be so much you want to know," said Niall.

"I know all I need to," said Hugo, disgust thick in every word. "You betrayed the Legend Hunters."

"I was trying to save them," Niall insisted.

"You became a weapon for Gantrua."

"No," said Niall. "I helped him gain power only so it would be concentrated on him, so there was only one leader to watch, so I could know every detail of his plans, every threat to this world. Everything he was plotting with Mr Glad, for example."

"You almost let that traitor destroy Darkmouth," exclaimed Hugo, incredulous.

"It wasn't supposed to be like that," Niall said urgently. "I didn't expect Glad to succeed in his plan. It was my idea to pass crystals through because I knew you were working on that great device to close up the gateways. Glad had told us. The crystals were to help you make the bomb work. All that time, I was trying to protect you as best I could."

"You betrayed Darkmouth."

"I was trying to be a Legend Hunter, even so far from my Blighted Village."

"You betrayed *me*," Hugo said. That statement echoed about the chamber, settled in the grim light of the Infested Side.

Finn felt the urgency of the ticking bomb inside him. He didn't know if he had power over it or if *it* had power over him. He tried to speak, but it came out as a meagre croak from his throat, so afraid was he of the blade pressed to it. Neither his father nor grandfather heard him.

"I left the map in the painting for you, son," said Niall.

"Stop calling me that," Hugo told him.

"I left in the hope that someday you might find it, learn about this cave. Protect it from those who would seek to use its power. Maybe even use it, if you wanted, to find me. To find the truth about me."

Finn tensed, the energy rippling across him. He spoke again. Louder. "Leave us, Dad."

"What, Finn?" his father asked.

"Go," Finn told him.

"I can't—"

There was a scrape of shoes on stones and the sound of

433

someone climbing through the rubble of the passageway towards the chamber.

"I said no one was to come in here," said Hugo. "I'll send you back out in a desiccated ball."

Finn's mother appeared in the chamber. She stopped as soon as she saw the set-up, gasped a little. "Finn."

"Mam," said Finn. He sensed Niall's breaths quicken a little, noticed a change.

"Does he want to..." Clara could hardly say the words. "...kill you?"

"No," said Niall.

"You were going to desiccate me in the tower," said Finn. "I'd never have been reanimated. No difference."

"No, I don't suppose there would have been to you." Niall sighed and glanced back through the hole to the Infested Side. "But there was a difference for me." He adjusted his grip on Finn's arm, shifted the position of the sword so that it almost felt like a relief to Finn to have it pressing somewhere else. His grandfather spoke almost directly into his ear. "It's the energy, yes?"

Finn nodded carefully.

"A charge," continued Niall. "Ready to go off."

Finn felt like the filament in a bulb about to burst into brightness. "Get out, Dad," he repeated.

"He thinks he can use this power given to him by the blood crystals," said Niall.

"I can," said Finn. "I did before. On the Infested Side."

"The Legends told me about it," said his father. "It will kill you."

"I survived last time."

"You weren't under tons of rock last time."

Finn hadn't thought of that. He glanced up at the roof of the cavern, just waiting to bury him. He felt defeated. But he could still feel the energy mounting inside him.

Niall drew him in tighter. "You know, son," he said to Hugo, "I could have lost any sense of the passing of the years in that place where there's hardly any difference between darkness and day."

"Stop it," said Finn's father.

"And the Legends, they have lifetimes that make ours seem no longer than the strike of a match. We come into this life, we leave it shortly after. But they live on, some of them for centuries. And they complain constantly about it. Never-ending gripes about their boredom. And that eats away at any sense of the days, the years, the decades. But I never lost count. Not one day. Not one minute."

"Enough," said Hugo.

"Thirty-two years," recounted Niall.

"Stop."

"One day."

"I'm warning you."

"And twenty-three hours. That's how long since I left Darkmouth. Since I left my family to find the boy, to save the world. And, over those long, long years, I have ignited, and I have destroyed, and I have filled those Legends with so much fear of me. And yet there's something they do not know."

He pushed his face forward fully into the light. The scraggle of his white whiskers. The sag in his skin. The scars. "It is gone. The energy. The power. All of it. Drained."

The sword was no longer pressing into Finn's skin, but was almost resting on his collarbone. He wondered if he should elbow his grandfather in the ribs and run for it.

"And now I am nothing. I'm not a weapon. I'm not a bomb. I am old skin. Crumbling bones. I can't go out there into Darkmouth. I can't go back to the Infested Side. I am trapped here. In this cave. Called a traitor to the Legend Hunters. A traitor to my son. And now a traitor to the Legends too. Of no use to anyone."

Niall fixed Hugo with a stare, his eyes blanched, a ghost. "But, while I am not the man you see in that

436

portrait, one thing never changed." He pulled Finn closer. "I am not a killer. I only ever wanted to stop the sky from falling apart. To protect a town our family has stood guard over for a thousand years. To be a Legend Hunter. First. Always."

He pressed his blade tight again, its tip touching Finn's chest. In reaction, the energy seemed to pool at that very point.

"Prove it," said Clara. "Let Finn go."

"I will, but first I must create a new path."

Niall whispered into Finn's ear, a death rattle in his voice. "This blade is not for harming you, but to release you. To release your energy. We will close this hole and you will live. But you will need to let go of the power. Are you ready for that?"

No, thought Finn. *I just want to go home now.*

"It's OK," said Niall. "I can help you. Help drain the power out of you and into the gateway. The rock won't kill you. I know a way."

Finn felt his heart beating very fast. "How do I know you're telling the truth?"

"You can't," said Niall. "But what choice do you have?"

Finn knew he was right. He was going to explode, one way or another. He couldn't hold it much longer.

"Go, Mam," he said. "Go, Dad."

They didn't leave the cave.

Finn wanted to shout at them to run, but he couldn't speak, couldn't hold the power back any more. The energy rushed through him, desperate to escape. The clock ticked down. The urge to explode was overwhelming.

Only *he* had the power to close off the hole between worlds. To stop all this.

"Are you scared?" his grandfather said softly.

"Yes," he said. Because Finn was very scared indeed.

"You are far braver than you know," said Niall, comforting, sympathetic. "Now let's end this. Together."

Niall pressed the sword to Finn's chest. The tiniest of pressures. Enough to just prick the skin.

A thin trickle of blood ran across the edge of the blade.

"Go, Mam!" he bellowed. "Get out, Dad. I can't—"

Inside Finn, a bomb went off.

64

It began again.

The atoms in Finn's body becoming sticks of dynamite. His veins a fizzing fuse along which fires ran until...

But this time there was no explosion. Instead, there was Niall Blacktongue's hand on his shoulder, his other palm on his elbow. Finn felt the energy boil to the top, overflow just as it had before.

Only the power was not being released but diverted. Finn's vision flared; a great noise filled his mind and, amid the agony of its grip, it took a second for him to understand that the power was draining from him and flowing instead into his grandfather.

Niall's whole body was arched, fighting to keep hold as energy jumped and flickered, trying to escape and explode. He spoke a mantra that gradually morphed into a shout of pain which rose until it filled the chamber.

The energy left Finn entirely and Niall collapsed to his knees at the entrance to the Infested Side, while Finn slumped against the cave wall, not caring about the scraping rock, but only that he was free again, the burden lifted. Empty.

The last echo of Niall Blacktongue's anguish faded in the cave.

Finn felt his mother lifting his face, checking him over, holding him by the shoulders, pushing up his chin so she could see into his eyes, asking him over and over, "Are you OK? Do you feel OK?" Until, eventually, Finn mustered the energy simply to nod in agreement and Clara let out a stuttered breath of relief.

Hugo towered over Niall Blacktongue, Desiccator pointed at him, tension so thick the cave didn't seem big enough to contain it.

Slowly, hands raised, Niall lifted himself from the floor, sand clinging to his cloak, threads of electricity running along his skin, sparking, crackling, as he pressed a hand against the cave wall.

Still Finn's father did not shoot, as if fighting with his own instincts.

Finn stood unsteadily, grabbing at the rock for support. His mother was trying to help him move from the cave.

Niall raised a hand to him, fingertips crackling with electricity. "When I left Darkmouth," he said, agonised, "it was to make a new path to the future. I hope I've done that, Finn. It's up to you to take it."

Niall sparked, a match striking, ready to burst into flame.

"I will use this power. Destroy this gateway. Destroy this cave. End this path to the Infested Side."

Hugo's Desiccator was still raised, but his finger was no longer on the trigger.

Niall dropped to his knees. Finn saw that his eyes were whirlpools of energy. Every vein glowing. Every neuron firing. He was looking at his son and grandson, Clara between them, each standing in the cold, grim light of the Infested Side. Finn saw him murmur a mantra before speaking through teeth clenched in pain.

"I am sorry."

Finn's father watched Niall for what felt like the longest time, but may only have been a second. He lowered his weapon. Finally, Hugo nodded, and Finn immediately recognised that this unspoken acceptance flooded Niall with contentment. A visible calmness even as he struggled with the energy rippling through him.

"There is so much to tell you," said Niall, tensing. "But no time. Leave. Now. My future ends here."

Hugo, Finn and Clara took one last lingering look at him. Then Hugo seized Finn by the shoulder, and took Clara's hand, and together they ran.

Finn, Hugo and Clara came out from the cave on to the beach, yelling at the crowd of Half-Hunters to get out of the way, to get into the water, off the cliff.

"Fire in the hole?" Steve asked as the trio ran past him.

"Just run," ordered Hugo.

"Fire in the hole!" shouted Steve and ran.

Nothing happened for a few seconds other than a beach and cliff full of bemused Half-Hunters hurriedly seeking protection. Eventually, from behind the rock at the headland, Estravon popped his head up from underneath his hands, carefully looked back at the cave and said, "Is something supposed to happen?"

There was a rumble. The entire cliff heaved a little, soil spilling from its edges as it settled again. The Half-Hunters still loitering on it took that as their cue to scarper in whatever direction seemed good.

Silence.

Nothing moved.

For a moment, it seemed that no explosion was—

And then light burst from the cave entrance, a crimson that briefly filled the beach, throwing everyone on it to the ground, hands over heads. The cliff lifted again, then slumped in the middle. Two wide cracks chased away in either direction from the epicentre until the grass collapsed, imploding suddenly, catastrophically, disappearing in a great cloud of dirt and rubble, a rumbling noise like the world falling in.

When it finally settled, the dust drifting up and out across the water, a cliff that had cast a shadow every day for many millennia was no more than a great pile of soil and stone.

Finn watched from where they had dived behind a rock on the beach, tried to process the scene. The destruction. The chaos. The fact that he was still alive. It was utterly, completely, bafflingly surreal. And yet the strangest thing of all was how normal that was beginning to feel.

Emmie emerged from where she had been hiding alongside him. "Whoa," she said. "Whoa."

That was pretty much the most articulate response possible.

Broonie popped up from behind her. "Now I know there's no limit to how bad my days can get."

"Is it safe?" Steve asked Hugo, but Finn's father didn't answer. Instead, he flicked open the clasps at the neck of his fighting suit to get some air, rubbed his face with the back of his hand and walked towards the rubble.

He turned, scanned the entire beach, every Half-Hunter who had come to claim his town, to take his home, to take his legacy, and waited for Clara to stop hugging Finn.

"I'm sorry about my clothes, Mam," Finn was saying to his mother. "And I left my bag behind with all the books in it and—"

"Oh, shhh," she said and gripped him tightly while he tried to breathe and to not look too embarrassed in front of Emmie.

When she finally let him go and went to embrace Finn's father, he wiped his forehead clean of her kisses and said to Emmie, "I wasn't even gone that long."

Emmie laughed at him. "This has been amazing. What a day! What a week! And we did it, Finn. We survived. We went into the Infested Side and we came back. And this is going to change everything. I mean, for you. And for me. And for everybody. And..." She stopped, looked at him. "And did I already mention that's a nice kitty T-shirt you're wearing?"

Finn wanted to die all over again.

Where the mighty mound of rubble met the beach, Hugo stopped, bent down and picked up a grass-fringed clump of soil, a worm wondering why it was suddenly dangling free. He threw it away and picked another to move aside.

Finn slowly jogged after him, bent down and did the same, flinging a clump of soil out of the way. "Dad," he said, because now was the time to say it. Now was the time to tell him that he wanted to be free of a future as a Legend Hunter. Free of prophecies and the end of the world. Free of any more of this. That he had got his dad back. That he had earned his freedom. That he just wanted to go off and be normal, go to school, grow up to be a vet in a town where the animals weren't murderous. "Dad, I..."

"I never doubted you, Finn. Not once," his father said, sifting through rubble. He stopped for a moment, looked at him. "OK, maybe once or twice when things were really bad." He smiled, just a small tired one, tinged with sadness, but still warm with pride. Then he resumed digging through the rocks. "We'll take a few days off, hey?

Get back at it after that. I've learned so many new moves over there..."

Finn let him talk. The time wasn't right to start telling him about how he wanted to be a vet. The time might never be right.

He had lost his father and found him again, and he couldn't yet believe it. He had found his grandfather and lost him again, and that was even more unbelievable. The thought almost overwhelmed him, but how must it have been for his own father? "Dad," he said. "Granddad..."

"I don't really want to talk about it," his father replied. "Not now anyway. Later. For sure. But it's complicated. Very complicated."

He pulled an orange life jacket from the rubble, put it aside and just kept digging.

Clara arrived, sleeves rolled up, to help out. "I could've married an accountant," she complained. "Or a dentist. Oh, I could have married any number of dentists. But no, I had to go and marry the last Legend Hunter on the planet. I should have listened to my mother."

Beneath Hugo's overgrown beard, there was a hint of a smile.

Emmie joined them, picking up a desiccated Legend with its hardened scales dusted in earth. After a dramatic sigh of frustration, Steve threw down his helmet and started digging too.

Half-Hunters began to move in, helping to clear the rubble and desiccated Legends, to push their way into whatever might remain of the cave, until people in various shades of armour and helmets, tattooed or clean, spiked or smooth, snaked in a line across the beach, passing debris along from one to the other.

One eager Half-Hunter, with a red Mohican welded on the top of his helmet, blue swirls adorning his fighting suit, muscled in between Hugo and Finn, the joints of his fighting suit grinding with rust, his eyes wider than a child on Christmas morning.

"Hi," he said. "I'm such a big fan."

Both Finn and his father kept pulling at the rubble.

"I hope you don't mind, but I have to ask," the Half-Hunter said to Hugo. "What exactly are we digging for?"

Hugo didn't pause, didn't even look at him, just kept pulling at rocks and clumps of soil as he said, "When you find him, you'll know."

"Thanks," Finn said to the Half-Hunter. "For coming to rescue us."

"Well, you know, that's not exactly what happened. To be honest, we all came here to claim Darkmouth as our own. That's the tradition once the last remaining Legend Hunter, you know..."

Hugo gave the Half-Hunter a laser-beam glare even while he continued to sift through soil and desiccated Legends.

"...dies," the Half-Hunter concluded. "But anyway you're alive. And Darkmouth is all yours again."

Finn's father pushed aside dirt-caked, earthy stones with his hands, threw a desiccated Fomorian over his shoulder, then stopped digging for a moment to look at Finn. "Not for much longer," he said. "Next time you want to take Darkmouth, you might have to take it from someone tougher than me."

Finn remained still for a moment until he realised his dad was talking about him. So many things had changed. Him being slow on the uptake was apparently not one of them.

"Ah yes, we're looking forward to the ceremony," the Half-Hunter was saying as the digging went on. "It'll be a big day. All the excitement, the music, the dozen golden monkeys."

Finn's mind had wandered. Tiredness was closing in on him. The enormity of what he had just been through beginning to squeeze his mind. He stood, wiped his brow with a filthy hand, looked at the industry on the beach and carnage surrounding it.

He had been into the Infested Side. And back. Again.

He had been blasted by crystals. Twice. He had ignited once. Almost done it a second time.

He had travelled through time. Fallen from a tower. Flown with Legends. Escaped from death.

He had been told he would end the world. End two worlds.

A breeze pushed at Finn's fringe as the sun disappeared behind an approaching cloud. He looked towards the newly revealed stretch of beach beyond the flattened cave. A new path lay ahead. Uneven, strewn with rocks, dangerous.

One thought hit him above all others.

"What do you mean, a dozen golden monkeys?"

On the beach, Estravon was sitting on the cool pebbles, taking in the scene. The damp sky, the foaming surf, the Half-Hunters crawling across the ruins of the cliff.

An alarm sounded. An electronic *bleep-bleep* on his wrist. He checked his watch, pressed the button to silence it. "That's the two days up," he muttered to himself, and picked at the ruins of his suit while shaking his head. "Lucky Legend Hunter, Hugo. Very lucky."

Estravon noticed someone standing beside him, a pair of legs stalled at the corner of his eye. He nodded towards the collapsed cliff.

"They should really be wearing hard hats," he said to his new companion.

The person didn't respond. Estravon turned and squinted up at the stranger, but the glare of the day was blinding to him after so long on the Infested Side,

and he couldn't see the face of the man he was talking to. All he could make out was a long coat over a suit and unkempt, greasy hair like long black strands of spaghetti.

"Rough day?" asked Estravon.

"I've had worse," said the man, his voice deep and unnatural, as if echoing from the bowels of the earth.

"Tell me about it," said Estravon. He watched Finn pick through the rubble, stopping briefly to rub his forehead, then stare into the middle distance as if lost in thought. "That boy," he tutted.

"Yes, that boy," said the man.

"You know him? Of course you do. Everyone knows him. The things they say about him? I doubted it all, but here I am, just about living proof. But that's the life we chose, huh?"

But the man was gone. Estravon hadn't seen or heard him go. He couldn't see him anywhere on the beach. Yet it seemed for a moment as if his shadow remained, fleetingly after he'd left. Estravon shook his head again. "I spent too much time over on the Infested Side," he said. "I need a good sleep."

Thin, barely there, a shadow drifted above the beach, above the crowd of Half-Hunters at the ruins of the cliff.

It rematerialised at the crack of fresh soil where the cliff had been sliced clean from the land, leaving a view of the town of Darkmouth, its roofs and alleyways huddled together for protection.

He formed slowly, surely, stretching his limbs in agony until solid again. Then he broke into a smile of such malevolence it killed a passing butterfly stone dead.

Mr Glad had been trapped between worlds. Pulled apart every time a gateway opened in that cave. Yet, as each of those gateways closed, he had been brought closer and closer to the world again. Until he was no longer at their mercy. They were at his.

He was back. Not from the dead. From somewhere far worse than that.

Mr Glad examined the empty air, peered at it as if catching sight of a particularly interesting molecule, and reached out a crooked finger. He picked at the invisible fabric, as if finding a loose stitch, revealing a small spot of golden light that hung, unmoving, in the air. With his nail, he picked at it again, tearing a narrow scar in the sky, through which Mr Glad could see the dark of the Infested Side.

He gazed into it for a while, then broke into a

vengeful smile. Quickly, he ran a hand over the light, folding the edges back together so that they sealed again.

A cloud of fine debris drifted high on the breeze, passing through Mr Glad. When it was gone, so was he.

Across Darkmouth, it began to rain.

THANK YOUS

I am indebted to everyone at HarperCollins *Children's Books* who has worked on this story and the *Darkmouth* series so far. Particular gratitude to my extraordinary editors, Nick Lake and Samantha Swinnerton in the UK, and Erica Sussman in the US.

Thanks to copy editor, Jane Tait, and her invaluable eye for detail. Thank you to interiors designer, Elorine Grant, and cover designers, Kate Clarke and Matt Kelly. Also thank you to Geraldine Stroud, Mary Byrne and Nicola Carthy in publicity, Hannah Bourne in marketing, Amy Knight in production, and Brigid Nelson and JP Hunting in sales, and to Tony Purdue in HarperCollins Ireland.

My particular thanks to Ann-Janine Murtagh, head of children's books at HarperCollins, for her invaluable support.

Thank you to my agent, Marianne Gunn O'Connor, for her continued belief, passion and relentless work.

Thanks to James De La Rue for illustrations that have become so important to the world of *Darkmouth*.

It takes a great many people to press a book in to the hands of readers, but it couldn't be done without all the great booksellers out there, so I'm very grateful to them.

Thank you to my family. Special love and thanks as always to Maeve, without whom this adventure would never have happened. And thank you to my wonderful children, Oisín, Caoimhe, Aisling and Laoise.

And, finally, thanks to all you great readers for stepping into the world of *Darkmouth*.

SHANE HEGARTY

DARKMOUTH

CHAOS DESCENDS

Finn's been through so much, he'll now be allowed do what he wants with the rest of his life, right?

Wrong.

Whether he likes it or not, he's going to be made a proper Legend Hunter. But people are disappearing, Legends are appearing where they shouldn't, Broonie's complaining, Emmie's got a secret – and an attack so big is coming that Finn has the weight of the world on his shoulders.

The weight of two worlds, actually.

COMING
FEBRUARY 2016

SHANE HEGARTY